Entanglements and Terrors

David Gerrold

For information address
David Gerrold at his official website:
www.gerrold.com

First edition

for
Gordon Van Gelder,
Charley Finlay,
and
Lisa Rogers,
With love.

Contents

Introduction

The introduction is where the author attempts to explain the book.

But mostly, it's all second-guessing.

When you're writing a story, you're not thinking about how to write a story, you're just writing. You're inside it. You're living it. You're looking through the hero's eyes, listening to what he hears, smelling, tasting, and feeling everything he experiences as well — and not just the physical sensations, the emotional ones as well. And you type, you attempt to get as much of that down onto the paper as you can.

Actually, that's an anachronism. Or at best, a metaphor to evoke the actual process. Because no one is getting anything onto paper anymore. You're staring into a 13- or 32-inch lightbulb, clacking away at a keyboard and making little crawly marks across a big glaring white space, hoping that they will make enough sense that somewhere, someday, some editor will be so desperate for something to publish that he'll even pay to publish *these* words.

These stories represent some of the best work I've published in the past two years. And this collection is a special edition, assembled specifically for sale at the 2015 World Science Fiction Convention. There—that's the explanation. I want to show off some of the stories I'm proudest of...and perhaps seduce you into looking for some of the other books and stories I've written.

Monsieur is a vampire story. Not the typical vampire story—it's more of a deconstruction of the whole vampire mythos. When I finished it, I realized there was more story to tell, so *Monsieur* ended up being the first chapter of *Jacob,* a much deeper exploration of just what it takes to be successful in the vampire world.

Monsieur has been simultaneously published in the September/October 2015 issue of *The Magazine of Fantasy & Science Fiction* and is reprinted here with their generous permission. I recommend you subscribe to the magazine. You won't be disappointed.

The Thing In The Back Yard—well, I could tell you what inspired this story, but then I'd be opening myself up to ill-will, a lawsuit, and another life-long feud. So instead, I'll say nothing about it except that it was a great deal of fun to write, as well as being a genuinely cathartic experience. It was first published in the September/October 2014 issue of *The Magazine of Fantasy & Science Fiction.* The last line was an accident. I wasn't planning it. It just happened when I arrived. But I will not apologize.

The Great Pan American Airship Mystery or How I Murdered Robert Benchley was originally planned for a deco-punk anthology, but because of length issues, it didn't make the cut. So I sent it to Sheila Williams at *Asimov's Science Fiction* and she bought it immediately. It was an opportunity to have some fun with an alternate vision of the twentieth century, one where giant airships sailed across pristine skies and George Gershwin lived a few years longer.

Finding Monstro was written for an online website, I don't remember which one—that's how well my filing system works. It takes place on a planet *almost* Earth-like. My own thinking is that there are no Earth-like planets, there are only lazy science fiction writers. I was thinking about a planet with an equator so hot it's uninhabitable—a possible future for the planet we live on—and how the colonists might deal with it. I stretched the laws of physics a bit, but not far enough to break them. There's another idea in this story too—I've been wondering about the relationship dynamics of an all-male colony. This is a very small piece of that thinking.

The Old Science Fiction Writer was first published in the November/December 2014 issue of *The Magazine of Fantasy & Science Fiction.* On the surface, it's just me being silly about the future, but there's more to it than that. I'm not going to spoil it by saying more.

The Bag Lady is a happy accident. Many years ago, decades even, George R.R. Martin invited me to be a part of an anthology about urban superheroes. I said I wanted to write about The Bag Lady. But I never could come up with a story and the *Wild Cards* universe occurred without my participation. However...

I was flying back from Canada last year, a three-hour flight, and I had an idea—I popped open my laptop and started typing. Before we began our descent, I had written the entire story. Okay, it's only 1400 words, but when I got to the end of it, there was nothing more to say. The moment is complete. I did submit it to *The Magazine of Fantasy & Science Fiction*, but they said it reminded them too much of something they'd published 32 years ago. (I will go to my grave wondering what that other story is/was.) But Mike Resnick picked it up for *Galaxy's Edge*.

And finally, *Entanglements*, first published in the May/June 2015 issue of *The Magazine of Fantasy & Science Fiction*. (See why I want you to subscribe? They keep buying stories from me.)

Entanglements is what I call a "transfusion story." There's this thing that writers say—well, some writers anyway—"Writing is easy, just sit down at the keyboard and open a vein." I've done that. A few times. I open a vein. And when the story is finished I need a transfusion.

I know when I've done it by how I feel when I get up from my desk and come back to this planet. I'm exhausted—more than exhausted, empty, drained. Emotionally numb. I walk around the house, restless—bored, annoyed, frustrated, unable to eat, unable to concentrate on anything at all—no books, no TV, no movies, not even music. So I clean the kitchen, I take the trash out, I sort some stuff, I take a shower, I do all those little things that require no real human engagement at all—the stuff you do when you're going through the motions of life while your self is recovering, recharging.

Entanglements left me trembling. It's a sneaky story. It snuck up on me, and I expect it will sneak up on you. I'm very proud of it and it's the justification for this whole collection. This book is an opportunity to put it in front of a wider audience.

And finally...the last piece in this book is a bonus preview of the opening chapters of *A Method For Madness*. This is here to entice impatient fans of *The War Against The Chtorr*. At the time of this writing, I am two, maybe six chapters away from finishing the book. By the time this collection is published, the book should be finished and in the hands of the publisher.

I'm grateful to the editors who've published my stories in their magazines—Gordon Van Gelder, C.c. Finlay, Sheila Williams, Mike Resnick, and all the others along the way. And a special shout-out to the best copy-editor in the business, Lisa Rogers. (She makes me look like a more polished wordsmith than I really am.)

And most of all, I'm thankful for people who read—that's *you*, the person holding this book—because it's people who read that give me the opportunity to have a life I love living.

I get to be a science fiction writer—and that's the best job in the world. A science fiction writer gets to go anywhere in space, anywhere in time, any dimension, any possibility—even things that are impossible. A science fiction writer is a literary timelord. Who wouldn't want that job?

—David Gerrold

Monsieur

Dark returns and I am awake.

The first few hours, I keep to myself, as usual. Since the invention of electricity, since the invention of gaslight, since the invention of candles and oil lamps, since the invention of fire, humans have rolled back the dark.

Not a problem. The first few hours, I keep to myself, listening.

Even the dark is filled with noise now.

Not so long ago, I could lie still and alone, drinking in the sounds of the world, crickets ticking away the heat of the day, owls questioning the darkness, and sometimes the skittering of tiny feet in the woodwork. Now, I sense all the different voices, both silent and raised, sometimes quietly intense, more often screeching—and underneath it all the distant howling of machines, everywhere tinny attempts at music as if to drown out all the other noises.

And the night is filled with dazzles now. Prowling fingers of light shear across the sheltering gloom, spreading shadows, shredding darkness.

But the dark is my world, not theirs. Eventually, even the bravest creatures return to their little boxes to hide, to slumber. The dark grows still again and I am free to walk the streets alone, tasting the air.

Sometimes, sometimes, long years of sometimes, I lie alone in silence, lost in dreamtime.

And sometimes I awake, curious again, hungry again. I move through the night alone, a faint and glimmering shadow.

And finally sometimes I seek out those last uncertain pools of life, those three-in-the-morning lonely outposts, the last diner or gas station on a lonely road, standing brave against the pressing dark.

I seek the gatherings of those who circle the glare. Like moths, they sparkle only for an instant, then fly into the light—they crackle into smoke and disappear.

•⊷══✦●◗◘◖●✦══⊶•

The pages work their way around the group and finally back to me. Mark and Larry nod their approval. Janice purses her lips, frowning over a phrase that bothers her, she'll return to it later. Her scrawny little brother utters the inevitable, "Real vampires don't sparkle," as if it's his own sudden profound insight. Everybody ignores him.

Jerome—the one who's actually been published, therefore he has *credential*—sucks at his coffee. "I like the rhythm. It sets a mood."

A couple others chime in with half-formed ideas, nothing useful, and I realize what I'm missing is the acknowledgment that the piece *works*. No one has actually said, "This is good. I want to read more."

And in that moment, I realize how much I hate writers' workshops.

We don't want honest criticism—that might hurt. What we want is a standing ovation and a glittering trophy shoved into our hands. We want validation. So we don't give honest criticism. We avoid the cruelty of candor. Not wanting to lose the illusion of friendship, we just play patty-cake with each other's bullshit and pretend we're real writers.

Camellia—not her real name, but the one she writes under—usually goes through each manuscript like a third grade teacher correcting punctuation. Her prose is methodically precise, perfectly bland. She grabs for the parsley and misses the meat and potatoes.

Jerome sits, he types, he sells. There's no secret to it, he says. Just sit, just type. He has a genius-level IQ and the social skills of a hyperactive beagle. But it's not arrogance, it's enthusiasm, getting that award nomination for his first short story was the first time he was ever validated for anything. He finally has evidence he's good at something. Self-esteem issues die hard. When you're small and smart in high school, you don't get girls, you get swirlies. If you're gay, you don't get girls anyway.

Patty writes fan fiction. That's the polite phrase. She doesn't bring pages to the meetings anymore. And she won't upload anything to the Facebook group either. Most of her stories end up with Kirk and Spock professing their undying love for each other. Sometimes one is hurt and the other comforts him. Sometimes they end up in bed, sharing the most embarrassing pillow talk before fucking each other's brains out. Larry was unimpressed and told her bluntly, "*Star Trek* is about reaching for the stars, not your vibrator." She hasn't spoken to him since. Occasionally, however, she still maintains that *everything* is fan fiction. She justifies that notion by arguing that all writers are reworking their personal fantasies into their stories.

Jerome says that women writing about male-male sex isn't all that different from men fantasizing about lesbians. Maybe that's the point. What Patty writes is for herself, not anyone else. And if that's true, then Larry is right too. Me—I'm not going there anymore. It's an argument without end.

Michael is working on an epic. He hasn't shared any of it. Mostly, he sits and grunts and offers insights that he borrowed from "the big guys." Michael has read every book on writing he can find. He wants to be perfect, he wants to write the greatest book ever. He's been working on his epic since middle school. His claim to fame is a letter he received from the editor of a major magazine after he submitted his fifty-page outline. The editor wrote back, "You should learn how to lance a boil before you attempt brain surgery."

Michael waves the letter around as if it's a validation. The editor wrote back. A personal note. No one has the heart to tell him he's had his legs cut off at the ankle with one of the most elegant cheap shots since Mark Twain (allegedly) said, "I did not attend the funeral but I sent a nice letter saying I approved of it."

Gil and Emma always come together, but they're not a couple. Gil rides a motorcycle so he dresses in leather. Emma wears skirts over jeans. Is that some kind of statement or does she have the fashion sense of a Republican? Maybe she's transgender—nobody is sure, nobody is impolite enough to ask—but she definitely has a feminist mission. Does it pass the Bechdel test? Is there unconscious sexism in the structure of the story or the way the characters are presented? Does it challenge the bubble of white male privilege or does it reinforce the patriarchy? Her stories aren't narratives. They're screeds about how the world would be better off without men. One day, Larry is going to punch her. And that will prove she's right about men and violence. It's not that anyone disagrees with her militancy—we wouldn't dare anyway—it's just that she can't talk about anything else.

Gil doesn't write. He comments. He annotates. He informs. He explains. He deconstructs. He is erudite. And that's why nothing in the world satisfies him. He only sees what's wrong. That's why no one will go to the movies with him. You come out laughing and joyous—"That was fun!"—and Gil will immediately begin speaking in that intense manner of his, explaining how the filmmakers conned us, manipulated us, and ultimately cheated us. All too often, he's right. And after he's through, you don't know if you want to punch Michael Bay or Steven Spielberg or Jar Jar Abrams. Or just Gil. Behind his back, Larry calls him "Mister Buzzkill."

Oh, and Blaze—why do women choose such silly names for themselves? Blaze is a dithering idiot. Not my words, Larry's. She's short, she's fat, and she loves to pretend she's a profound thinker. She speaks in that meticulous fannish way, halfway between Asperger's and booorrrring, annotating aloud every meticulous detail of the minutiae of her existence. Today she pretends she's a writer. Next week she'll pretend to be an artist. The week after that, I don't know yet—but eventually she'll cycle back to pretending she's a writer. We had to ask her not to bring her guitar—that was when she was pretending to be a filker. She sings almost as well as she plays. She knows two chords.

Me? I'm the guy who...I don't know. I'm still trying to figure it out.

I want to be the guy who takes this business serious. At least, that's the way I see myself in my own personal movie. That means I'm the quiet shy guy. The listener. The observer. How do others see me? I'm the spear-carrier, sometimes the sidekick, occasionally the comic relief in their movies.

It also means I'm *that* guy—you know, the one that everyone else explains things to, so the audience will get it. They see me as the stupid one. I am surrounded by self-appointed explainers.

In the movie, when you need some necessary exposition, there's always Murray the Explainer. He's an archetype, like Morgan Freeman always plays The Magic Negro. He's usually a scientist, more often a computer nerd who types fast, sometimes a specialist of some kind, like a paleontologist or an expert in epidemiology.

Murray the Explainer is never the hero. He's always scenery. In my case, all those Murrays are also a lot of useless and annoying noise. There was a time when I appreciated the attention. Now, not so much. So I've learned how to smile and nod.

Maybe I'm being arrogant—

Nope, there's no maybe at all in that. I am arrogant. It's part of the job. Whatsisname, that guy who spoke at the college last month—he said writing *is* arrogant. You have to be at the very top of the arrogance ladder to believe that what you write is so important that trees should be chopped down.

"What about those of us who only publish eBooks?"

"Even more so—you're burning coal to create electricity. You're contributing to the heat-death of the planet. That's even more arrogant."

So okay, I'm arrogant. Arrogant enough to have a derogatory opinion of dilettantes and dabblers, doodlers and dawdlers, and especially the danglers who don't do anything useful at all, just hang on like dingleberries. And every bit as useful. They suck the energy out of the room. I take this shit serious. If I'm going to kill a tree—or a planet—I had damn well better make sure it's worth it.

It's not about putting words onto paper—not anymore anyway. Now it's marks on a screen. The last time I printed something out, it was a term project. But it's not the words—it's the thought-pictures, the moment, the mood, the feelings, the experience. It's time-telepathy. A storyteller takes something out of his head and eventually it finds its way into yours. But that's not enough for me. It can't be just a moment of distraction—the story has to do something else, something more. Maybe it could be a little piece of *truth*.

And that's really the bottom line. Who the hell am I to enlighten anyone? I can barely boil a cup of ramen.

In my existential moods, I ask myself why—why is any of this important? Why am I investing all this effort? Why am I doing this?

Because it's a great way to be with people without having to be with people...?

I don't know.

Except—and this is something Michael shared once and it stuck with me ever since. He said that people who read, especially people who read a lot, have more empathy than people who don't read. It's his theory that empathy is a necessary condition for true sentience and from there, true sapience. It sounds good. I like it. It's a useful justification to hang onto while I figure out the real reasons. And if he's right, maybe someday I'll see what enlightenment looks like.

Anyway.

The coffee shop stays open all night, so it doesn't matter how late we stay. Sometimes we sit and argue until two in the morning. Sometimes we don't. Sometimes we even go home and write. Sometimes I open up my laptop and type a few notes to myself, maybe even a whole paragraph, and later on—when I realize I've done five or six pages—I look up and see I'm all alone. The others have left.

Tonight, I'm not alone. The new guy is still here. The one in the black hoodie. I don't know his name. He said it when we shook hands. His hand was very cold. I remember that, but I forgot his name. I close the laptop. "Can I ask you something?"

He shrugs.

"I don't mean to be rude, but I have to ask—are you an albino?"

He shakes his head. A hint of a smile flickers in his eyes. "No. I'm just extremely allergic to sunlight. It's a very rare condition."

"Ah." Jacob—that's his name, now I remember. "You don't say much. Do you write?"

He scratches his cheek with one well-manicured nail, thinking it over. "No, I don't write. But I'm interested in writers."

"Why?"

"Why not?"

"No, I mean—I guess this is a strange thing to say, but my experience of writers? I mean, even myself. Especially myself. We're pretty screwed up as people. We're too fat or too skinny, too short or too tall. We're awkward, we're weird, we're dancing with insanity, with two left feet. And you don't even want to know about all the weird sexual experimentation—"

"Precisely," Jacob says. "That's *exactly* what makes writers interesting." He moves his chair closer to mine, he leans forward, stares into my eyes. "People. Think about it. The great mass of men lead lives of quiet domestication. Like animals in feeding pens, they shuffle meekly from one cubicle to the next, school, school, school, work, work, work—until they die. But writers..." Now he smiles. "Writers—the good ones, anyway—are always looking, listening, sniffing, tasting, touching, experiencing the whole world with all their senses. They're exploring, discovering, learning, sharing. They're pushing the limits of what they know. They're going out beyond the safety of the firelight into the darkness. They're going into the risk zone. They're breaking taboos. The good writers—they're *interesting* specifically because they're *not* safe and comfortable and normal."

"Yeah. That makes sense. It's the kind of thing you hope is true. If you're a writer."

"It is true. The evidence is there."

"So..." I push my empty coffee cup to the edge of the table, just in time to catch Millie, the waitress, passing by with a fresh pot. She refills my mug, Jacob's too. I face him again. "So, what I wrote—? It's crap, right?"

He shakes his head. "No. It's just...naïve."

"Naïve? Why do you say that?"

"Because it is." He leans back in his chair, hooking one arm over the top of it. "I used to be an existentialist—that's the polite way of saying, 'I don't care and I don't care that I don't care.' But there's a way of looking at the world. 'What is, is. What isn't, isn't.' As if that means something. It doesn't. Or, if you dig even deeper—'Life is empty and meaningless. And it doesn't mean anything that it doesn't mean anything.' You like that kind of crap? It sounds profound, doesn't it? It's not. It's just a clever way of disassociating yourself. If you don't have to care, you don't have to take responsibility."

He holds up a hand to stop me from replying. It's a very pale hand and I can't help but stare at it. "No, there's more. Let me finish." And my attention returns to his eyes. They're intense.

"The whole point of that word salad is to say that if you want life to have meaning, you have to make it up yourself. Because you're God inside your own universe of experience. So if you follow that train of thought toward its illogical solipsistic end point, everybody is alone."

I can't help myself. I ask, "So what does this have to do with vampires?"

"Everything," he says. "Being a vampire is the ultimate loneliness. Everyone you know grows old and dies. You might be immortal, but you're alone."

"But you can make other vampires, can't you? To keep you company?"

"You've never been married, have you?"

"No."

"After the first fifty or sixty years, you've had enough. You're just waiting for her to die. Now think about what it would be like if neither of you could die and you're stuck with each other for eternity...." He pauses. "When you get to the point where you can finish each other's sentences, when you know each other's jokes, when all you have are each other's memories, when you can tell each other's stories, when there's absolutely nothing new to say to each other—"

"But if you love her—?"

"Really? What's love?" Jacob asks.

"Uh—"

"Yeah. That's my point."

"I always thought love was when two people fit together so well they become two parts of a larger whole."

"Like Romeo and Juliet? Two addlepated teenagers fall in lust and by the time they're through three days later, six people are dead—Mercutio is stabbed, Tybalt is stabbed, Paris is stabbed, Romeo poisons himself,

Juliet stabs herself, and Lady Montagu dies of a broken heart. Not the best demonstration of a healthy relationship, is it?"

"Now you're just being cynical."

"Am I? Are you arguing that the hormonal responses of two barely post-adolescent persons are a strong foundation for a lifetime relationship? Think about it. Do you really want to spend eternity with this person?"

"Uh—yeah. Okay. I see your point. But not every relationship has to be permanent, right? I mean, you make new friends all your life, don't you? As you grow older, as you meet new people, as you move through new circumstances—wouldn't the same be true for vampires? You could make new...I don't know, what would you call it?—relationships?—without necessarily having to turn them into immortal companions, right?"

"True. And you can get a new dog, but it's not the same dog, is it?"

"Oh." That one I knew. Too well.

Jacob says, "Let me finish my earlier thought. One of my favorite philosophers holds that everything is a conversation. Everything. There is no *is*. There's only the 'is' that we assign to things. Let me say that another way. Maybe there really is an objective reality, but we're not designed to experience it. So all that any of us really knows is our own subjective experience, our own conversation about what is. So there's no 'is,' there's only the *is* we speak. And when we speak it, that makes it real—for the person speaking and for the person listening, at least for as long as he's listening. What do you call it? Taking a thought out of your head and putting it into someone else's? You do it when you speak. But you also do it when you write. And if you're really really good at it, your *is* becomes the other person's *is*."

"And you're telling me this because...?"

"Because you asked me why I said your story—your fragment of a story—is naïve, and I said, 'Because it is.' And no, I don't mean like a subjective *is*. I mean it like an objective, can't-be-argued-with 'is.'"

"Okay. You say it's naïve. Why?"

Jacob nodded. "What do you know about vampires?"

"The same thing everybody knows. They're—"

"Right. You know nothing. Because until a vampire sits down and writes a memoir—a real vampire, a real memoir, not a work of fiction—you know nothing. No one knows anything. It's all make-believe."

"And you know better?"

"Do you?" Jacob's gaze is piercing. He studies me. "Have you ever met a vampire? Has anyone?"

"They're fictitious creatures. It's all made up."

"Ahh."

"So everybody creates their own *is*. About vampires, I mean."

Jacob nods agreement. "Now you're getting it. But—" He stabs the air with a forefinger and his eyes flash with a conspiratorial gleam. "What if vampires actually exist? What if there's something real underneath all those stories—some condition that people have misunderstood for centuries?"

"Yeah, and what if there were no rhetorical questions?"

He ignores it. Properly so.

"Here's what's wrong with most vampire stories," Jacob says. "Most of the time, anyway. The writer isn't telling us about vampires. He's telling us what *he thinks* vampires might be. He's telling us what he believes, what he fears, what he wants. He—or she—hasn't really thought about the experience of being a vampire."

"And you have?"

"I'm not a writer. You are. What's interesting about your pages, your little fragment, is that you're trying to put yourself into the experience. Other writers—" He shrugs. "They're trying to redefine the experience in their own terms."

"Maybe I'm doing the same thing...?"

"Maybe. Maybe not. Walk it out and see. Tell me what you think a vampire is."

"Well, traditionally—"

"No, not traditionally. Realistically."

"Umm, okay." I lean back in my chair. Visions of Dracula dance in my head.

"Here's a clue. Think about the ecosystem."

"Oh, well in that case." I lean forward again. "It's obvious. The vampire is the apex predator." Frowning, trying to remember all those Discovery channel documentaries. "That means you need at least...damn I don't remember, but its hundreds of herbivores, maybe thousands, just to maintain a healthy breeding population *and* support the carnivore families that feed on them. The size of the herbivore population determines how many carnivores can survive. But it's more than that—you need the carnivores to weed out the sick and elderly, the slow and feeble. The carnivores help keep the herbivore population healthy."

"Uh-huh." Jacob looked pleased. "You're on the right track. Forget vampires for a minute and think about ecosystems a bit more."

"Okay, I'm thinking."

"Who's the apex predator on Earth right now? I mean, without vampires."

"We are. Humans. We're eating the planet down to the bone. One day there won't be enough for everyone and we'll have riots, wars, and eventually a massive population crash."

"Unless—?"

"There is no unless."

"Yes, there is. Think about it."

"Oh, okay. Gigantic industrial farms. Not the sprawling acreage that uses up land, but city-farms. Forty-story greenhouse towers. Hydroponics. Meat-tanks. Stuff like that."

"Yes, if humans get hungry enough, that's what they'll build, because the market will make it profitable. And yes, you will get that hungry, so it's inevitable. What did you have for dinner?"

"A hamburger."

"Where did it come from?"

I laugh and point toward the kitchen.

"Before that—?"

"Probably that huge cattle feedlot up north—"

"Uh-huh. So now look at it from the point of view of the cow. They're in bovine paradise—they get to be part of a huge successful herd, tens of thousands of friends and companions, with lots and lots of good food for everybody to eat, they're encouraged to stuff themselves and be happy, and best of all, they don't have to worry about predators—wolves, coyotes, mountain lions, bears, or even bad weather. They have a nice warm barn in the evening, they get vaccinated against all kinds of diseases, and they get inspected regularly to keep them healthy. A very low-stress existence. Eat all you want and never have a stampede. From the cow's perspective, it's a nice life."

"Until you end up a hamburger."

Jacob smiles. "Well yes, there is that—but the evidence of modern civilization is that most people have already made that trade."

"Really?"

"Really."

"So you're saying the human population is a giant feedlot managed by vampires?"

He grins, a quick flash of his very white teeth. "Parts of it, yes. We still have a lot of wilderness left. For those who still like the hunt."

"Ha ha. Very funny. So you're a vampire?"

"Oops. Did I say that out loud?" He laughs, too easy.

"Yeah, you did."

Jacob waves it away. "There's no such thing, remember?" Then, more seriously, "Don't panic. This is just a thought experiment. For your story."

I notice he dodged the denial.

I type something into the laptop. *Vampires. Apex predators. Feedlots.* Then to him, "So, okay—if there are seven billion people on the planet—"

"Seven point five—"

"—how many vampires will that support?"

Jacob leans back in his chair, steeples his fingers. "You're asking the wrong question. No. You're asking that question before you have all the information you need to answer it. First you have to establish the life cycle of the vampire."

"The what—?"

"What I said. The life cycle. The traditional idea—the Dracula fantasy—is that if you drink a vampire's blood, you become a vampire too. What does that suggest?"

"An infection."

"Obviously."

"So it's a disease—a disease of the blood."

"Uh-huh. And...?"

"If it's a disease, then it's not supernatural. It would have specific symptoms and conditions. And also...maybe it's curable. Stoker hinted that it was—with transfusions."

"Specific symptoms and conditions?" Jacob looks at me expectantly. "Like, for instance?"

"Um, okay. Well, anything that would help contribute to the mythology. The vampire mythos says that vampires have great strength. And we know that the human body is capable of impossible feats of strength. It's called hysterical strength, it's what happens with whacked out PCP-users, so that gives us some idea of what the human body can do when it's pumped full of...well, whatever it takes to create that kind of enhanced ability. So, if I were speculating—oh, I *am* speculating—I'd guess that the condition lets the individual trigger his hysterical strength on demand. It wouldn't just be muscle strength, it would mean faster reflexes too. All kinds of physical abilities would be boosted—climbing, running, lifting, fighting, but probably not flying. That's too much of a stretch."

"Not bad." Jacob nods. "Can you extrapolate the rest of it?"

"Sure. It's obvious—well, obvious to anyone who knows anything about physiology. That's a lot of work for a body to do. So any kind of super-strength must use up a lot of energy—like a cheetah can only run so far before his body temperature rises dangerously, then he has to stop. So, I'd say that someone with this condition would have only short bursts of super-strength available, then he'd have to stop and recover, as if he'd been running a marathon. Ahh—that's it. Maybe super-strength uses up so much energy that the body needs a really huge amount of recovery. Maybe the person would have to go into some kind of deep dormancy so his body can rebuild its reserves of energy, a sleep so deep he can't be roused, at least not easily—it would look like death. He'd need a safe place—a place where no one would find him and disturb him."

"Like a crypt?"

"I was thinking more like a dark basement or maybe a bedchamber with heavy curtains. Okay, yes—a coffin would be ideal. Oh, wait—that suggests something else. If the vampire needs a quiet dark resting place, that would mean he has extremely heightened senses, to the point of sensory overload—I think it's called hyperesthesia. So he'd want a chamber that's very dark and very quiet. A coffin in a basement would be a good place for a prolonged state of recovery."

I'm on fire with the idea now. Jacob waits for me to continue.

"Y'know—that could explain Poe's story, 'The Fall of the House of Usher.' Both Madeline and Roderick are infected, only Madeline much more seriously. Roderick knows what's coming. He knows she's not dead, but he lies to the narrator and says that she is. He really does love his sister—he wants her to die in her coffin because he wants to spare her the horror he believes must inevitably follow—"

"Nice," says Jacob.

"I don't know if Poe was aware of the vampire mythos. He never wrote a vampire story, did he?"

Jacob shakes his head. "Not that I know of."

"But he might have been aware of the symptoms. It would explain a lot. I know he had a fear of being buried alive. And madness—" I lean forward, frowning. Another thought.

"What?"

"I'm thinking that...well, it makes sense to me...I mean, think about it. If the condition, whatever it is, creates enhanced strength, then it would also enhance the person's reflexes, which means it affects the nervous system too. That would account for the hyperesthesia...."

"And...?"

"And that would probably—I'm just guessing here, but I think it would probably trigger hallucinogenic episodes as well, most often related to the bursts of super-strength, but maybe other times as well—like when the person gets hungry. I mean *really* hungry. I imagine the condition would require a lot of energy to sustain itself, and that would probably mean incredible cravings—so let's say some kind of hunger-induced hallucinations. Maybe to a primitive mind that would feel otherworldly—maybe the hallucinations have a chemical component, so they feel like an irresistible hunger for blood. Or flesh. But like I said, I'm guessing now."

"Those are good guesses. They're consistent."

"With the facts?"

"With each other. Anything else?"

"Um. Well, if the person has hyperesthesia, that would show up as... um, a..."

"Yes...?"

"A severe allergy to sunlight—" I stop.

Jacob grins. Again with the teeth. I'm not sure I like that. "Um."

Jacob reaches over and gently pushes my laptop shut. "Let's go for a walk," he says. "A nice walk in the dark." Seeing my expression, he adds, "Oh, don't be silly. I just had a steak sandwich and coffee. I'm good for now." He tosses some bills on the table, paying for both of us.

I slide the computer into my knapsack and follow him out to the parking lot, past the light to the park beyond, under the trees where the night is even darker—here, there's only a trace of moonlight to hint at shape and form.

"Let's talk," he says.

"Isn't that what we've been doing?"

Jacob stops and looks at me. "Mostly, you've been talking. Now, it's my turn." Surrounded by the shadows, he seems to glow. "You're not the first to figure it out—that it's not a supernatural thing. Some of us are scientists. Some of us asked to be...*turned*. So they would have enough time. So they could study the condition from the inside."

"Is it curable?"

"You're assuming we might want that. I'm not sure any of us do." Jacob adds, "Our research is secret, so our resources are necessarily limited. But... we're beginning to understand ourselves. And our condition.

"It's a parasitic symbiosis, an infectious mutation, a transformational phenomenon, none of that and all of that. Remember that movie, the one with the big green pods? You fall asleep for a while and then, when you wake up, you're *different*—it's like that. Only it isn't."

He sits down on a stone bench. "You did miss one thing, though. It does extend the lifespan. We're not immortal, but for all practical purposes we might as well be. We age so slowly it's imperceptible."

"May I ask—how old are you?"

He pats the bench next to him. An invitation. I sit.

"I am very young," he says. "I was born in Seattle. In 1858. My mother died in childbirth. My father drowned at sea. He was a fisherman, his boat sank in a storm. I was an orphan at thirteen. I became a street rat. And a peg-boy—"

"I'm not familiar with the term—"

"Be grateful." He pauses.

I was...used by men. It kept me alive.

You might find this hard to believe, but many of them were kind—even tender. Later, when I grew older, the customers were rougher. So...I went into another line of work. One day—well, let's just say I wasn't as good at picking pockets as I thought I was. I chose the wrong target—or maybe the right target. I thought he was just another old man, a strange one because he moved so slowly, but—I found out the hard way that he could move a lot faster than me. Later on, I understood why, but the moment it happened I was paralyzed. He had a grip like an iron bear-trap, but he wasn't angry. He was amused. He pulled me around in front of him and stared into my face and said, "I admire your courage."

I was too shocked to say anything. I didn't have to. He leaned down and whispered into my ear. "I will give you a choice. Would you like to share my dinner? Or *be* my dinner?"

I don't know how I knew, but I knew he meant it, every word. Something in his voice, not the sound of it, but the way he said it. He had a very soft voice, almost womanly, very musical. I think that's why I went with him. His voice.

He took me to a place down by the wharf where the fishing boats came in. I hadn't been anywhere near there since my father died. It wasn't that I feared the docks, I just associated them with bad luck.

But that night it was a different world, bright with gas lamps and cigars, painted whores and boisterous sailors. And us—tucked away in an upholstered retreat on the second floor of an ancient but still expensive eatery at the shadowy end of the boardwalk. I had salmon and scallops and a big bowl of crab chowder, potatoes and beer and finished up with cake and coffee—more food in one place than I'd ever seen in my life.

He ate too, but not as much. Mostly, he watched me. I figured he'd probably want me to share his bed later. It wouldn't be the first time I'd been picked up on the street. It was a rougher life than sitting on a peg, but the pay was better. You didn't have to give half of it to the whoremaster. And I had already figured that if this man was as gentle as his voice, it wouldn't be so bad. You can get pretty good at recognizing who's safe and who isn't—although sometimes they fool you. With Monsieur—that's what he told me to call him—I wasn't sure, but I belonged to him now, for as long as he wanted me. At least it would be a bed.

———————

"And that was when he turned you?"

"Oh, hell no." Jacob laughs. "No. My...transformation came later, much later."

"I don't understand—"

"Of course you don't. It's a trope that lazy writers use—that the people of the dark are so eager to recruit they have no sense of taste, pardon the pun. Maybe you don't give much consideration to your choice of meals—or life partners—but the men of The Community do. Especially where eternity is involved. There's patience, even wisdom. The careful distinctions of time and possibility. That's something else you haven't thought about. Once again, the mythology has obscured the reality."

I retreat to the safe question. "What am I missing?"

"Only the obvious. Probably because you're too young to see it, the same way I was. Stop and think what it means to have an extended life-span. You were smart enough to recognize the hallucinatory aspects of the condition—are you smart enough to work out the rest of it?

"What do you think the world looks like to someone who moves through it unchanging? Meanwhile, everything whirls around you, decade after decade—a century passes, another starts, and you're still young and vibrant, still hungry for experience. What do you do? Seek out endless pleasure? At first, maybe. But you have no idea how quickly that becomes boring, a relentless merry-go-round of sensation. No thanks. Delight and wonder are spices that add flavor to life, they are not the stuff of life itself. A hard lesson for children to learn.

"No. Here's what you do instead. You read voraciously, you attend concerts and seminars, you explore the details of the city, you scour the libraries and museums, you take courses at the university, you travel and observe, you seek out knowledge and understanding—and you watch for people of intelligence and insight. All those things for which you have no time—suddenly, you have all the time you could want.

"Do you know why it's such a pity that human beings are so short-lived? It takes you too long to figure out how to live—and just about the time you do, you die, and all your preciously gained knowledge and experience dies with you. You can spend a lifetime becoming an expert in science or medicine, history or philosophy—and then, in the blink of an eye, you're gone, *it's* gone, all that learning disappears from the world. Lost forever.

"Do you want to know what the real hunger is? Not blood—that's for beginners. No, the real hunger is for knowledge. Experience. Insight. Enlightenment. Levels of understanding that surpass what's possible in a single lifetime—levels so far beyond simple mastery they have no name. That's the only real justification for...for *this*." He holds up his hands, pale in the moonlight. "Yes, I'm hungry. But for the deeper sustenance of the soul. So I ask you now—why would I, or anyone else so blessed, so cursed—why would any of us want to spend even the most fleeing of moments with an unfinished, inexperienced, incredibly naïve adolescent? A teenage girl or boy? Ignorant, uneducated, and mostly uninteresting. Why? Where's the attraction in that? Her beauty? At best, it would be a passing fancy, a casual engagement, a distraction, a diversion, a bit of novelty. But a relationship? A life-partner? Please. Endless romance is an adolescent masturbation fantasy."

Jacob stops and takes a breath. He steps in close to me, eyes hard. "Does it happen? Yes. Sometimes. And the results are usually horrific. Turning a child creates a monster. An adolescent—the condition affects their hormones—they become caught in a tangle of uncontrollable lust, they have to create other monsters like themselves for their blood-orgies. It's not romance, it's insanity. Those are the ones who end up with stakes through their hearts, with their heads cut off, buried at crossroads, burned alive—those are the ones who created the mythos, the crazy ones."

He holds up his hands again. "Look. See the way I shine in the dark? Yes, we *do* glow." He laughs. "But it's the way we reflect light, that's all. I'll share a secret with you—it's not so secret anymore—but we're changing the narrative.

"It used to be, we wanted the world to dismiss the tales as ignorance and superstition, unworthy of serious scientific inquiry. That worked, to a degree, and it allowed us to stay safely undiscovered in the shadows, but it also made us objects of fear. Predators. Enemies.

"Not too long ago, a generation perhaps, you wouldn't have accepted my invitation. You wouldn't have walked into the darkness willingly with me. We would not have sat and talked. No, you would have retreated, repelled, horrified. Instead of curiosity, you would have been alone, with nothing but your fears and inhibitions. And I—I also would have been alone. You would have learned nothing from me and I would have learned nothing from you. Both of us—we would have been denied the discovery of each other.

"But today, I and others like myself—we are objects of sympathy, people are interested in us, people identify with us. A few even care about us. A generation from now, maybe two, who knows? Perhaps we will someday have our own pride parade down Bourbon Street—at midnight, of course. It will be an interesting time. However...I do not see myself coming out of the coffin any time soon. Based on the hysteria of you short-timers, I think it likely I will be safer remaining in the shadows." Jacob falls silent, considering a future I won't live to see.

Finally, I ask, "So if Monsieur didn't want to turn you—?"

Jacob shakes his head and smiles, remembering.

Shall I describe him now? Yes, I will.

He was not what you would call tall, but he was a good height for the time with a stocky build, like one who had worked with his body for most of his life. But his skin was curiously pale and his hands had returned to the softness of an easier life.

His eyes were paradoxically both dark and gleaming at the same time. His features were even, neither coarse nor soft, neither rugged nor feminine, but with a hint of all those qualities, depending on the light as well as his expression.

Mostly, however, he appeared to have an undefinable attraction. The more he spoke, the more I wanted to listen to him. The more I looked into his face, the more I wanted to continue looking.

We talked. I should say that mostly I talked. He asked questions. I hadn't realized I'd lived through so much hardship, but he extracted my entire life story in a very short time. Even the worst parts. The parts I didn't want to discuss. He had that power to draw it out.

Later, I realized Monsieur had been interviewing me, studying me. Finally, over cake and coffee, apparently satisfied, he offered me a job. Room and board and a few dollars a week. He needed someone to manage his house during the day. He said he could not bear the sunlight, so his waking and sleeping hours were inverted from those of other people.

He needed a daykeeper, someone to manage the minutiae of the place while he retreated from the glaring eye of the sun. At first I was skeptical—who wouldn't have been? But winter was coming in hard and my resources were already meager. And Monsieur wasn't bad-looking, he was clean, and he seemed gentle enough. How could I not be tempted?

He reassured me at great length that his intentions were honorable. He needed a responsible and resourceful individual to administer the housekeeping of the day, bring in the mail, accept deliveries from the local grocers, sign for occasional shipments, that kind of thing—and firmly turn away all morning and afternoon inquiries. "Do you have an appointment? No? Well, please leave your card. Monsieur will get back to you at his pleasure." Or, "Monsieur is resting now and cannot be disturbed. Please return after sunset. Monsieur will see you then." I had to bathe every day, wear clean clothes, and never leave the house while the sun was up. At sunset, I prepared the tea.

But that was the easy part. There was another requirement, much more challenging. Every day I had to read a book from his library, any book I chose. He had an amazing collection, most shipped from New York and London. It was difficult at first. I could make out the words, but what they meant was often a puzzle.

In the evening, Monsieur would come down from his chambers—I was forbidden to enter his rooms during the day—and we would sit together and discuss what I had read. He was a patient tutor. I struggled a lot at first, but soon I began to realize that all these books—they were a kind of treasure. They were letters from the past, tales of far away people and their adventures.

I admit to some laziness at first—I didn't have the discipline for parsing the sense of the most intricate sentences I encountered, nor did I have the patience to go scouring through the dictionary to discover the meanings of words I didn't recognize, and too many of the experiences detailed in the books were incomprehensible to me—but all that ended quickly.

If I hadn't kept up with my reading, if I hadn't paid close enough attention to the volume to manage a real conversation about it, Monsieur would catch me out quickly. The first time it happened, he made it clear that keeping up with my reading was the most important part of the job. He didn't want a houseboy—he wanted a companion worthy of his intelligence. Very gently, he asked me—if I didn't like reading, would I be happier returning to the street? Because if I wasn't going to read, if I wasn't going to hold up my end of the conversation in the evenings, why should he keep me around? I never skipped a day of reading after that. I still struggled, but as time passed my struggles eased. I slowly grew more skilled. Eventually, my daily pursuits in the library ceased to be an onerous chore and became an enthusiastic challenge.

In the evening, when Monsieur was satisfied that I had learned something from the day's reading, even if it was only the smallest insight, we would go out to dinner. I knew he enjoyed teaching me—but the other part of it was that he did not want to leave the house until after the evening bustle of the streets had subsided. Eventually, I came to look forward to our conversations. Monsieur was revealing to me that there were farther horizons in the world than I had ever realized before.

Sometime later, after he was satisfied that I was capable of study, Monsieur arranged for tutors, all kinds. They taught me history and philosophy and the manners of a gentleman. He bought me clothes to match my new demeanor. I learned to speak French, play the piano, and even studied a bit of medicine, such as it was in those days.

It was a heady time, it was the grand fruition of the Enlightenment—the world was changing, recognizing the advancements of science and industry. It was ironic as well—because this great Enlightenment had also encouraged the people of the dark to turn their attentions inward and begin studying themselves. Ourselves. That was when a few brave souls even made themselves known to certain men of medicine. It was foolish and courageous, but necessary.

But—I digress.

Monsieur was grooming me, first to be his keeper, later his companion. But for most of that time, I think I was merely his...his pet. His guard dog of the moment. I don't think he had any plans to turn me at the beginning. Later on, I was an interesting experiment. Could a daykeeper be brought up?

From time to time, Monsieur would entertain visitors, gentlemen like himself. I would lay out meats and cheeses, wineglasses and decanters of port or sherry, most of which they left untouched. Sometimes they allowed me to stay in the room and listen to their conversations, but I didn't enjoy that much. The way they treated me, it felt like they were patronizing me, as if I were a child—or worse, some kind of marvelously well-trained animal, a specimen for their amusement.

I recall one of these gentlemen remarking that it was both dangerous and foolish for Monsieur to trust me so implicitly. Another agreed, but said he could understand the attraction. He spoke about me as if I was merely an object on display, something without comprehension or feelings—as if I was not even in the room. His companions nodded knowingly.

Later, after they left, usually in the last thoughtful hours before dawn, Monsieur would excuse their unconscious rudeness, explaining that they had come from different times and different places, and did not yet understand the new world as well as he did.

Sometimes we visited the homes of one or another of these same gentlemen. It made me realize that Monsieur was an exception to the rule. Their apartments were dark and curiously bare of the details of daily existence, as if the rooms were maintained solely for appearance's sake. Some of the men shared accommodations and their homes were meticulously immaculate. This was my first clue to the heightened sense of smell that all these individuals enjoyed—or suffered from. You cannot imagine how badly a city can smell if it is not well tended. Two or three of Monsieur's acquaintances had housemen of their own, mostly to manage the same chores I had. One looked at me skeptically, as if he disapproved of my existence. Another gave me a conspiratorial wink, as if we both shared the same secret—but a secret I did not yet know.

But for the most part, Monsieur and I lived a life apart from that particular social circle. While he never specifically said so, it did appear to me that he took little pleasure in these occasional gatherings, attending more of necessity than affection. I did not know then what they discussed in private, but it was quickly evident that these gentlemen also shared the same disability as Monsieur. Later, when I was allowed to attend myself— as the newest member of the club, so to speak—I finally understood his disaffection. But I also found it a useful colloquium, a seminar of mutual purpose, a school for survival in a world of massive disagreement. But at the time, I knew nothing of this. Only later.

At least once a month, usually in the darkest part of the lunar cycle, Monsieur's behavior changed. He'd get erratic and unpredictable. For several evenings in a row, as the hours lengthened toward midnight, he would become restless. He'd start to pace, he'd be irritable and unapproachable. I learned to recognize the signs and remain as unobtrusive as possible.

Finally, almost in anger, he would reach for his great dark coat and walking stick. At first I offered to accompany him, insisting that it wasn't safe for anyone of wealth to be out alone in the city, especially not this late at night, but Monsieur always dismissed my concerns, similarly rejecting my offer to join him, saying that he needed to take the night air by himself. He bade me stay in my room, get a good night's rest, and not to worry, no harm could ever come to him. I couldn't help but notice the strange way he phrased that. No harm *could* ever come to him. Not *would*, but *could*.

Sometimes I waited up for him—usually to his great displeasure. Because sometimes he came home disheveled. Once, his clothes were viciously torn and I thought I saw blood on his shirt, but he waved me away, saying it was nothing for me to concern myself about, as he stumbled up to his room.

On other evenings, when we stayed home together, he often displayed a curious tenderness. Sometimes he visited me in the bath, often bathing me like a father would with his only child. His touch was affectionate, never untoward, but he seemed fascinated with the appearance of my flesh, openly admiring the rosy color of my skin, made even more red by the heat of the bath water—though I had become much paler now for spending so much time indoors. It was a curious behavior on his part, yes, but I'd experienced much worse at the hands of lesser men, and after a while I came to enjoy his attentions as a sign of his affection.

I had been with Monsieur for almost three years and I was beginning to feel safe, even comfortable, perhaps for the first time in my life—but I had also begun to experience a growing unease. I was feeling incomplete, if that is even the right word. Perhaps it was an emotion without a name.

Monsieur must have sensed my disquiet for he asked me one evening what troubled me. It was a cold, rainy night, we were sitting in front of the fire and I felt bold enough to ask Monsieur why he had brought me into his house if he found me so unattractive. He looked astonished and asked me what I meant by such a question. I told him that he had never once placed a hand on me, never once invited me to share his bed, never once even asked me to remove my shirt. The only time he expressed any interest at all in my nakedness was when he visited me in the bath.

It puzzled me greatly. At the beginning, and for sometime thereafter, I believed he had chosen me because he recognized my nature—but now I had no idea why he'd brought me into his household. I could only assume that whatever interest he might once have enjoyed, had faded with time—or worse, perhaps he now found my nature somehow embarrassing or even abhorrent. He would not be the first to feel that way. Prior to my engagement with Monsieur, I had met and serviced gentlemen who sought out the pleasures of boys or other men, but pretended to the more typical interest in female bodies—

I did not get to finish. Monsieur interrupted me with that great gentle laugh of his. He reached over and placed his hand on my arm and reassured me—no, that was not the case. First, he told me not to be ashamed of my nature. Many men prefer the company of other men, women hold no attraction for them. He gave me the key to the locked bookcase and told me to read some of the histories of ancient Greece and Rome. And medieval Japan as well. He said that as I read more, I would learn that I was in august company. I shared the same nature as Plato and Socrates, Michelangelo and Leonardo. Great thinkers, magnificent artists. I should be proud of that shared spirit.

So why then did Monsieur not caress me or fondle me? Did he not share my nature? Did he not appreciate it? Again, he laughed. "Dearest boy," he said, "I find you painfully attractive. There is nothing I would like more than to lie in your arms and enjoy the sweetness of your kiss. But I must not. It would not be fair to you."

"Not fair? Please, Monsieur," I begged. "I would be your willing servant in all things. Even in your bed."

"And I would have you be just that, if I could," he said. "But I dare not. For were I to be so foolish, I would do you irreparable harm. And I care about you too much to inflict that kind of grief on you. Trust me, Jacob."

I fell to my knees before him, sobbing. I buried my head in his lap and cried at great length. Monsieur said nothing. He merely sat and stroked my hair, which now fell down past my shoulders, I'd never had a haircut, Monsieur had never allowed me to. He just stroked my hair and waited until my grief subsided.

Finally, I looked up at him, met his dispassionate gaze, and begged him as if I were begging for my life. Perhaps I was and didn't know it, but I was so overwhelmed with emotion I felt as if I might go mad if he wouldn't tell me the truth of why we couldn't consummate our passion, why we had to impose such impossible restraints upon ourselves. If I surprised Monsieur with my desperate outburst, I surprised myself even more. I had never felt such desire for another person in my entire life.

———————————

Jacob interrupts himself. "Oh, yes—that's something else you missed—the attraction."

"Huh?" I had been so caught up in his narrative, it was almost a shock to return to the present.

"The monthly excursions—you know what those were for, of course. No, we don't have to feed every night—we don't have to feed at all, in fact—but we do have a lunar cycle of our own, and in those days, before anti-depressants and mood-altering substances, we were too often overwhelmed by the hormonal storms of our bodies—our own bipolar madness. That part has never made it into popular lore, has it? Of course not—real biology complicates things. The facts get in the way of masturbation fantasies, eh?

"But that's key to understanding the *other* thing—our unnatural pheromones. Yes, we have pheromones. It's part of the condition, and they're strongest at those times of the month when we're hungriest. It's a chemical lure that serves to overpower any fear you might experience. You experience it as irresistible attraction. Male or female. The more you are exposed to one of us, the more you are—oh, what's a good word here—enchanted? Fascinated? Enthralled? Captivated? *Held.* From the predator's point of view, it's a very useful adaptation, wouldn't you agree?"

Jacob smiles. He shows his teeth. The chill of panic starts in my groin, rises like a wave, spreads up through my belly and my chest, expanding outward in a rush, but almost immediately it turns into a surge of heat—or something—all the way up into my throat and my face and finally to my eyes. I wipe moisture off my cheeks.

Jacob reaches over and delicately touches the top button on my shirt with one incredibly well-manicured nail. Without a word, I fumble it open. I'm ready to undo the next one when Jacob leans back, smiling but wagging his finger at me as well. "See, what I mean?"

I swallow hard. Regret as much as relief.

Jacob gives me a look—is it pity? "That's just the barest intimation of what I was feeling for Monsieur."

<hr />

Monsieur must have been moved by my tears, because he said, "Jacob, my son—yes, that is how I regard you, as the son I wish I could have had. You have given me more happiness than I ever believed I deserved. I have trusted you with my well-being for almost three years now, a blink of an eye for me, half a lifetime for you. It is time for you to understand just how much I trust you.

"'You know that I cannot abide bright lights of any kind. I must avoid the daylight because I have a condition of the blood. There are other disabilities as well, far more severe, and I shall discuss those with you as it becomes necessary. But for the moment, dearest boy, please understand that my candor on this matter is a gift of enormous trust—were I to succumb to my attraction for you, were we to consummate our passion, you would very likely be exposed to suffer the same disabilities in time. I simply cannot risk that. I dare not burden you with this condition, not at this stage of your life. Not yet. As much as you have begged me for physical attention, I must with even more intensity beg you to resist—resist with all your heart and soul, as if your very life depends on it, because it does. My refusal is not a rejection of your spirit, dearest Jacob, but an affirmation of it"

Of course, his words only increased my distress. I was heartbroken—now that I had spoken my affection and Monsieur had spoken his as well, now that I knew the depth of his feelings, the situation was even more untenable.

I was caught up in his pheromones, of course. But Monsieur understood all too well why he dared not expose me. At that stage of my life, still barely a teenager, I would have become a monster stuck in a post-adolescent hormonal storm, a captive of my own relentless lust. I would have created monsters around me.

Such an event was not unknown to The Community, that regular gathering of Monsieur's associates. In the past, The Community had acted quickly to destroy such monsters before a plague of hungry desires could flame out of control.

But Monsieur had not yet shared any of that with me. Perhaps he thought I would imagine him insane and go to the authorities. Perhaps he feared it would destroy my affection for him. Instead, he simply assured me it was for my own good that we not share a bed. Despite my hormone-driven pleas, he insisted. I even told him that I would not mind sharing his disability, but—he argued just as fervently—who could we trust to protect the house and the both of us during the day?

It has been repeated so many times and in so many places that knowledge is power that most people believe the statement without ever questioning it. But my experience demonstrated to me that it couldn't possibly be true. Not always. Certainly not here.

Some knowledge drains you of power, leaves you feeling empty and helpless. Staying in the same house with Monsieur became intolerable—I spent long hours in distress, my mind churning, even to the point of considering that if I wanted to preserve what was left of my sanity, I should leave his house forever.

Monsieur could not have been unaware of my anguish. He was suffering considerable misery of his own. Night after night, he went out into the darkness, returning only with the first rays of dawn, as feverish and wild-eyed as an escapee from an asylum. I had never seen him so crazed. When I asked him if there was anything I could do, he only glared at me.

When I cried out in alarm, he flung me back against the wall in anger or some other unidentifiable emotion. He gave me a look of such intense rage I did not dare to speak.

The next evening, as soon as the last rays of the sun disappeared from the drawing room, Monsieur came rushing downstairs, wearing only his dressing gown, disheveled and grief-stricken. He grabbed me at the bottom step, clasped both my hands in his, and begged my forgiveness for his fury of the previous night. He had no excuse, he said, only that his condition, as he called it, sometimes drove him into fits of madness, an uncontrollable lunacy. He believed he had been managing it well, but obviously he'd become overconfident—last night had vividly revealed that he had not maintained himself as well as he had hoped. He was so terribly, terribly sorry that I had suffered the brunt of his fury that I felt his anguish as my own.

I forgave him, of course. How could I not? But as we sat together at the bottom of the stairs, alternately apologizing and forgiving each other, it was crushingly obvious how much we both were struggling with the situation. We whirled about a common center of turmoil—the same way the Earth and the Moon rotate around a common center of gravity. But because the Earth has much greater mass, that center of gravity is actually located a thousand miles deep beneath the surface of the planet, so while the Moon swings around this world, the combined center of gravity follows it, circling inside the planet's core, relentlessly stirring the mantle—and so, the Earth wobbles in its orbit.

That was the effect I had on Monsieur, disturbing him in his own eternal course. Like the Moon, I rotated around him, always keeping the same face to his ever-changing moods, my presence pulling him first in one direction, then another. Around and around we circled, a strange and terrible dance in darkness. He held me in his gravity and I disturbed his core.

Finally, late one night, as I rested sad and alone in my bath—even after the water had lost all warmth, I felt no urge to withdraw—I realized that Monsieur had done me no favors. All the tutors, all the lessons had produced only one terrible result—I had grown educated enough to experience true despair. I knew too much of life, too much of the world, to accept anything less than all of it—and all of it was what I could not have.

As I lay there, lost in the slow dissolution of my soul, my thoughts devoid of purpose, my mind wandered into territories I believed I had left behind. Suspicion overwhelmed me. I began to wonder on Monsieur's intentions when he left on his solitary walks. Unaware of his true nocturnal purposes, I could only imagine him tangled in the arms of some other street boy, I still saw them from time to time, whenever Monsieur and I went out together. Monsieur must have noticed them as well with his extraordinary awareness, but even to an ordinary mortal the boys of the street were unavoidable— they postured languidly against a lamppost here or the corner of a building there, not-so-discreetly advertising their availability.

Show a bit of calf, bare a sleeveless arm, it was enough—the nocturnal dances were a healthy business in those days. If a boy had looks, if he was wise enough to avoid the ravages of disease, he could survive a while, until he finally grew strong enough to find a place on a fishing boat or cargo vessel or some other useful trade. In that business, a young man's attractiveness dissipated quickly.

I'm sure the boys noticed us as well. Those few who might have remembered me from my days among them must have assumed that I was now serving only a single wealthy patron as his personal toy, but I had no desire to explain or justify my situation to anyone, so I ignored them. But as I said, they could not have escaped the notice of Monsieur.

But when I examined my jealous thoughts, holding them up to the cold light of logic, I fell into a most curious argument with myself. If Monsieur would not want to risk passing his condition on to me, then surely he wouldn't want to expose any of the boys on the street either—but if he had no affection for those fellows, why would he care if they were exposed or not? And if he wasn't out there looking for a bit of horizontal refreshment, then what was he looking for? I did not know about the possible creation of monsters at the time, or I would have been reassured that he was not soliciting the custom of the street.

Once again, Jacob interrupts his narrative, giving me a sly smile.

"Yes, now I know what Monsieur was doing. He was feeding. Unable to satisfy his sexual appetites, his blood lust had surged. Flared. Fortunately, Seattle was a rough seaport then. It still is. Dead bodies were not uncommon. But...Monsieur was careful. He did not need the city plunged into the same kind of panic that later paralyzed London when Jack the Ripper roamed free. I'm sure he feasted well. I am equally sure they never found the bodies..."

"Jack the Ripper—?"

"Sloppy," Jacob says. "Very sloppy."

On that particular night, as the stillness stretched into the last hours before dawn, as I lay cold in my bath, waiting for I don't know what— perhaps even death would have been welcome—finally I heard the sound of the front door and footsteps on the stair. Monsieur had returned.

It was his custom to check to see if I was awake. Sometimes we would share a bit of bread and sausage, cheese and wine before he retired. This night, not finding me in my bed, he came to the bathroom next. Discovering me unexpectedly in the tub, he became alarmed. He put a hand into the water and withdrew it quickly, startled. "My God, it's colder than me. How long have you been lying here?"

"I don't know," I said. "Forever, I think."

My reply further alarmed him—as it revealed my dissociated state of mind. Without regard for my nakedness, Monsieur pulled me to my feet, lifted me from the tub, and wrapped a heavy towel around me. He grabbed another and vigorously rubbed me until my skin was red—my hair, my neck, my shoulders, my arms and back and chest, lower down as well.

When he was finally satisfied that I was dry enough and warm enough, he swaddled me in his own dressing gown. He scooped me up in his arms— I'd known he was strong, I hadn't known he was *that* strong—and carried me to my bed. Once he had settled me among the pillows, he looked at me very sternly. "We cannot continue like this, Jacob, can we?" No, we cannot, I agreed.

He sat down on the edge of the bed. I remember every detail of the moment—how the mattress creaked, how it gave beneath his weight, how I felt myself pulled toward him. He looked away from me then, studied the wainscoting of the wall, stared beyond it as if he was seeing something a thousand miles away.

In the silence that followed, a flurry of emotions swept through me. I felt cautious and skeptical, hopeful and afraid—because even as I feared what he might say next, I hoped for the strength of his wisdom.

And yet, at the same time—I was also beginning to fear Monsieur. Despite his own erratic behaviors, more so now than ever, I still believed in him. But I did not trust his friends. I didn't like the hungry way that some of them looked at me. And if these strange men were his friends, then what did that say about Monsieur? We are known by our friends, are we not?

Finally, Monsieur turned back to me, with such an expression of sadness on his face that I immediately wanted to pull him to me, but I had long since learned not to engage in such open and enthusiastic expressions of affection, for he always pulled back, alarmed. But tonight, he surprised me. He reached out and took my hands, holding them gently between both of his. "Let me ask you this, dear Jacob. Have you given any thought to your future?"

I didn't answer his question, I couldn't—because the future was all that I could think about. That black unknown tomorrow I had been fearing for so long had pushed me beyond anguish into despair. I was facing the terrifying reality that I would finally have to leave this house. Although I had experienced so much comfort and wonder here when I was younger, now there was only distress. The tension between us had become unbearable.

But I couldn't tell him the truth. I couldn't speak at all. Instead, the tears rolled down my cheeks unabated.

I'm certain Monsieur must have understood the source of my despair. If ever it was possible for one person to read another's thoughts, Monsieur must have known mine as clearly as if they were engraved in fire. My feelings were betrayed by the pageant of my expressions.

"Dearest Jacob," he began, "you cannot have missed the confusion and disarray I have been experiencing in my own soul. I have been considering this problem at some length. And—" He stopped himself. The words were painful, even for him. "I have no choice in this. It is for both our sakes. No stop, don't speak—" He put a finger across my lips to keep me from protesting. "Please, Jacob. Let me finish."

I bowed my head in submission. One of the lessons Monsieur had been trying so hard to teach me was that of thinking before speaking. Too often, he said, we open our mouths and release the words that are floating at the very surface of our feelings. We would be better served by holding our tongues and considering our words before we uttered them. We might then make wiser choices. His point was that we must never speak from our emotions, because such outbursts were never rational and rarely wise to voice aloud. This was one of those moments—my protests would have been from my heart, not my brain, even though my brain had already reached the same inevitable conclusion. But I felt I had to protest anyway—because I feared the words that would certainly follow. Monsieur speaking them aloud would give finality to the decision and I wasn't prepared for that. Not yet.

Monsieur waited until I regained some small measure of composure. "Jacob, do not pretend with me. You understand as well as I. We cannot be together anymore. I must send you away from here before we destroy each other.

"Stop now. Stop and listen. Please, Jacob. I need you to understand something. All this time, all these years—these three short years, watching you grow toward manhood, watching you discover the vast horizons of the world around you—they have been a revelation to me. This was something I never expected to have, because of my condition—the opportunity to nurture a child and see him become a worthwhile adult. Do you think I am without feelings? Do you really think I *want* to send you away?"

I didn't answer. I couldn't. He spoke the truth. I hadn't considered his feelings at all, only my own.

"Remember how I caught you? Did you ever wonder how easy it was for me? You thought you were stalking me? On the contrary. I saw you studying me even before you knew what you intended. I watched you with some amusement. Your oh-so-casual approach, your studied nonchalance. You were a terrible thief, Jacob. It's a good thing you did not pursue that career or you would have spent much of the last three years behind bars."

I started to protest. "That's not true. I was—"

Clumsy. And slow. Inept." Monsieur finished the sentence for me, leaving no room for argument. He stared into my eyes. "I saved your life. That wasn't my immediate intention, but I admit I was charmed by your ambition—and yes, amused by you as well. I watched you follow me from a distance and I wondered if that single-minded determination could be put to some practical use. I suspected you might have a heart of some value. Yes, Jacob, you were an experiment—at first. I was curious what you might become if you were nurtured. Later, I realized you were something more. Much more. My mistake. Had I foreseen the journey we would find ourselves embarked upon, had I realized the inevitability of this moment, my rational self would have...would have taken the easier course."

He fell silent a moment, looked away, looked back. "There were opportunities along the way. Many. And I will admit, there were moments when I argued with myself—what am I doing? Why am I letting myself care? My companions in The Community—they made eloquent arguments against you, that you represented an unprecedented danger to myself, first one kind of danger, then another. Not just betrayal, but worse.

"I didn't listen. I thought I knew better. And I believed that if you ever betrayed my trust, I would be able to deal with that situation swiftly and dispassionately. You would have simply disappeared. This is Seattle. No one wonders, no one worries if a street boy vanishes. It happens almost every day. But—

His expression softened as he remembered. "But you never gave me cause. You surprised me, Jacob. More than that, you have shown yourself to be a rare and precious delicacy. I am as proud of you as if I had given birth to you myself.

"You will recall that last month I had my attorney visit. You were not party to that meeting, but I gave him very specific instructions for your future. One of the things I instructed him to do was redraft my will. No, Jacob, don't panic. I am in no danger of death—certainly not any time soon, and probably not for a much longer time than either of us can imagine.

But accidents do happen and I wish to have you provided for in such a case. Should anything untoward happen to me, you will inherit this house and the contents of my various bank accounts. But I promise you that is extremely unlikely. It turns out that my disability, my condition, also makes me very hard to kill. Not impossible, just difficult.

"'But that is not what I need to discuss with you tonight. I have given much thought to our situation and I have come to a decision. It is the right decision. It will be the best thing for both of us. It will not be easy at first, not for you, not for me, but it will be necessary.

"It is time for you to attend the university.

"My attorney has made arrangements with his associates in Boston. They have secured rooms for you near the university and they will manage an endowment that I have provided so that you will have a dependable income. You will not want for the necessities of life. You will have cash in your pocket, enough so that you can enjoy comfortable meals and wear fashionable suits and present yourself as a fine gentleman wherever you go. You will have a line of credit at the largest bookstore in the city. And your tuition at the university will also be guaranteed for as long as you choose to attend. You will have letters of reference from all of your tutors, so the question of your admission will not be an issue.

"There are no conditions on this endowment. You may take it or leave it, as you choose. No, wait—do not answer yet. I said there are no conditions. But I do have a request. Several requests, in fact.

"First, I request that you avoid any actions or behaviors that would bring you to the attention of the police. You must not allow yourself to be tempted to return to your childish habits. I doubt that you will, but I would be terribly disappointed if you did.

"Second, I request that you keep yourself free of disease. You know the ones I mean. I cannot forbid you to enjoy the pleasures of physical intimacy—that would be cruel and inhumane. I ask only that you choose your partners wisely. If you find a partner worthy of your most supreme affections, you will have my blessing. You deserve a lifetime of happiness, it is such a rare commodity. No, Jacob, please let me finish. I know what you're going to say, it is not necessary, and I cannot have you bound by an impossible promise, it would only make you unhappy and resentful.

"Third, and this is the most important of my requests—I request that you study ferociously at the university, whatever interests you the most. Philosophy, history, science, economics, medicine, law—any or all of those things would please me. But not religion. There is no profit in that. It is an intellectual dead end. But study anything else, everything else, and study it with enthusiasm and passion. Make yourself knowledgeable. Make yourself wise. Make yourself an expert in all the things that will give you power to manipulate the circumstances of the world.

"My fourth request is that you write to me regularly—but no more than once a month. I do not want you to feel beholden, and as you know, I am not one for letters, but I would like to keep apprised of your progress in your studies and your observations of the lives around you. From time to time, I may offer my own advice and suggestions to you. You may heed my words or disregard them as you wish.

"And that brings me to my fifth request. I request that you stay away from this house and my acquaintance for at least ten years. You may not return before your twenty-seventh birthday. You may return any time after that—but only if you have not found a permanent partner to share your life. Because under such a circumstance, a return visit would be disruptive to everyone involved.

"If I am not living in this house, and I do not think I will be, despite the many pleasant hours we have shared here, I will not be hard to find. My representatives will have a sealed envelope for you, with information on how to contact me if I have relocated. It is very likely that I will have. With my...condition, I find it necessary to move at least once a decade."

When he finished, I did not speak for a very long time. There was too much to assimilate. Finally, I said, "I will go. I will obey all your conditions—"

"Not conditions. Requests."

"But—"

He touched my cheek. "What is it, Jacob?"

"May I make a request as well?"

He nodded.

"I request that—no, that is not fair. Never mind." I waved it away as if I had not spoken.

Monsieur smiled. "I know what you were going to ask. You were going to ask me not to bring some other boy into this house, not to replace you with another. And I know why you stopped yourself as well—because you realized that would have been an unfair thing to ask.

"You don't have to worry, Jacob. It's not in my nature to bring boys into my house, one after the other, fall in love with them—and then send them off to university. You have been...a unique adventure. I do not think my heart could stand another such."

I nodded and smiled, feeling better already that he understood me so well. A thought occurred to me. "But Monsieur—without me here, who will take care of you?"

He shook his head. "You needn't worry about that either. The gentlemen of The Community are not without resources. We have acquired a small team of trusted associates who understand us and who tend to our specific daytime needs. I shall arrange matters with them. If necessary, I can close up this house and stay at—well, never mind, you don't need to know about that now. I will be all right."

A week later, I boarded a ship for San Francisco. From there, I traveled east on the newly completed transcontinental railroad to New York, a challenging and rigorous journey, two weeks long. But finally I arrived and found myself caught up in the heat and bustle of an amazing city—so amazing I was tempted to abandon my journey to Boston and stay there instead. But after seeing the condition of the young men strolling the streets, I knew I should not succumb to that idea. I headed north and a few days later completed my enrollment in the university.

Jacob stops talking. Lost in thought, perhaps, remembering a world that no longer exists in memory and barely exists in photographs.

"I think I understand—"

"Yes. He was waiting for me to ripen. He was waiting for me to become a worthy companion. He could have had me any time, but he loved me too much for that. Instead, he wanted me to have enough experience of life that I would learn to be my own man, so that each of us would have our own wealth of experience and knowledge to share. He wanted me to earn my immortality. He needed me to become a true partner—interesting enough to be worthy of a life together.

"But more than that, he wanted—perhaps even needed—a companion with proficiency. The world was changing faster than The Community could keep up. Monsieur recognized that. Staying current in science and medicine and economics is a necessary survival skill for an immortal. And style as well. Think about it—being out of fashion is dangerous. It makes you conspicuous."

"Ahh." A glance at my watch. "Dawn is coming."

"I know. I can already smell the changes in the air."

"I want to hear the rest of your story."

"Yes, of course you do. You want me to tell you how his letters suddenly ceased, and how I came back to Seattle to discover he had died in a fire—a daytime arson. You want to know about my inheritance and how I found The Community again, and how I finally did get turned, and who the arsonists were and what happened to them afterward, and why I had to leave Seattle.

"And after that, you'll want to hear about my experiences in Europe during the Great War. For a person like myself, a war can be marvelous fun. You'll certainly want to know what it's like to kill and feed. All you short-timers ask about that. But most of all, more than anything else, you'll have me speak about how I choose my...victims. Yes, I suppose that's an accurate word."

Jacob touches my arm. I do not recoil. I do not pull back.

"I'm only immortal. I'm not immoral. I don't feed on innocents. Neither do most of the other gentlemen of The Community. Here's a clue. Have you noticed something about this part of the world? Have you noticed there has been a significant decline in violent crimes? Think about that and wonder.

"One more thing," he says. "A secret—about the monsters, why they happen. Young blood tastes better. More than that, the younger the blood, the more alive it makes us, the more it keeps us vibrant. So yes, that was the initial attraction for Monsieur. He saw me as a puppy, a tasty snack. And yes—that also explains why so many of the monsters are so quick to create more. They can't help themselves—they don't know the difference between feeding and fucking. And that, my friend, is why the rest of us work so hard to keep them from happening and kill them when they do." He flashes his teeth. "And they taste good too. Vampire blood is the best."

A nervous laugh. And then I realize he isn't joking.

"Oh."

"Yes," he says. "Now you know what's wrong with your stories. All of you."

He stands. I stand quickly to keep up.

"Will I see you again?"

"I don't know. Will you?"

"I, uh—"

He cocks his head curiously. "You what?" Before I can answer, he waves the question away. "Never mind. I know what you were going to ask. You always do, all of you. The answer is no. Not today. And maybe never. Today was just...an interview."

"An interview? Did I pass?"

"Maybe."

"And what do I get if I do?"

He smiles. "Maybe someday, I'll check back and see what you've become."

"That's it?"

"That's all there is. Right now, anyway. I'm waiting to see how the fruit ripens."

And then he's gone, disappearing into the last of the darkness, as if he's made of shadow himself.

I expect someday I'll see Jacob again. I wonder what he'll offer. I wonder if I'll accept.

I toss the pages across the table at the others. "And that, my dear little puppies—*that* is how you tell a vampire story."

The Thing
In The Back Yard

That Pesky Dan Goodman is not a bad person. He has a good heart. He's well-intentioned. And I just might kill him anyway. Every time he wanders through my life, the unintended consequences are always disastrous.

Always.

I ran into him at Bob's Big Boy in Toluca Lake. It's a local landmark. Weekends, the parking lot is filled with classic cars and the wait time for a table is an hour. It's a coffee shop decorated with as much history and ambience as Los Angeles is capable of—plaques and photos dating all the way back to 1936. The food ranges in quality from meh to meh-plus. Be grateful it won't kill you. But this is one of the few places that still knows how to make the classic Big Boy double-deck hamburger, of which all other double-deck hamburgers (including the Big Mac) are mere imitations.

For me, the Big Boy hamburger is comfort food, because Bob's is where my dad used to take me on special occasions. We called it "Big Bob's." So it's where I take my son when we need a special night. I don't always order the Big Boy anymore, because now it falls into the category of one of those things that you eat until you hate yourself. The food coma hits before you can get to the parking lot.

Never mind. This time, I had an afternoon meeting in Burbank. I was feeling a bit peckish—that's a strange word to me, an English term, I don't really get it, but never mind, I've always wanted to use it in a sentence and now that I've done so, I can die happy. It'll never happen again.

I was hungry and I stopped in for a salad. I like their blue cheese dressing. Or is it bleu cheese? However you spell it, it's only good when it's fresh.

And that's when and where and why That Pesky Dan Goodman found me. But then, he always finds me in restaurants. This is why I carry antacids with me. And too often, the meeting ends with me picking up the check for both of us. I think he has a tracking device in my wallet.

He plopped himself down opposite. "May I join you?"

"You just did." I looked square across at him. "And no, you may not nominate me for the presidency of the Los Angeles Science Fantasy Society or the Board of Directors of any other organization. And whatever else you're going to ask, the answer is already no. So don't bother asking."

He said, "Okay." And maybe I was going to be lucky. Maybe the conversation was over. But he waved at the waiter. "I'll have an iced tea, please."

Back to me. "You look annoyed about something."

"Yeah, a little—"

I was annoyed—annoyed at having my private time interrupted. I politely closed my laptop, I'd finish proofreading the manuscript later. But I was too courteous to say that I was annoyed at the intrusion. That was my first mistake.

"Can I help?"

And this is how the Goodman trap is sprung—with some innocent remark that leads into what looks like a harmless conversation. And I, not watching where I'm going, step right into the bear trap hidden beneath the pine needles.

"We've been having a burglary problem. We think we know who it is, but we can't prove it."

"How are they getting in?"

"The alley in back. They're coming over the wall. Three meter high cinder block affair, but there's a telephone pole at one corner, so all someone has to do is climb it."

"I'm sorry to hear that. I hope you didn't lose anything important."

"We had a PlayStation stolen. Some CDs and DVDs. Those are replaceable. But they took my Z1U."

"Ouch. What's a Z1U?"

"Six years ago, it was one of the best professional-level HD video cameras you could buy. Five kilobucks. It's still a great camera. Or would be if I still had it. Now I've got a box of tapes that I have no way to transfer to the hard drive. It'll cost another two or three thousand dollars to pick up a used or refurbished one."

"You said you know who it is. Can't you get it back?"

"We can't prove it. We think it's one of my son's friends. Ex-friends. Someone the dog knows."

"Dogzilla?"

"Yeah. She only bites strangers. She bit one guy who tried to sneak in our back gate while we were cleaning out the garage. A week later, he had the gall to come to my front door with his doctor's bill—until I showed him the video surveillance. He was definitely on my property."

"So you've got a dog, you've got video, and you've still got stuff disappearing?"

"Yeah."

"You need an on-site security force."

"I wish—"

There. That was the sound of the steel jaws of the trap snapping shut, but I was too busy stuffing salad into my face to hear the clank.

"Hmm," said Goodman. That should have been my second warning. The way he said, "Hmm."

"What?"

"Nothing," he said. "Just a weird idea."

"Not garden gnomes," I said.

"No. Not garden gnomes. They're very territorial. And if you have cats or small dogs, they don't get along. Especially if the dog pees on one." He sipped at his iced tea. "And while they're great for rodent control, unless you bring in an armed squadron they're lousy at security." Another sip. "And then there's the noise problem. They drink too much and they like to party all night long. That's if you have only male gnomes. If you bring in a few female gnomes, the party usually gets quiet sometime after midnight. Although...on a quiet night, you can still hear a lot of grunting and moaning."

"You're speaking from experience?"

"I live in Burbank. You know all those bungalow units they built in the twenties and thirties? Where all the little old ladies live now? They think gnomes are cute. That's what they get when they're not allowed to have more than three cats. They put out gnomes."

"Oh, yeah."

"One year, the gnomes and the lawn flamingos next door got into a terrible fight—" He shook his head. "The SWAT team had to come in and impound them all. No one was injured, but it could have been a lot worse."

"There's probably a story in that."

"Disney already owns it. Scheduled for summer after next. Working title is *Gnome on the Range*. But that might change. Anyway—" He paused while the waiter refilled his tea. "—let's talk about your problem."

"Right. No gnomes."

"Do you have a running stream on your property? A koi pond? A pool? With a waterfall?"

"I've got a pool. No waterfall. Why?"

"Fairies. They like water, even one of those little Zen waterfalls would be enough. You could bring in a few fairies."

"And what good would that do? It'd be like having sociopathic dragonflies with ADHD."

"More like cosplay hummingbirds, but yes, fairies can be problematic. On the other hand, if they like you, your flowers bloom, the birds don't eat the fruit off your trees, stuff like that. They bring you a lot of good luck. Little things mostly. They get along with some cats and dogs, but it depends on the animal. It also depends on the person. If they don't like you, you bump your shins a lot, bees sting you, and it's a bad idea to go barefoot. Unless you're looking for Legos."

"Sounds like a high-maintenance relationship. That's not me. I raised a teenager, remember? That put me eight years behind schedule. And still counting."

That Pesky Dan Goodman grinned. "You knew the job was dangerous when you took it."

"No, I didn't. They don't put warning labels on children. And nobody says don't do it. 'It'll be fun,' they say. 'You'll be good at it,' they say. 'Your life won't be complete without children.' Hah! Ask a parent and they'll tell you—'You go to strangle them in their crib and they're so cute when they're sleeping, you think, well maybe just one more day.' Hah! And then they turn into teenagers. The whole thing was my mother's revenge. 'I can hardly wait till you have kids of your own—' It's like living with a chronic disease."

"But you love your kid—"

"Of course, I do. He's a Martian, but he's *my* Martian. And he's all the good luck I need. So I don't want fairies, thank you."

"No. You need something bigger."

"Uhh, no thanks. Do you know how much it costs to feed Dogzilla? What are you suggesting?" I should have shut my mouth after the second sentence. I should have gnawed off my leg and hopped away on the other. I should have paid the bill and run for the exit.

"There's more to the ecosystem than fairies and gnomes, you know."

"My neighborhood isn't zoned for dragons," I said. "Not even fire-lizards."

"No, I was thinking of something more...more down-to-earth."

"More down-to-earth? I'm not sure I like the sound of that. What are you suggesting? Zombies? Ghouls? No thanks. I had a vampire for a roommate once. Not fun. Not fun at all."

"Really...?"

"Long story. Some other time." I added, "Day sleeper."

"Of course. Anyway, I have this friend. A young guy, just starting out in life. His name is Emmett-Murray."

"Is he a redhead?"

"Very funny. No. He's half-troll. On his mother's side."

"Huh?"

"I said, he's half-troll—"

"I heard you. It's still sinking in. What was his father?"

"Human, he says."

"Hard to believe. Have you ever seen a female troll?"

"Don't be judgmental. It takes all kinds."

"Pesky. Look at me. I'm not as stupid as I look. You might want to Google how trolls mate. I have. That's why I don't write horror stories. There's nothing that can scare me anymore." I looked across at him. "Have you met the father?"

"He's deceased."

"Ah. Never mind. You just explained it."

Peskydang waved it off. "Anyway, Emmett-Murray needs a place to stay."

"Not in my house."

"No. Your back yard. You have a pool, a garden. You have a lawn. You have a lot of space there. And Emmett-Murray doesn't take up much room. He's only about yay-high." Pesky held a hand at waist-level. "He's a little guy, practically a munchkin."

"Yeah? Have you ever seen a munchkin eat?"

"Don't be racist."

"I'm not. I'm just—Never mind. I can't win that argument."

"Let me bring him by. You'll meet him."

"No, really. I don't see how—"

Pesky held up a hand to stop me. "Just meet him. Trust me on this."

"Last time I trusted you, I nearly got my passport revoked—"

"Clerical error. You did get it straightened out, didn't you?"

"Only because my sister is on first-name terms with our congressman."

"Well, there, you see? No harm, no foul."

"I don't think you're getting my point."

"Sure I am. You need security. Emmett-Murray needs a quiet little corner. You won't even know he's there."

"No, I really don't think this is a good idea—"

"It's a *great* idea, I'll bring him by Saturday. No obligation. Just meet him, he's a sweetheart. You'll love him."

"Pesky—"

"Oops. Look at the time. Gotta run. See you this weekend. Trust me, this is a win-win for everybody."

"I've heard that before, too—"

But he had already slid out of the booth. Leaving me with the check. Again.

And that's how I ended up with a troll—a half-troll—living in my back yard.

To be fair, Emmett-Murray was a cute little guy. He looked a bit like a munchkin, a bit like a gnome, but mostly like a Mini-Me Sasquatch. He stood waist-high, barely a smidge over a meter tall. And he had the kind of cabbage-patch grumpy-face that made him almost adorable. He was *cute.*

And I'm a sucker for cute.

They arrived after sunset. Peskydang thought it best to be discreet, so I let them in through the back gate, the one that opens onto the alley. Pesky made introductions. Emmett-Murray didn't offer to shake hands. He'd already learned how fragile human bones could be. He just held up a paw in a high-five gesture. I gave it a friendly slap.

"Thank you," he said, "for letting me stay with you." He spoke with an endearing froggy-gravelly voice.

"Um, that hasn't been decided yet—"

"I promise I'll take care of your gopher problem. And I won't eat your dog."

"Uh, thanks. That's reassuring."

"I can dig a hole over there, behind the tree, for my poop."

Pesky interrupted, holding up a large orange box. "I think he'd rather you use these hazmat bags."

"Oh, okay. I can do that."

"See?" said Pesky. "No problem at all."

Emmett-Murray puffed up his chest. "I can growl ferociously at anyone trying to come over your fence. How's this?" He opened his mouth as wide as he could—kind of like one of those kitchen trash cans where you step on the pedal and the whole top flips open—and let loose with a sound somewhere between an air-raid siren and a grizzly bear on the receiving end of unlubricated and unwelcome anal intercourse.

The transformer on the power pole exploded in a shower of sparks. And all of the avocados blasted sideways off the tree, ripe or not, splattering across the yard and the wall and the side of the garage. Several splashed into the pool where the water was already roiling in uneasy waves. Dogzilla, who had been cautiously sniffing from a distance, yelped and ran, disappearing with a crash through the doggy door into the house, probably ending up cowering in the far corner under the bed.

"Um, look, guys. I don't think this is such a good idea—"

"Oh, the dog will get used to him. Emmett-Murray likes dogs."

"That's what I'm afraid of—"

"Oh, no. I won't eat your dog. I already promised."

"Yes, that's very reassuring. Pesky, can I have a word with you, please?" I led him aside to a place I hoped was out of earshot. I glanced back. Emmett-Murray was sniffing the corner of yard. "Pesky, I know you have a big heart. I don't. I need my privacy."

"Only for a few days, a week at most. Two. Until we can find something more permanent for him."

"How about your place?"

"I'm only allowed a cat. Maybe two if they're clean. You know that."

"I really can't do this—"

"Only for a little while. You'll never know he's here. He'll dig himself into the ground and look like just another boulder in your rock garden."

"Right. A big shaggy boulder."

"But think about it. Your burglar will come over the fence, Emmie will open his mouth, he'll let loose one of those roars, and that'll be the last you'll ever have to worry about theft—"

We were interrupted by sirens. Three cruisers, a fire engine, and an ambulance. Two minutes. Impressive. The cops came carefully through the back gate, guns drawn, shouting. "Police!" and "Freeze!" A chopper moved into position, circling overhead, its finger of light prowling across the yard.

Officer McBride recognized me immediately. "You good?"

"False alarm," I replied.

McBride shouted back over his shoulder, "Clear!"

"Can I lower my hands?"

He nodded and holstered his gun. The other cops holstered theirs, but slower.

"How's the boy?" McBride asked.

"Keeping his nose clean."

"Good. Glad to hear he survived his teens. You, too. Some doubt there for a while."

"Yep," I agreed.

Abruptly, the chopper's beam found the darkest corner of the yard and stayed there, revealing Emmett-Murray—illuminating him in stark relief as he pawed quietly at the ground. The cops froze. All six of them. Their hands went back to their guns. McBride spoke first. "Is that—? What is that?"

"It's a half-troll. On his mother's side."

"Is it yours?"

"Uh, no. He's just visiting."

"But he's on your property. And it looks like he's digging a burrow."

"Oh, um—"

Another officer stepped up. I recognized her face, didn't remember her name. I had to glance at her name-badge. Benson. She didn't look friendly.

"Do you have a license for that troll?"

"He's not mine."

"He's in your yard."

"Okay, fine. Do you want to take him away?"

Officer Benson glanced around to the other officers. To the firemen. To the paramedics crowding in beside them. They all shook their heads. She looked back to me. "All right...." She took a breath. She went to McBride and the two of them whispered together for a few moments. Finally, she returned. "We're not going to do anything tonight. We'll give you some time to sort this out, but we'll be back in 30 days. If he's not licensed by then—"

"You'll take him then?"

"—you'll be subject to civil penalties and fines."

"He's not mine."

"He's in your yard."

"Not by my choice." I looked around. Pesky was nowhere to be seen. Houdini could not have effected a better escape.

"You realize we're going to have to report this."

"I know."

She handed me her card. "I have to give you my number. It's policy. I hope you don't need to use it. I really do not want to come back."

By the time the police finally left, Emmett-Murray had dug himself a nice little burrow. He was almost invisible. And I was emotionally exhausted. Okay, maybe a few days. I could earn some karma points. I'd track down Pesky tomorrow and have him find another placement for Emmett-Murray, but for the moment not even the cops were coming into my back yard.

I had to admit, there was a certain sense of security in that.

And what with one thing and another, I couldn't find That Pesky Dan Goodman even if I laid out a trail of hundred dollar bills and jelly doughnuts. His phone message said he was off on another retreat—a very appropriate word in this case.

So I told myself I'd been through worse and reminded myself of my mantra for difficult situations. Grit (my teeth) and bear it.

There were adjustments to be made, of course.

I didn't warn our regular pool man in time. The new pool guy charged an extra $50 a month.

Dogzilla refused to go in the back yard again. That meant she had to be taken out front to pee. And that meant I had to interrupt my schedule several times a day to make sure she could go. On a leash. Because "Come back now" and "Go inside" were no longer in her vocabulary. And she spent a lot of time curled up in her blanket. Whimpering.

And now, there were some very odd smells coming from the back yard, like someone barbecuing a skunk, or a Volkswagen. On those days, we closed all the windows and turned the fans to high. It helped. A little.

One week passed, then another. Pesky remained unreachable. But he'd told the truth about one thing. Little Emmett-Murray kept mostly to himself. Except for the strange smells and the weird howling noises at three in the morning and the occasional unexplained seismic thump and the weird mound growing in the corner where he burrowed and the dead patches of grass around it, we never would have known he was there.

I live on a dead-end street for the quiet. And most of my neighbors are fairly calm people—especially since the six wannabe terrorists in the house to the north grew up and moved away.

On the other side of the alley behind my back wall, there's a two story office building. The windows of the dentist's office provide a pretty clear view down into my yard, so I do my skinny-dipping at night. I can float on my back and watch the stars—although there are nowhere near as many visible anymore due to light pollution.

I hadn't seen little Emmett-Murray since he'd burrowed in. I assumed he was still hibernating or whatever it was he was doing when he was curled up like a rock. But no, he wasn't hibernating.

After a deep underwater lap, starting at the shallow end and heading diagonally across the length of the pool, I breached at the far side, grabbing a serious breath—and screamed in surprise at the unexpected thing that was standing there.

Little Emmett was not so little anymore. He was a huge dark lump, a hulking blob. I fell back into the water, shrieking and floundering, came up choking and gasping, grabbed for the deck, and coughed out a couple of soup bowls of chlorine and phlegm.

"Are you all right?" he gravelled.

"Uh, yeah. I'm fine. I will be. Thanks for asking. You just startled me."

From my vantage point, treading water in the deep end, Little Emmett looked to be chest-high now. He'd lost a lot of his baby fur, leaving behind a patchy mass of uneven hair and oily skin. He looked like an orangutan with mange. Only not as attractive. His posture was ominous and his features were solidifying into a disturbing frown. Almost a glare.

I felt suddenly uneasy. I kicked away from the side, turned over, and swam quickly back to the shallow end. I could feel his eyes on me the whole distance. I grabbed my towel, wrapped it around me quickly, and dripped all the way to the back door of the house and into the kitchen. "That was weird," I said to no one. "Just weird."

I grabbed my phone, dialed with shaking hands, but Pesky was still in retreat. Not a retreat, more of a rout. His message started with that annoying *doo-dah-dee* disconnect tone to discourage automatic-dialers, then went to a deep radio-announcer voice saying, "Thank you for calling. All of our operators are busy right now. Your call is important to us and will be answered in the order received. Click-buzzzzzz." Ha-ha. Very cute. And as useful as a bronze tribble.

By the time Pesky got back from wherever he was retreating to, three weeks had passed and Little Emmett was almost as tall as I was. Pesky came by, looked at him, and nodded approvingly. "Ahh, yes. I get it. He's thriving."

"Thriving?"

"Of course. You should understand. When a child, or any young mammal, is placed in an emotionally sterile environment, they don't grow as fast as they would if they were being nurtured by an appropriate caregiver. It's called 'failure to thrive.'"

"So you're saying I'm a good parent for a troll?"

"Half-troll. On his mother's side. And yes."

"I've had nothing to do with him. I ignore him. In fact, I resent him. I resent the fact that he's here." I turned to Emmett-Murray. "Don't take it personally. It's not about you. It's about the loss of my privacy." Back to That Pesky Dan Goodman. "I resent that you plopped him into my back yard, *against my wishes*, and then disappeared for a month—"

"Three weeks and two days. And yes, resenting him was exactly what he needed. In his previous placement, they were cuddling him. You don't cuddle trolls."

"They're not exactly cuddle toys, you know."

"The more you resented him in your back yard, the bigger he grew. Now you have a *real* security system."

"I didn't want him here in the first place."

"You needed him. He needed you. It's a perfect match. Stop complaining. That could be dangerous. Trolls are subject to gigantism."

"So you want me to love him—?"

"If you don't want him to outgrow your yard, yes, that would be a good idea. You should be happy. Your collection of Mickey Mouse Fantasia figurines is safer than ever."

"That's not the issue—"

"Well, it should be. You had a problem. I found you a solution. Now you can stop worrying about burglars. You should be thanking me. You're an ungrateful ass."

"Yes, I am. I want him out of here. The dog is terrified to go out. She's peeing in the house. And the neighbors are complaining. And in a week, the police will be back with citations and warrants and subpoenas and god knows what else. You said this placement was only temporary until you found something more permanent for him."

"Okay, okay!" Pesky backed away, holding up his hands as if to ward me off. "Just don't piss him off." Behind me, I could feel the subsonic rumble of Emmett-Murray growling.

"What about pissing me off? Look!" I pointed around the yard. "He leaves footprints five centimeters deep already."

Pesky frowned. "What is that in inches?"

"Two. Two inches deep."

"I wish you hadn't gone metric—"

"Liberia, Myanmar, and the United States are the only three countries that haven't. I'm learning how to think international." I caught my breath. "And I wish you'd stop changing the subject. Look at my yard. He's cracked the pool decking in three places. His burrow is turning into a small mountain. And he's uprooted what's left of the avocado tree. This is—this is—this is just—" I threw my hands in the air in a gesture of helplessness. "I admit it, I've run out of words."

"I get it," said Pesky. "You're frustrated—"

"Frustrated? Is that what you think this is?"

"Glrgh—"

Slowly, I removed my hands from Pesky's throat. "I want him out of here. I want him out of here now. I want my life and my privacy back. I never asked for him. I never asked for this—" I waved my hand around at the war zone that used to be my back yard. "This was all because you don't understand the word *no!*"

"All right, I'll see what I can do—"

"No. You'll do it. Tonight—"

"Tomorrow at the latest. Do you know how hard it is to place a troll—"

"Half-troll," I corrected. "On his mother's side. And I want him out of here."

Pesky looked past my shoulder. "Did you hear that, Emmett-Murray?"

"But I don't want to leave," he whined. Like a garbage disposal eating marbles. "I like it here."

"I can see that," Pesky said. "But I'll bet I can find you a place where people hate you even more."

"I don't know," grumbled Emmett-Murray. He pointed at me. "This one treats me right. The way I want to be treated."

"Oh, crap. I give up. What do I have to do? Burn the house down?"

"I wouldn't advise it," Pesky started to say—but Emmett-Murray interrupted quickly, clapping his huge hands in delight, booming like a Kodo drummer. "Would you? Would you? I like fires. Big fires. The bigger the better."

"No, no no no no no no. Out of the question. Don't even think about it. Don't even think about thinking about it. Pesky, get him out of here!"

Pesky looked helpless. "I'll have to rent a truck—"

"I'll help you pay for it!" I stalked back to the house, grumbling and swearing in every language I knew, including several dialects of Pascal, Java, C++, and Assembler.

Grabbed the laptop and started Googling. Eviction. Ejectment. Pest control. Troll removal. Exterminators—

The problem was that despite my being the property owner, I had limited legal rights. There's this thing about squatters. They're like vampires. If you invite them in, you're doomed. With trolls, it's even worse because trolls are considered an endangered species. So you're not allowed to interfere with their existence in any way, shape, manner, or form.

And while I hadn't exactly invited Emmett-Murray in—Pesky had mostly abandoned him here—there was an implied contract in existence. Security services in exchange for a place to burrow. According to some of the horror stories on the Web, a good lawyer could establish that Emmett-Murray had more right to stay on my land than I did. As long as he deterred intruders, he was fulfilling his obligation.

Essentially, this: if a troll doesn't want to leave, there's not much you can do about it. And the more you nurture a troll—the more you resent him—the more he thrives, the bigger he gets. You can go out on the patio and stand and stare and hate him intensely and watch him grow five centimeters per hour.

The police came by on the thirtieth day. Pesky still hadn't found a truck rental that would haul a troll for less than three thousand dollars, and another thousand in mandatory insurance—and at the rate Emmett-Murray was growing, we had to find something soon or even an eighteen-wheeler cattle-hauler wasn't going to be big enough. Officer Benson knocked on the front door, McBride stood politely behind her. She had a clipboard with a thick sheaf of papers.

She started off with "maintaining a public nuisance" and ended up with "failure to remove hazardous waste material." She added complaints from the neighbors and then worked her way through a long litany of legal horrors, including damage to the local sewage system and other utilities, various zoning abuses, endangering the neighborhood, failure to secure appropriate licenses and permits, failure to neuter—Oh, yeah? You try it! Be my guest!—failure to abide by state animal control regulations, violations of the Endangered Species Act, and various federal statutes, regulations, and restrictions, all warranting further investigation by the Environmental Protection Agency.

"Sign here, please." She pushed the clipboard and a pen toward me. "Your signature acknowledges that you have been served and that you understand the consequences of failure to comply."

"I've been trying to comply—" I stopped myself. "Look, I acknowledge that what I have in my back yard is a suburban horror story, okay? I'm afraid to leave my house because he says he likes fires. I called my lawyer. She hung up on me. I can't find another lawyer. They just laugh and say, 'Whoa. You *do* have a problem.' So what do you suggest? What can I *do?* I mean, aside from just abandoning the house and fleeing out of state—"

"That won't help. You can be extradited." She sighed. "I'm not unsympathetic but you let him burrow in. The responsibility is yours."

"I didn't *let* him. He was abandoned here. Doesn't the state have some agency or something? Some way to remove him? I mean, this can't be the first time a troll has settled in somewhere he's not welcome."

She shuffled her papers. "According to this, he's only a half-troll—"

"On his mother's side, I know."

"—and that complicates things. Is he covered by the laws of the reservation? Or is he covered by human laws? It depends on his tribe, whether or not they want to take responsibility. Usually, they don't. It depends on his parentage and his DNA. It depends on a lot of things. The legal processes could drag on for years. The law is still trying to sort these issues out and until we get a Supreme Court ruling, nobody can say for sure."

I sagged. Beaten.

Officer Benson wasn't without feelings. She saw how close to despair I was. She looked to McBride. He nodded. She turned back to me.

"Look," she said. "I'm not supposed to say this. This is off the record, okay?"

"Okay."

"But if you can get him to leave on his own, all this paperwork" —she held up the thick sheaf of forms— "all of this would magically disappear. Because nobody really wants to pursue this. Because pursuing it would mean some agency or other would have to take responsibility. And nobody wants to go there. So, if you can figure out a solution to this problem, if you can get him to leave on his own, you're pretty much off the hook." Then she added, "Just don't file a missing-troll report. Please? Because nobody's going to go looking for him. I can guarantee that."

I took a deep breath. I even made an effort to straighten and meet her gaze. "Thank you. Thank you for that."

"But you gotta do it quickly." Again, she held up the clipboard. "Once this stuff starts working its way through the system—it'll be death by a thousand paper cuts. Dipped in battery acid."

"Okay, yes. Thank you."

As soon as they left, I tried calling Pesky—

Doo-dah-dee! "Thank you for calling. All of our operators are busy right now—"

The thing I hate about cell phones is that you cannot slam them down into the cradle when you are frustrated. You can slam them down onto the countertop, but that just shatters the screen. It's (you should pardon the pun) counter-productive.

By now, little Emmett-Murray was three meters tall. His hair, what was left of it, was coarse and patchy—and curly. He looked like he was covered with a bad case of pubic hair. His expression had hardened into a permanent glower. Most of the time, he was a large lump burrowed into the earth—the cinder block wall separating my yard from the next was leaning precariously outward and would probably topple into the neighbor's patio in a day or three—but occasionally Emmett-Murray could be seen wandering restlessly around the yard, frowning and rumbling and squinty-glaring at the ground.

It wasn't like he was searching for something. It was more like he was pacing out his territory. From time to time, he would stop and stare at the cinder block wall, as if he could stare right through it, as if he wanted to knock it down, as if he wanted to own the neighbors' yards too.

Back to the laptop—to Google troll behaviors.

Oh, crap.

I did not sleep that night. I didn't even try going to bed. I just paced around the house—the human version of Emmett-Murray's restless circuit.

"I'm smart," I told myself. "I'm smarter than the average troll. I should be able to solve this. This isn't the worst thing that ever happened in my life—" I had to stop for a moment and consider that sentence. No, it wasn't the worst thing I'd ever experienced. Not even in the top five. "And I'm still standing. So I should be able to handle this. I'm smart enough, right? Right? I just have to outthink the situation."

See, that's the thing about writing. On paper, the pauses don't show. In real life, it's a never-ending series of long pauses. It's a maze of twisty little passages, with dead ends, locked doors, and pitfalls. Not to mention the occasional concealed tiger-pit with punji sticks at the bottom. You keep banging your head, your whole body, into barriers of all kinds—floors, ceilings, brick walls, until either they or you break open and you find something that looks like a solution. Writers are people who believe there is always a solution. (Successful writers, anyway. Unsuccessful ones never find one, so they never finish. Among other reasons.)

The point is, the reality of a situation is never as malleable as the description of it.

Okay, start with the obvious. Deal with it head-on.

I went out into the back yard. It looked gloomier than ever—twilight even though it was only afternoon. Do trolls have so much antigravitas that even photons avoid them? Emmett-Murray was standing motionless before the cinder block wall that separated the back yard from the alley, staring at it, frowning, rumbling to himself. I could feel the vibrations of the ground through the soles of my boots. I now had to wear heavy boots to go out into the back yard.

"Don't like wall," Emmett-Murray said. "Blocks my view." He looked a lot bulkier than he had just two or three days before. Pesky would have said he was filling out nicely.

"I need the wall," I said. "Please don't knock it down."

"It's in the way." He assembled his sentence slowly.

That was the other thing—the bigger a troll gets, the more he hardens. His brain processes get slower. His language abilities deteriorate.

"Umm, Emmett?"

He swiveled his huge head around to look down at me, his expression frozen in ferocity. "Yah?"

"Look, I know I did you a big favor, letting you stay here. But I need— um, I'm going to—I need to do some remodeling now. So I have to ask you to leave. Please. You'll have to find some other place to stay."

He ignored me. He looked at what was left of my house behind me. The roof over the patio had collapsed sometime during the night and the kitchen wall now sagged as if it was melting. "House blocks my view too."

"Did you hear me? I'm asking you to leave. Please."

He looked down at me again, an expression both implacable and challenging. Ugly. "I like it here."

"Emmett, you can't stay."

"Yes, I can." He frowned in thought. "You can't...make me go. I have... rights. We made a deal. I have to keep my word."

"I didn't make any deal. Pesky did—"

"Still counts. I have...a job."

My neck was starting to hurt from looking up at him. "But I have rights too, Emmett. I'm the property owner. And you can't stay here without my permission."

He shook his head. "I like it here." He turned away, as if that was his final word on the subject.

"Emmett—?"

"Go away now, you. No more talk." He stared at the back wall again. "Ugly, very ugly."

Okay...

So that wasn't going to work.

I headed back into the house. I had to go around the side to get to the front, because the back door wouldn't open anymore—because the kitchen wall was leaning sideways and the door was jammed in its frame.

I made myself a cup of tea.

While the tea was cooling, I fixed myself a rum and Coke. Malibu coconut rum and a twist of lime. You put the lime in the coconut, you drink it all up. It's called a Hairy Nilsson. If you use diet Coke, it's a half-Nilsson.

The tea remained forgotten in the microwave.

I stood there in my kitchen, in the dark, leaning against the now-crumbling marble counter, brooding, thinking, pondering, considering, rationalizing, hating—

That was the problem. The more I hated him, the more he thrived.

I should stop hating him.

Right.

I should go out, give him a big effusive hug, pinch his cheeks and tell him he has a *shana punim* and gush like a fanboy at a *Star Trek* convention. If I did that every day, how long would it take for him to grow disgusted?

No. It wouldn't work. He'd know it was an act. He'd just get taller. How big do trolls grow anyway? Some researchers claimed that trolls could grow as tall as five to eight meters. The Norwegians said the ancestral beasts were even bigger.

The noise of the back wall coming down startled me out of my reverie.

"It was in the way," Emmett-Murray explained. "It blocked my view. Of the alley." He thought for a moment, scratching himself in various places. "I will stack the blocks for you. So you can use them again."

"Thank you," I mumbled. And staggered back around to the front of the house and inside.

I was not insured for a troll infestation. And trolls were not considered an act of god either. Hell, no. It didn't matter. The insurance company had already sent me a notice of cancellation anyway. As soon as the damage started spreading to the neighbors' lots, the lawsuits would be inevitable.

Maybe I could get my lot rezoned as a troll-ranch? No, that wouldn't work. A pig-farmer would be more popular in this neighborhood—and the last one had left seventy-four years ago.

Flashes from the back yard caught my attention. I peered out the window in the broken back door. A carload of teenagers was just easing past the hole in the wall. Two of them were leaning out and snapping pictures with their cell phones.

"I should charge them for that—" I started to say.

And stopped cold.

Halloween was only two weeks away—

And this neighborhood took Halloween seriously. There were at least half a dozen haunted houses advertised all over the valley. And the agricultural college had a corn maze and hayrides and other harvest-themed events. There were at least a dozen costume stores within walking distance—one in every strip mall, it seemed.

Maybe—

Almost—

Ideas do not leap fully formed from my skull like Athena bursting from the forehead of Zeus. (If only...)

But I always know when I'm on to something. The internal fireworks start going off like cosmic popcorn. In this case, it was the Fourth of July. There were too many possibilities. I had to sit down and list them all, crossing off the ones that were too much work as well as the ones that would probably not be cost-effective.

Flyers. Internet postings. Facebook. Possibly a couple of videos on YouTube—maybe they'd go viral. I didn't need a lot, just enough to establish the right narrative. Obvious in retrospect. I should have realized it from the beginning.

First thing, I needed a good photograph. Not too hard to obtain. I could shoot out through the window of the back door. Emmett-Murray was silhouetted standing in the rubble of the cinder block wall, backlit by the security lights on the building across the alley. A great angle, brooding and mysterious. I just hoped he wasn't thinking about how the building blocked his view of the boulevard.

Next, a little tinkering in Photoshop. Bring up the contrast, adjust the colors—turn the orange of the argon lamp into a futuristic glow for the background, then darken the hulking off-center shape in the foreground with blackened indigo. Then the title across the top in dripping crimson. The Lonely Troll! It came out looking like a movie poster.

Now, the text, in white below.

"Feared and hated! Trapped in a hostile world. Unloved and unwanted. Lost in an uncaring city! All he ever wanted was a hug, a simple moment of kindness! Just a little bit of love!

"Come and visit the Lonely Troll. Show him he's not alone any more. Show him that there are still people in the world who can open their hearts to those who are different. Bring your children. Reawaken the heart of the troll!"

And then, below that: "FREE TO THE PUBLIC! HALLOWEEN WEEK ONLY! Starting a half-hour after sunset! Donations gratefully accepted. All proceeds will go to the creation and maintenance of a permanent loving home for this poor misunderstood beast." Then a map directing people to come up the alley.

I uploaded the flyer to my website, to Facebook, to Twitter, to Tumblr, and even Grindr. What the hell. I invited people to share it everywhere.

Then I went onto the website of the local print shop and ordered five hundred matching flyers. I'd paper the neighborhood.

I also ordered a couple arrow-shaped banners to put up, one on each side of the hole in the wall. "The Lonely Troll!"

Plus several large signs that said: "Have your picture taken with The Lonely Troll! Only $25!"

And then a couple more signs that said: "Hugs! $100! At your own risk. Please ask permission before hugging the Lonely Troll."

I could pick those up tomorrow, while taping up flyers. No. I had a better idea. I'd pay the neighborhood kids to post the flyers everywhere. And they could hand them out at the mall and at the college too. That would work. If we ran out of flyers, I'd order another five hundred. And five hundred more after that.

Finally, the hugest banner of all. "All You Need Is Love!"

And one last thing. Music. I'd load the stereo system with a selection of Disney songs—"Hakuna Matata", "A Spoonful Of Sugar", "Can You Feel The Love Tonight", "You've Got A Friend In Me," and of course, "It's A Small World." I'd crank up the speakers to eleven.

One last thing. I went digging for the card Officer Benson had given me. She answered on the second ring. "Is he gone?"

"Not yet. But..." I took a breath. "I just wanted to let you know that there will probably be some increased traffic in the alley behind my house, starting tomorrow night. We might need a police presence to, um, monitor the situation—"

"Now what?"

"I'm holding a fund-raiser for Emmett-Murray. To help him find a loving home. Oh, hell, any home, loving or not. Just as long as it's far far away."

"Do you have a permit?" she asked.

"Haven't even considered it," I answered.

"You could be cited."

"Do you really want to shut this down? And have him stuck here?"

Silence.

"I see your point. Have a good time. I'll let the rest of the division know."

It worked.

Every night, the crowds cheered as Emmett-Murray emerged from his burrow. Emmett-Murray's expression went from hateful to sullen to confused to fearful. The crowd interpreted it as loneliness. I enrolled a couple of friends to help me with logistics and we moved through the crowd every ten or fifteen minutes collecting donations in huge Mason jars. I couldn't believe how eager people were to stuff fives and tens and even twenties into the jars.

On the second night, people started throwing flowers and bouquets. Little children ran to hug his legs. Teenage girls lined up to kiss him on the cheek. Grown men studied him warily, then grinned reluctantly and waved.

People waited patiently in long lines for family pictures. Little children wanted to be photographed sitting on his shoulders, grown-ups wanted to perch on his knee. Emmett-Murray rumbled in distress. He lowered his head sadly. He looked to me for explanation, obviously unhappy, moving himself back and forth in slow confusion. "This is all for you, Emmett-Murray! You've transformed the neighborhood. This is your party! It's to honor you and show you how much you're loved!"

By the third night, I was even believing it myself. I didn't have time to count the money, I just dumped it into a huge black trash bag and stuffed it under my bed.

On the fourth evening, as the silent firestorm of sunset faded from the west, the largest crowd of all had gathered. They waited impatiently, filling the alley in both directions. Several police cars, a fire engine, an ambulance, and a few fully suited members of the SWAT team were also in attendance, but the crowd was peaceful. I recognized a few faces. People were coming back every night now. Many were carrying home-made "We love you!" signs as well as flowers and even stuffed animals.

But Emmett-Murray did not come out of his burrow.

After a bit, the crowd started chanting. And singing. "We love you, Emmett! Oh yes we do! We love you, Emmett. Please don't be blue!" It was wonderful.

I got down on my hands and knees and crawled as deep into the burrow as my nose would allow. The stink was incredible. My eyes were watering so hard, I could barely see. "Emmett, you have to come out now."

"I don't wanna."

"I know, but you gotta."

"No."

"Pesky will be very unhappy. So will I."

"Good."

Oops. Wrong thing to say. Try a different tactic—

"Emmett, listen to me. It's very important that you come out now and see all the people."

"No. I said no."

"If you don't, they'll just start singing louder. They won't go away. They'll be here all night."

"All night?"

"Yes. All night. Until dawn. They came to see you and they won't leave until you come out."

"If I come out, they'll go away?"

"Not right away, but yes, they will. They just want to see you."

"No. They'll want to hug me too."

"We'll tell them no hugs tonight, okay?"

"No hugs? You promise?"

"No hugs. I promise. Just some pictures. And songs. And maybe some flowers too."

"You promise they'll go away?"

"I promise. But you'll have to come out and see them. Fifteen minutes.
And then I'll tell them you're very tired. Okay?"

"Fifteen minutes, that's all."

"I promise."

"I don't wanna."

"I know. But they won't go away until you do."

Long stinky silence. The singing outside grew louder.

"Okay. As soon as they stop singing."

"Okay, but if you don't come out, they'll start singing "It's A Small
World" again."

Emmett-Murray didn't answer.

I backed out of the burrow, brushed off as much of the dirt as I could,
then held up my hands to silence the crowd. "He's coming. He is. But he's
asked for quiet. No singing, please. Okay?"

The crowd quieted down expectantly.

We waited. And waited. And waited.

I walked to the burrow and called down. "Emmett? Emmett-Murray?"

A deep unhappy rumble, but the ground began shuddering and I knew
he was crawling up the tunnel to the surface.

When he finally emerged, the crowd couldn't help themselves. They
cheered loudly! Hundreds of flashes sparkled from every direction,
blinding me, blinding Emmett. He held up a huge paw in front of his eyes
and flinched. It was like being onstage with the Beatles. The shrieking was
pretty intense as well.

It was wonderful. I kept Emmett-Murray in front of the crowd for
an hour and a half before I let him crawl back down into his burrow. My
helpers and I circulated through the crowd and filled three huge trash bags
with eager donations. I stuffed them under the bed with the rest.

On the fifth night, Emmett-Murray was gone.

He didn't leave a forwarding address.

The burrow was cold and empty.

Reluctantly, I pulled down the banners and the posters. As the crowd
gathered, I stood on a ladder and held up my hands for silence. "Emmett-
Murray has gone. I can't really speak for him, but I know he was deeply
affected by all your love and affection. It was overwhelming—but it was
also very stressful. All the lights and noise and attention. As you know,

trolls are very private and very sensitive. They don't deal well with crowds. As much as Emmett-Murray appreciated your attention, your flowers and signs and stuffed animals and songs, it was also very embarrassing for him, so he's moved on to a quieter place. Speaking for myself, we're enormously grateful for all the donations, of course. We're going to use some of it to rebuild this wall as a shrine to Emmett-Murray, and whatever other repairs have to be made in the neighborhood, and the rest, whatever's left over, we'll pass on to the local troll reservation. I'm sure Emmett would approve. I'll circulate among you one last time..."

All totaled up, we had over seventeen thousand dollars in donations, enough to repair most of the damage to the back yard.

We filled in the burrow—the contractor had to bring in several truckloads of dirt and gravel, we had no idea where most of the dirt had disappeared to, had Emmett-Murray just eaten it? That would have explained some of the mystery of his bulk. We laid a concrete deck over the top.

I was able to get a reasonable price for repairing the back wall and the patio. The kitchen wall and door had to be completely rebuilt as well. After the last bill was paid, I sent the remaining two hundred and fifty dollars to the Federal Agency for Troll Affairs.

I won't say that things are completely back to normal. Dogzilla still won't go into the back yard to pee. But my therapist says that if I stay on the medication, the nightmares will eventually subside. I'm down to only one or two a week now.

The good news? That Pesky Dan Goodman is still respecting the restraining order.

And Officers Benson and McBride invited me to their wedding.

From time to time, curious people stop by and ask if I've heard anything about Emmett-Murray or why he left. "No, sorry, I can't say."

But if I'm having a good day, I say, "Ask not for whom the troll bailed..."

The Great Pan American Airship Mystery
or
Why I Murdered Robert Benchley

After all is said and done, I blame Nikola Tesla.

It's his fault.

Because—if we're going to talk about cause and effect, then we have to go all way the back to the original cause.

No, Nikola Tesla did not set out to invent an efficient method of low-cost helium extraction, it was a side-effect of his coal-fusion research, but if he hadn't discovered it, no one else would have. At least not in our lifetimes.

Tesla often gave away many of his discoveries, but not this one—he patented the helium extraction process. The technology that followed created so many new industries and opportunities for profit that it pushed Tesla's own company into the Fortune 500 within 18 months.

Knowing that Tesla was unlikely to invest in lawyers and lawsuits, patent violations started cropping up everywhere. The Third Reich, for instance, began extracting their own helium from the Ruhr, the large coal fields located in the west of Germany in North Rhine-Westphalia—they used the helium to lift over a dozen huge vessels, all modeled after the luxurious Hindenburg.

Not to be outdone, the United States Congress created the National Aeronautics Studies Administration—NASA for short—to fund research and development in aerial transport.

Three years later, in June of 1937, The Great Pan American Airship Line began operations at their expansive new terminal on Welfare Island. Due to rising international tensions, as well as considerable domestic pressures against foreign competition, the trans-Atlantic German airships would be restricted to the airfield at Lakehurst, New Jersey.

To demonstrate America's commitment to a new age of aerial transportation, Pan Am announced the inaugural journey of their magnificent new flagship would be a coast-to-coast celebrity cruise. They held a nationwide contest to choose the name of the vessel they had nicknamed The Big Lady, and three lucky contestants would win berths on the first trip to prove that economical air travel for everyone was now a reality.

At 11:33 am on Thursday morning, June 3rd, 1937, First Lady, Eleanor Roosevelt officially christened the vessel in a grand ceremony and the Pan American flagship *Liberty* lifted majestically into the air while the United States Marine Band played *America, The Beautiful.* The Chorus of St. Patrick's Cathedral accompanied and WNBC broadcast the event on nationwide radio. RCA also broadcast an experimental television signal originating from the top of the Empire State Building. Receivers at Grand Central Terminal showed a grainy image of the *Liberty*'s liftoff, although most people could have simply stepped outside onto 42nd street or Fifth Avenue for a better view.

Three times larger than the Hindenburg, she was a gleaming silver illusion. She circled Manhattan island three times while tugboats below thumped their horns, fireboats howled their sirens and sprayed jets of water, and Mayor La Guardia read a poem of salute by Robert Frost on the WNBC radio station.

Most people assumed that circling Manhattan was a salute to the city. Actually, it was an opportunity for Captain Bradley to test all the systems of the airship, one after the other, and reassure himself that everything was operating up to spec. It was a second shakedown cruise, unofficial but necessary. Coming around Battery Park for the third time, finally satisfied that the ship was handling the way he wanted, he spun the wheel to the left and the "Big Lady"—her affectionate nickname—turned gracefully to port. She was now officially on her way. We passed over the Statue of Liberty and out across New Jersey..

Aboard the vessel, a host of Broadway and Hollywood celebrities waved to the crowds below. George Jessel, Al Jolson, George and Ira Gershwin, and George M. Cohan, waved from the portside windows. Dorothy Parker, F. Scott Fitzgerald, Robert Benchley, George S. Kaufman, Heywood Broun, Alexander Woollcott, and several other members of the notorious Algonquin Round Table waved from the starboard side. Also aboard were Charles Lindbergh, Amelia Earhart, and William "Billy" Mitchell. 65-year-old Orville Wright had been invited as well, but had politely declined. He still believed the foolish idea that heavier-than-air vessels would become the primary vehicle of modern air travel and felt it would be hypocritical to lend his name or support to this journey. Tesla had also declined the invitation, saying there was nothing in San Francisco to interest him right now.

Less notable, several high-ranking members of the army and navy were also among the complement of passengers, but much less conspicuous. They seemed more concerned with the operational aspects of the *Liberty* than with the promotional aspects of the journey.

Pan Am's official statements asserted that the average air-speed of the Big Lady would be 85 miles per hour, and that the non-stop voyage would take no more than 36 hours. The Big Lady would be going around the south end of the Rocky Mountains rather than over. But some of the engineers were betting that Captain Bradley would push the engines hard, hoping to average more than 100mph—as well as crossing *over* the peaks to give the passengers a spectacular view of the mountaintops, ultimately arriving at San Francisco at 10:30 A.M. the next day, a journey of only 26 hours. If that did happen, then despite traveling more than 24 hours, we would still arrive an hour earlier than our departure time, an artifact of our westward passage through three time zones.

Heading west over New Jersey, many of the passengers still crowded the windows and speculated about the crowds below. Tiny people came running out of their houses and their businesses, shouting and pointing and staring skyward. They cheered and hollered and waved. When the shadow of the *Liberty* passed over, some of them panicked. We saw a few small children crying, they were carried inside by their reassuring mothers— where they promptly leaned out of the upstairs windows to stare again.

After a half-hour or so, after the second or third tray of drinks had been passed around, the Gershwins commandeered the piano in the salon and started playing. Later, Oscar Levant took over the piano, providing accompaniment for Cohan, Jessel, and Jolson as they worked their inebriated way through an impromptu medley of popular songs.

When they finally tired out, Jack Benny, and Fred Allen began trading quips—it started with Fred Allen asking Jack Benny why he hated the violin so much that he kept playing it. Benny responded with an observation that bags under Fred Allen's eyes were so big they required their own porters. Allen replied that Jack Benny couldn't ad-lib a belch after a plate of Hungarian goulash. Benny promptly turned to him and grumped, "You wouldn't say that if my writers were here."

I wished his writers were aboard as well. I would have loved to have met them. I assumed they would be very funny men.

I was—at that time—a guest relations steward aboard the *Liberty*. My job was to keep the customers happy for the nearly two days it would take to travel the 2600 miles from New York to San Francisco—actually a bit more, because our course would zig-zag a bit to fly over several important cities and landmarks. That meant maintaining the well-being of everyone onboard who assumed they were entitled to special treatment—and that was everyone onboard. In the case of my specific charges, that mostly involved keeping them drunk enough to be cheerful, but not so drunk as to be uncontrollable. Passed-out was not an option.

But holding a tray of martinis was not my career goal. I intended to bootstrap my career by writing a memoir of this adventure. I planned to sell articles wherever I could to establish a name for myself.

I was already making notes for a profile of the celebrity doings for *Life Magazine*, a revealing slice of salacious gossip for *The New Yorker*, a report on the amenities of a flying hotel for *Popular Science*, a complementary article about the maintenance of the onboard necessities for *Scientific American*, a description of how well the six electric propellors performed for *Popular Mechanics*, and possibly even—I'd have to do it under a pen name—a futuristic story for *Astounding* about a giant passenger vessel journeying through outer space to Venus or Mars—I just needed a plot.

I had to trade a few favors, including a couple of sexual ones (that was fun), but I did get myself assigned to take care of the Algonquin Round Table crowd—that might have happened anyway. It turned out they were a boisterous group, hard to deal with, and none of the other stewards wanted to acommodate them and all of their shenanigans. A couple of the Algonquin group were putting away enough booze that their breaths had become flammable. I expected—hoped—that after they settled in and became comfortable that they would start discussing important literary issues.

Lunch was delayed because of the unscheduled performances—none of the staff were brave enough to interrupt the entertainers, the rest of the passengers would have dropped us out the nearest window, so we didn't serve until we were well over eastern Pennsylvania and Oscar Levant remarked, "You can smell the cheese even from up here."

We weren't that high, he could have been right. The *Liberty* cruised below the clouds, usually only three or four hundred feet above the ground, mostly so passengers could have a great view of the landscape, but she was engineered to go much higher. Tanks of pressurized helium gas were stored along her keel to inflate additional lifting ballonets when more altitude was needed—such as flying over a mountain. To descend again, the extra helium would be released, or pumped back into the storage tanks. Large tanks of water were also used for ballast. This was the same water that passengers would use for washing. If the *Liberty* needed altitude quickly, it could be released in a massive shower. By the time it hit the ground, it would be little more than a mist. At worst, a momentary drizzle.

The *Liberty* carried 200 passengers and 85 crewmembers. By comparison, a Hindenburg-class ship could carry only 72 passengers and required 62 crewmembers to manage the journey. The *Liberty* had been designed to carry 400 souls, but Pan Am was using the inaugural journey to demonstrate the large cargo carrying capacity of the *Liberty* as well. A half-dozen new Fords were stored in her hold. None of the military officers would discuss it, but more than once I saw them scribbling numbers on yellow pads and arguing about balancing the weights of tanks, trucks, cannons, troops, and supplies.

Cross-country shipping by railroad could take anywhere from three days to two weeks, depending on how much you wanted to pay. For some industries, air transport would be both faster and cheaper—like fresh fruits and vegetables from the California fields to the New York markets. And then there were those lucrative mail contracts to consider.

After lunch, some of the passengers retired to their cabins to rest up for the rigors of dinner. The cabins were spacious and well-equipped, deliberately more luxurious than those found on any ocean-liner where space would be at a premium. The opposite was true aboard the *Liberty*. Here, weight was the limiting factor, not space.

Only the control gondola hung below the body of the craft, I'd delivered coffee and sandwiches to it on our training flight, it was a broad comfortable platform. All the other passenger and crew spaces were inside the *Liberty*'s envelope. Because a massive framework of aluminum girders and steel tension cables was needed to provide a stable structure for the huge array of giant lift bags, there was also considerable space beneath the ballonets for accommodations. There was almost too much space.

When Tallulah Bankhead boarded, she looked around the lobby and asked the nearest steward—me—"What time does this place reach San Francisco?" She had the most amazing voice, as deep and husky as a velvet martini. Then she stared into my eyes and asked, "Who do I have to fuck to get a drink?" You can bet that sent me scurrying.

The interior of the airship and all of her trim and accessories, were decorated in the latest Art Deco style—Streamline Moderne—very light and bright, all minimalist and futuristic, exactly the statement Pan Am wanted to make. Willliam F. Lamb, one of the principle designers of the Empire State Building, had supervised the design of the passenger spaces of the airship. He was also onboard, somewhere.

A broad salon stretched across the front of the aircraft, outlined by a terrifyingly open horseshoe of glass. This was the main gathering place for the passengers. It was almost too sprawling, too wide, too open, it felt cavernous. Huge windows stretched across the front of the deck and circled wide around both sides—that and the high ceiling gave the whole chamber a broad spacious feeling, much like Hollywood's conception of a blissful afterlife.

A second level of walkways circled the high windows so every passenger could have a grand view without ever having to crowd. All of them would be able to observe the ground easily through the large downward-angled panes. The sheer size of those glass walls made it feel as if we were not within a vessel, but simply drifting along on an airy platform, as removed from the mundane cares of the world as the gods of Olympus—well, we were—but the sense of a heavenly condition was deliberate. We floated gracefully across the sky, trailing a massive shadow across the ground below, a visible reminder of the *Liberty*'s astonishing size.

Across the main floor of the salon, there were step-up levels for service areas and step-down levels of various sizes for gatherings of passengers to discuss common interests. The chairs and couches were upholstered in muted shades of red, silver, and blue—all very Pan American. The floor was carpeted in a lighter blue, a reflection of the sky. The walls were eggshell-white with gold trim. Silvery murals portrayed Lady Liberty in a variety of heroic poses.

Just aft of the salon was spacious dining hall. Behind that was a selection of smaller spaces, a cozier bar, a reading room, a smoking lounge for gentlemen, and a corresponding lounge reserved especially for the ladies. For overseas flights, the billiards room would be converted to a small casino. Further back, the airship contained a motion picture theater, a gymnasium, a quiet reading room stocked with many current magazines and a selection of popular books, even a bowling alley and a tennis court, and other lightweight amenities to alleviate the tedium of a long voyage. There was almost too much acreage on the main deck. The designers had run out of ideas before they had run out of space.

The original blueprints had included a swimming pool, with the water in it doubling as ballast. At the last moment, the airline had postponed the installation. It wasn't the weight of the water that concerned the engineers, it was the weight of the support structure of the pool and all the additional plumbing and pumps and filters needed to maintain it. The pool hadn't been completely ruled out, but the accountants at Pan Am had successfully argued that the loadweight could be more profitably used for cargo, and the company was still weighing the pros and cons.

After Pennsylvania, we headed across Lake Erie. Captain Bradley diverted course slightly south so that people all across the northern shore of Ohio—Cleveland, Lorain, Sandusky, and finally Toledo—could see the *Liberty* and cheer and wave. Beneath us, more boats tooted their horns and people waved flags and banners to catch our attention. Many of the passengers went to the windows to wave back.

But not the Round Table group. They had gathered themselves near the bar again and were proceeding to work their way through pitchers of martinis, as well as a heated discussion of something they called, "writer's block." That sounded promising. As a burgeoning author myself, I hoped to learn some of the wisdom of the sages, especially the hard part. How do you get the words onto the page?

Sometime after lunch, Dorothy Parker sent a radiogram to her editor: "I have not forgotten you. I have only forgotten to write the article."

Two hours later, her editor wired back. I brought the radiogram to her myself. She plucked it from the tray, took a puff off her cigarette, and opened it nonchalantly. I had never seen anyone open a radiogram so nonchalantly before. She must have received so many of them in her career that she took them for granted. She looked around at the rest of the group. "He says," she said, and read it aloud. "'Put down the damn martini and find a typewriter. Benchley has one. He never goes anywhere without it, even if he has no intention of using it.'" She frowned across the table. "Is that true, Robert?"

Benchley had the good grace to look embarrassed. "Well, yes. It's impossible to procrastinate properly without a typewriter."

Mrs. Parker looked up at me, still waiting with the tray held out. "Are you waiting for a tip?"

Yes, ma'am. But I didn't say it aloud. "Will there be a reply?"

"No. Yes. Send this back. 'Benchley and typewriter defenestrated over—" She frowned. "Where are we? Oh, it doesn't matter. Defenestrate him over someplace interesting. No, make that boring. Oh, never mind. He'll have to look up defenestrate and he hates looking things up. Begone now."

I bewent.

I bewent all the way back to my station next to the bar. As much as I would have liked to eavesdrop on their conversation, it would have been rude—and against the rules. I was only allowed to approach if summoned by a gesture, or if I was emptying ash trays.

Nevertheless, snatches of conversation still floated over to the bar, enough to suggest that the topic of writer's block was still circling the conversation like a maiden aunt.

Because lunch had been delayed for more than an hour, dinner was also delayed, but only thirty minutes. We were over the northern part of Indiana when the sun touched the horizon ahead of us. Oscar Levant advised against looking out the windows at the broad plains of Indiana. "It's only the people we fly over."

The entire meal service was scheduled for ninety minutes. Soup, salad, fish, three kinds of carvery meat, dessert, coffee, and after-dinner drinks. The Algonquin crew managed to stretch it out to two and a half hours. By the time they finally heaved themselves laboriously from their chairs, it was nine o'clock and we were approaching the Chicago flyover. The city was a bright sprawl of lights ahead, searchlights sweeping the sky.

As we approached, we could hear music coming from a band on the pier, but the distance kept it from being clear or identifiable. It sounded like a badly-tuned radio. According to Fred Allen it was "an excited crowd of bagpipers, accordion-players, and Jack Benny fans." Beside him, Benny replied, "I'm having trouble seeing your fans, Fred. Are there any?"

Over the city, we were blinded by searchlights hitting us from the ground, they blazed up at us from everywhere, especially along the shoreline and the major boulevards. "It looks like a dozen Hollywood premieres," said Bankhead. "Louis B. Mayer should see this. He'd crap his pants." She pronounced it "Louie."

"I wonder what it looks like from down there," said a tiny woman, one of the contest winners. The winners had been picked by their weight, a fact not made known to the general public.

I took the opportunity to answer. "Did you see the glow in the water as we passed over the lake? That was our lights. The entire airship is outlined with Nikola Tesla's new illuminators—the ones that give off almost no heat. He calls them light-emitting-diodes. They print them on some thin panels of glass. From the ground the *Liberty* looks like a great silver spoon, blazing across the sky. The airship's name is spelled out in lights like a Broadway star—only bigger than any marquee on broadway. Each letter is 24 feet high."

Beside her, a nondescript little man—the publisher of a pulp science fiction magazine, *Thrilling Wonder Stories*—spoke up. "Imagine if we could put a news-marquee on the side of the airship, like the one in Times Square. We could display messages to the people below." He thought a moment. "Or perhaps we could put projectors inside the skin of the dirigible and show motion pictures on her sides. Of course, the skin of the ship would have to be translucent enough for the movie to show through. Perhaps someday we'll have airships anchored above cities, projecting television programs to thousands of people at once."

He frowned, another thought crossing his mind. "That would use a lot of elecricity, wouldn't it?" Still frowning, he added, "I wonder if Professor Tesla's wonderful diodes could somehow be reversed to turn light into electricity? You could put rows of panels across the top of the airship and power its engines off sunlight all day long. Hmmm." He pulled out a notebook and hurriedly scribbled his thoughts into it. "Perhaps I'll write a sequel. Ralph 124C42+...." He wandered off, lost in thought.

The woman, the one who'd won her passage in a contest, said, "What a strange little man. Is he an inventor?"

"His name is Gernsback. He's a science fiction writer."

She frowned in confusion. "Science fiction? What's that?"

"Pulp fiction. The silly kind. The kind you don't want to let your little boy read. Rocket ships to the moon. Giant mechanical brains. Robots. Silly things like that."

She made a face. "Oh, that terrible stuff. No, we'd never let Jeffty read that trash."

By ten, the Algonquins had reclaimed their place in the salon and another pitcher of martinis was meeting its olive-strewn fate.

"Do they ever stop?" the evening bartender whispered to me.

"I don't know. I think Broun—or is that Woollcott?—got up to pee once. The rest of them must have iron kidneys."

Between emptying ashtrays, retrieving pitchers and replacing them with full ones, occasionally delivering and sending radiograms, and always being as unobtrusive as possible, I managed to glean a sense of their evolving conversation. Tallulah Bankhead's remark about Louis B. Mayer had sparked a conversation about writing for the movies, something that both Dorothy Parker and F. Scott Fitzgerald had dabbled with.

Before long, they were plotting a film of their own—or perhaps just plotting. The story involved, of course, a beautiful Broadway star traveling aboard a gleaming new airship when a terrible murder occurs. For the better part of an hour, the group argued about who to murder, perhaps someone in their own group? That ended abruptly when Bankhead declared, "Dahling, you can't murder a writer. Nobody will notice. It has to be someone important."

Oh, good grief. Didn't they realize? The writers are the *most important* people in Hollywood. If it isn't on the page, it isn't on the stage! You have to take it seriously!

But instead, they wasted another hour of discussion about who might be worth murdering. The comedians were quickly dismissed, so were Jolson, Jessel, and Cohan. The Algonquins finally settled on George Gershwin as a suitable victim, then moved on to speculating about the identity of the murderer and what possible motive he (or she?) might have for killing America's most gifted composer.

"Possibly his brother, Ira?"

"What motive?"

"Over a girl maybe...?"

"How tawdry. How boring. Besides...."

"No, dear. George isn't gay. He's been bedding all those women—"

"—yes, trying to prove he's a man."

"What a wonderful way to prove it." That was Oscar Levant, who'd been passing by, but stopped for the gossip.

I didn't hear the end of that discussion, there were several other late-night gatherings that needed my attention, but none as interesting. The next time I passed by, they were arguing about writer's block again. That was something I really wanted to hear about—how did the great ones get past it?

It was either Broun or Woollcott—I never could figure out which was which—who said, "Oh, there's a very easy trick to break a block."

Benchley was already glowing with inebriation, had been since liftoff, but he looked across the table with all the interest he could muster. "What?" he said.

"Quite simple. You put a sheet of paper in the typewriter and you type the word 'The.' The human mind abhors a vacuum. It is incapable of leaving the sentence unfinished. You will find yourself typing something to complete the sentence almost immediately."

"Yes, dear fellow," said Benchley, "but what about the sentence that follows it? And the next after that? And the next and the next?"

The other one—Woollcott or Broun, or maybe it was George S. Kaufman—spoke up then. "Pablo Picasso says that all art is recovery from the first line. He was talking about drawing, of course, but I believe that's true of writing as well. Once you have that first sentence on the page, the rest will follow."

Benchley had already written quite a bit about his ability to procrastinate—that only the pressure of a deadline inspired true creativity—but in this group of trusted colleagues, he could admit that sometimes writing was difficult. Not the typing itself, but getting the right words in the right order. Others agreed. "There's an elegance that we aspire to achieve, but the limitations of our own selves remains our greatest challenge."

Benchley put his martini glass down. It was already empty anyway. "The..." he said. "The...." And then, "The the the the the." He nodded. "Yes. The...." And then he leapt up from his chair. "It's an admirable idea. I shall now proceed to test it." And he staggered off in search of his cabin.

The others went back to discussing murder, now arguing whether Jack Warner or Louis B. Mayer might be a better victim. There would be no shortage of suspects or motives. I did catch one line in passing. "No, not Walt Disney. If he doesn't like an actor, he tears him up."

By midnight, we were crossing Kansas—a dry state, it had the most restrictive alcohol laws in the nation. Legally, once we were in the state's airspace we were forbidden to serve liquor. When the company announced the flight itinerary of the *Liberty*, the Attorney General of the state had sent a letter of inquiry to Pan American's lawyers asking if the state's liquor laws would be observed while the *Liberty* was flying over the state. Pan Am's lawyers had promptly sent back a note assuring the Attorney General that state officials, including county sheriffs, were free to board, inspect, and serve any necessary warrants on any Pan Am aircraft flying over the state of Kansas. So far, none had done so.

Captain Bradley had altered the course a few degrees south to avoid a rumbling storm system spreading across the Dakotas and down toward Nebraska where it would probably turn into tornado weather. The big chart in the salon was automatically updated every fifteen minutes. It showed our location and also demonstrated that we were averaging 93 miles per hour, so we were ahead of schedule, but nowhere near the 100 miles per hour that some had predicted. The figures were also available in knots for the aviators aboard. Of which, I was not one.

Along about 1:30 in the morning, the Algonquins finally started making noises that suggested they might be through for the evening. Two other stewards and I had to escort several of them to their cabins. When the last one had finally been tucked in, we looked at each other in exhaustion. "When do any of those people actually find time to do any of the things they're supposed to be famous for?"

We secured all the windows, checking to make sure that none were left open to the night, we couldn't risk a drunken passenger falling out, then adjourned to our separate bunks. Crew's quarters were nowhere near as luxurious as the passengers', but we each had a private space, a sink, and a shower—and a window! It was an uncommon luxury. Eventually, on a full flight with 400 passengers, we'd be doubling up, two crewmembers to a cabin.

The cabins on the *Liberty* had what they called "picture windows." The windows in the salon were even larger, as broad as those in front of Macy's department store. By contrast, the windows on a passenger plane were little more than portholes—even on the newest aircraft under construction that Boeing was building in Washington state.

Pan Am had ordered six of those airplanes—the Boeing 314 Clipper long-range flying boat—for trans-oceanic flights. But with the success of the *Liberty*'s maiden voyage almost certainly assured, those planes might end up going to the army instead. Britain's Royal Air Force had also expressed an interest in picking up those contracts if Pan Am cancelled—as expected.

Unlike an airplane, it's easy to sleep aboard the *Liberty*. Her electrical propellors are so silent, and so distant from the passenger cabins, you can barely feel any vibration, just a gentle susuruss. Unlike the clattering internal combustion engines that keep airplanes aloft, the *Liberty*'s engines run on the same electricity that powers the lights and runs the radios. Everything aboard the airship runs off Professor Tesla's marvelous new graphite-and-lithium batteries. The batteries were kept charged by three diesel generators.

Although technically I was on a 24-hour shift, in practice I would not be needed until at least 10am, maybe later, if the Algonquins slept in—as expected—but I was already up and ready to go at 8:30am.

We were already over the northwest corner of New Mexico, and on course to pass over the Grand Canyon, then Boulder Dam, only two years old and already providing electricity for much of the southwest, then past Las Vegas, a small desert resort town, up over the Sierras, and eventually north up the coast toward an early evening arrival in San Francisco. Passengers could expect a glorious California sunset as we landed.

The course of the airship was primarily determined by weather, but the airline wanted everyone in the country talking about the airship. That meant flying over as many cities as possible so the people on the ground could see the *Liberty*. It also meant flying over the most spectacular scenery below so that passengers could take photographs to show their friends and families.

Of course, *Life Magazine* had photographers aboard the aircraft as well, two of them, and more stationed on the ground all along the route as well. We'd lifted off on Thursday, June 3rd. The next issue of the magazine would appear on Monday, June 7th. We were guaranteed the cover, of course, and would likely have at least four pages of departure pictures, showing liftoff from the field as well as more photos of the airship over New York, then probably six pages of enroute photos, especially aerial views of various landmarks, and another four pages for the arrival and landing.

According to the flight plan, we would head up the California coast, then sail in over the brand-new Golden Gate Bridge for even more spectacular photo opportunities. The bridge had opened on Thursday, May 27th, exactly a week before our liftoff, so it was a grand occasion to demonstrate America's growing industrial future, the strength and know-how that was bringing us back from the Great Depression.

After crossing over the bridge, the *Liberty* would circle the entire bay so people in Sausalito, Berkeley, and Oakland could also get a good look at the *Liberty*, then back across the bay to the Pan Am terminal at San Francisco Municipal Airport. We expected to see large crowds everywhere, but especially at the airfield where a motorcade awaited.

Governor Frank Merriam would be there to welcome us. He'd dedicated the bridge the week before, kissing every baby he could find. This week, he'd certainly make sure that the photographers would get pictures of him with George Gershwin and Al Jolson and Jack Benny—but not Tallulah Bankhead, she was developing an unsavory reputation among Republican voters, and Merriam needed all the good press he could get— he had a tough election coming up next year.

Not all of our celebrity passengers were placing themselves where photographers might find them, some actually found the photographers a nuisance, but the photographers themselves were having no shortage of photo opportunities. Even if they couldn't find Gershwin at the piano or Cohan and Jessel and Jolson mugging together, there were always the huge, downward-angled windows. They had already taken enough aerial photos for a dozen special issues and were now arguing which side of the Salon would be best for photos when we crossed the Golden Gate Bridge. The two *Life Magazine* photographers had the best plan, they would station themselves one on each side.

Most of the Algonquins slept through breakfast. Not surprising. But they missed a great view of the Grand Canyon from the air. That Gernsback fellow, the one who published *Thrilling Wonder Stories*, speculated aloud, "I suppose that's what the canals on Mars must look like, only larger, to be visible from Earth. What a grand civilization the Martians must have. We must make friends with them somehow."

Amazing, what some people thought about. I couldn't imagine anyone taking that science fiction stuff seriously.

The Algonquins did show up for lunch, one by one staggering bleary-eyed into the dining hall. Not the best argument for the life of a writer. These people were famous. They were role-models. Why weren't they acting like it? I was beginning to hate them.

They had the best job in the world—they were the caretakers of culture, the shapers of opinion—and they were behaving like common drunks. But if writing is one of the best jobs in the world, it's also one of the hardest—it's all decision-making, all day long. This word or that one, over and over and over again, all the way to the end of the sentence. And even if you get to the end of a sentence, you still have to start again at the beginning of the next. It's exhausting.

Maybe that's why writers drink—to escape having to make any more decisions, except perhaps how many olives in the martini. Or maybe a twist of onion instead.

And maybe what I was seeing was only an aberration. I couldn't expect these people to be brilliant and noteworthy everywhere, all the time, could I? This was a vacation for them, a break from the stress. Maybe they just needed to recharge their creative batteries? Who was I to judge?

They took their coffee in the salon, along with a pile of fresh pastries that quickly disappeared. I circled regularly, alternating between brewing fresh pots of coffee and refilling their cups. They were now arguing about the best way to murder Louis B. Mayer. Throwing him out the window of the airship was quickly discarded. If there's no body to discover, you lose the scene where the French maid screams in horror.

That led to a discussion of why the maid had to be French. Woollcott—by now, I was pretty sure it was Woollcott—noted that a young French maid was always going to be more fun to look at than a dumpy English maid. Bankhead responded that the dumpy English maid was a great part for a good character actress, and good contrast. "What she means," Dorothy Parker pointedly observed, "is that the star should be the prettiest one. Not upstaged by the ingenue."

Woollcott was undeterred. "Ah, but I have the perfect young actress—"

"Of course, you think she's perfect. She's sleeping with you and you're vain."

Bankhead leaned in. "Not perfect. Desperate." Then she added, "On the other hand, if you actually believe her orgasm, we should cast her, that proves she's a real actress." Turning to the rest, she said, "What if the producer's body is found inside one of the—what do you call them—the big balloons that hold all that nice helium?" She turned to me and stroked my arm suggestively.

"Lift bags," I said. "Or ballonets."

"Oh, ballonets. I like that. How very French. There's a bit of French sophistication for you, dear. Without all that messy business of having to buy a maid's costume. We shall find Louis B. Mayer's body in a ballonet. Suffocated because there's no oxygen. All blue in the face. Perhaps he has even been screaming. But no one could hear him."

"Umm, if I may—" I politely lifted a hand.

The actress looked at me, her hand still on my arm. "Yes, dear boy?"

"If he were in the ballonet screaming, the helium would affect his voice, make it higher pitched. It's the density of the gas." She frowned in puzzlement. I demonstrated. "He'd sound like this. *Help me! Help me!*"

The entire group fell out laughing. "Oh my god, that's priceless. Can you imagine Louis B. Mayer sounding like Mickey Mouse?"

"More like Betty Boop."

"Makes me think—maybe we should do this as a comedy."

"Somebody go find Jack Benny. He's got the best writers—"

"We'd have to put him in the picture—"

"Oh, right. Never mind."

"But if it's a comedy—"

"Who says it has to be a comedy—?"

"If we're murdering Louis B., it will be—"

"No, not a comedy, but certainly a feel-good movie. We could get Capra to direct—"

"No, we should get whatsisname, that little round English fellow, the one who does all those suspense movies—"

"I've met him." Bankhead shuddered. "I have no intention of working for him. He's..." She searched for the word, finally found it. "He's creepy."

She squeezed my arm, "Not you, dear boy," and finally let go, but not before giving me the kind of delicious look that made me wish the dirigible was a lot slower so we'd have one more night in the air.

"I have a question..." I was pretty sure that was Heywood Broun now. Maybe. "How do we get him into the lift bag? If we slice it open, doesn't the gas escape? Wouldn't that create a risk of explosion?"

"No, that's hydrogen. Helium doesn't explode. Isn't that right, steward?" They all turned to me as if I was the expert.

"Yes, that's correct, sir. Hydrogen is too dangerous. But helium is perfectly safe."

"But the gas would still escape, wouldn't it?"

"Well, yes. But the lift bags are very big. You could cut a slice near the bottom, shove a person in, then seal it again with duct tape. We use it to repair small rips. They do happen sometimes, so there are rolls of tape everywhere—in all of the tool kits and there are tool kits everywhere in the frame, for the convenience of the engineers. So that wouldn't be a problem. Unless the victim struggled. You'd have to knock him out."

"Or get him so drunk he passes out—" Parker pointed to Benchley who was quietly snoring in his chair.

"No, we can't murder Benchley. He still owes me money."

"Well, we can't murder Louis B. either then. He owes me a picture."

"Yes, but now that we have a plan, we'll have to murder the steward too, because he knows too much. We could practice on him. Would you like a martini, lad?"

"I don't drink, sir," I said, and excused myself to refill the coffee pot again. When I returned, they had decided that murdering a steward had no inherent drama. A murder mystery is only riveting if the victim is important. "So, you're safe, dear boy," Bankhead reassured me. "You're not important enough to kill. Don't take it too hard."

"Thank you," I said, noncommittally.

"Somebody wake up Benchley—"

"Why? He'll just start talking—"

"He's snoring!"

"You'd rather have him talking?"

And so it went. Somebody looked at me and asked why I was carrying a coffee pot instead of a martini pitcher, and they were off again. But they still weren't talking about writing. Or anything relating to the literary world. I didn't understand it. Every other profession, the people in it talk shop. These people, they just drank. They did wake up Benchley in time to see the huge white slab of Boulder Dam. "Impressive! You could project movies on it!"

"It's a long drive from Los Angeles. It'd better be one hell of a flick."

Then they retired back to their chairs in the salon. "Las Vegas? Nothing there to see. Just a wide spot in the road. It'll never amount to anything."

Somebody remembered that Benchley had been procrastinating his way through a writer's block—until somebody told him to go type the word 'The' on a blank sheet of paper. Dorothy Parker puffed on her cigarette and asked, "So how did that work, Robert?"

Benchley frowned. "How did what work?"

"The great 'The' experiment, remember?"

"Oh, that. Yes. Thank you." He frowned again. "Well..." He cleared his throat, preparing himself for an extended explanation. "One has to be well-prepared for the task, you know. Procrastination is not for the faint-hearted. It takes genuine commitment. You cannot just sit and do nothing. You must make it appear as if you are preparing to do something. A pipe is very useful in that regard. It requires a great deal of attention. It's an excellent way to look like you are preparing to get busy. Lighting a pipe demands a specific ritual, an elaborate ritual, a very time-consuming ritual.

There is the selection of tobacco, followed by the process of delicately filling the bowl, pinch by pinch, then the tamping. One cannot tamp the tobacco too firmly or it will be hard to light. Likewise, one cannot leave the leaves too loose or they will simply burn up. Then there is the application of the fire. As soon as the match has been applied to the tobacco, the smoke is over. This necessitates refilling, relighting, and oh, yes—reknocking. The knocking out of a pipe is as important as the smoking. You have to have the appropriate surface to knock the pipe on. Not just any table will do. No, knocking the pipe is a whole other ritual, you see, all part of the process, and if you leave any part of it out, you're simply not serious about procrastinating."

"Yes, you've bored us with this story before." Kaufman yawned. "You really must write it and sell it someday so we won't have to listen to it again. But we didn't ask you how to procrastinate. Most of us already know how to do that, we've each developed our own specific set of skills. What we want to know is how well the experiment worked?"

"What experiment?"

"The one where you typed the word 'The' on a blank sheet of paper—remember?"

"Oh, that experiment. It worked very well. You were right. I typed the word 'The' and almost immediately, the rest of the words came flowing out as easily as if poured from a pitcher of martinis. Of which, I will have one, if you please, steward." To the rest, he said, "It's still sitting in my typewriter. Feel free to look."

Unable to resist the invitation, the rest of them scrambled to their feet and headed for the corridor, leaving Benchley behind with a martini glass held high in his hand. He saluted me with it, knocked it back, then held it up again for a refill.

When the group returned from Benchley's cabin, filing back in like children after recess, they were smiling and nodding to each other, but they were already talking about something else. Benchley waited expectantly for their reactions. Parker glowered at him as she seated herself. "Too clever by half." A couple of others shook their heads as if Benchley had punned in public—a good pun, but still a pun, the literary equivalent of a fart. Bankhead gave him a scowl of approval. The one I'd identified as Kaufman parked himself, nodded and admitted, "Nice."

I was curious too, but I couldn't leave my station. By then we were coming out over the California coast, and following U.S. Route 101 north.

It ran all the way from Mexico to Canada, with portions of the route known as El Camino Real—"The Royal Road."

The Spanish had built their 21 missions in California each one a single day's travel from the next, so journeying missionaries would always have a safe place to rest each evening. Many of the state's coastal towns and cities still retained the names of the original missions: San Diego, San Juan Capistrano, San Gabriel, Santa Catalina, Santa Ysabel, San Pedro, San Fernando, Santa Clarita, Santa Barbara, Santa Clara, San Luis Obispo, Santa Inez, Santa Cruz, San Jose, San Francisco, and a few more that always fell out of my head. How did I know all of this? Because it was part of Pan Am's training for stewards. Passengers would always have questions about the scenery below. It was the stewards' job to provide accurate answers. Any question we couldn't answer was added to the training guide.

The rest of the journey was pretty much without incident. The Algonquins, exhausted from all their drinking, had given up their plans to murder Louis B. Mayer. For some reason, they were now muttering imprecations against several New York critics—individuals who were not aboard. "Murdering a critic would only be poetic justice—" Bankhead said, "They've murdered so many shows."

Benchley cleared his throat loudly. "I am a critic too, you know."

"When you're writing, yes. But most people know you as a humorist."

"I resent that," he replied, but without much emotion. He was giving more of his attention to his martini.

"Besides, you're too nice to murder."

"I resent that even more."

"We can't murder a critic. There would be too many suspects to make the plot workable."

"There would be even more suspects if you killed Louis B. Mayer."

"True, that. Maybe we *should* kill Benchley. Some people like him. That makes it even more of a mystery. Why would someone want to kill Robert Benchley."

"I can think of—" Kaufman quickly counted off on his fingers. "—four reasons."

"Besides that—"

"I think the question isn't *why*, but *who*." Bankhead looked to me. "Oh, hello, dah-ling, bring those martinis over here. Tell me—would you like to murder Robert Benchley?"

Before I could answer, Dorothy Parker said, "Oh, no, no, no. He's not important enough—"

"But he's adorable enough. No one would ever suspect him. I know—" She waved her martini glass for effect, but to give her credit she didn't spill a drop. The woman could hold her liquor. "I'll tell you exactly why he wants to kill Robert Benchley. He's a frustrated young writer and he's jealous—that's it! Jealous of all of us! Robert is just the first. Before the journey is over, he'll kill every one of us. It'll be just like Agatha Christie. *Ten Little Indians.* Only on an airship." She turned to me. "Would you like that, dah-ling?"

As deadpan as I could manage, "It's against airline policy to kill passengers. It might be bad for business."

Bankhead guffawed like a choking foghorn. Quickly recovering herself, she turned to the rest, "You see, darlings. He's perfect! Nobody would ever suspect him."

Kaufman shook his head. "No, no, no. It won't work. He's scenery. The murderer has to be a lead, not a second banana. But I do like the idea of killing Benchley. There's a sadistic kind of elegance to it. Although once he's dead, you lose some of your best opportunities for comic relief."

Woollcott added, "Having the steward be the killer is too much like 'the butler did it.'"

"Has the butler *ever* done it?" Parker asked. "I mean, how can it be a cliché if nobody's ever written it? Maybe that's how we make it work. If Benchley is the victim, then the other suspects have to be us. And here we are saying, 'Oh, it couldn't be the butler, that's too obvious—and it's the butler all along.' But we never considered it because we don't like clichés."

Silence, while they all considered it. I waited patiently to find out if I was going to be a murderer or not.

"Well..." said Kaufman, "We'd have to build up his part a bit. I do like the line about it being against airline policy to kill passengers. Notice he didn't say he wouldn't do it—only that it's against airline policy. Nice bit of misdirection there."

"That little lecture about the Spanish missions—and all those other bits of triva too. Electrical engines and lift bags and why helium makes your voice squeaky. We can use all of that—we'll play him up as stiff and boring. He'll be a dry comic presence for the first two acts. In act three, we reveal his seething core of resentment against those with real talent."

Bankhead slid her hand up my arm. "What do you think, dah-ling?"

I couldn't say what I was thinking. Fortunately, I was rescued by the chime announcing afternoon tea. Having missed breakfast, having drunk most of their lunch, the Algonquins agreed among themselves almost immediately that food was as good an excuse as any to relocate. They rose almost as one and headed for the dining hall, where trays of sandwiches and salads were being set out.

F. Scott Fitzgerald was the last to follow, still holding a glass of whiskey. He stopped and frowned at me, as if trying to figure something out. "Why would you want to murder Benchley?" he asked, very seriously. "I think I'd be a much better victim, don't you?"

"A very good point, sir. Shall I help you to your table?"

A southerly headwind slowed the *Liberty*, so we observed sunset while still passing over Santa Cruz. On the starboard side, we could see The Giant Dipper roller coaster, the highlight of the Beach Boardwalk amusement park. There were colored lights flashing, people shouting and pointing, and carousel music. After that, the hills darkened quickly, a color somewhere between emerald and blackened indigo.

On the port side, the sun went fireburst orange, then sullen crimson as it dipped into the horizon. For a few magic moments, the ocean glimmered with golden highlights across the surface of the waves. Several of the photographers got into a heated discussion about the limitations of monochrome and whether or not Kodak's new color film—called Kodachrome, of course—would ever be able to capture the dynamic range of such a view.

The Algonquin group's tea stretched on so long, they decided to remain in the dining hall and wait for dinner, now planned as a gracious evening affair over the San Francisco Bay, followed by a joyous welcome at San Francisco Municipal Airport—and apparently, I was no longer an accessory to their murder plot, which might have been just as well, because I had already begun considering several better mechanisms of violence, including a way to frame Hugo Gernsback for the entire affair.

No, these people were not a good influence. Any last thoughts I had still been nurturing about the glamor of writing had begun to evaporate somewhere after their second pitcher of martinis. What was left was a sodden residue, about as appetizing as the last forgotten olive in Dorothy Parker's glass.

But while they were at dinner...when no one was around, I took advantage of the opportunity to let myself into Benchley's cabin, ostensibly to make sure he had clean towels and a last full bottle of gin.

His typewriter sat on the desk, a tidy stack of paper next to it. In the machine, a single sheet. I had to look.

There, at the top of the page, a single sentence.

The hell with it.

Now I did have a reason to kill him.
It was too late for this voyage.
I got him on the return trip.

Finding Monstro

I gave up. I peeled off my shirt and mopped my armpits with it. I wasn't the first. It was hot in here.

There's this thing called "compare and despair." Some men don't like taking off their clothes in front of other men, especially when other men are larger. Men don't like to feel small. That's me. I'm not scrawny, but you won't find my picture on a calendar either.

But it was hot inside the boat, too hot for pride, so I took off my shirt and poured cold water down my bare chest. That would help for a while.

Felcher whistled, as he did every time I pulled off my shirt—and I ignored him, as I did every time he whistled. His real name was Felger, but that wasn't what we called him. Felcher knew I was married, but Jose wasn't on this mission, so to Felcher, that made me a target for flirting.

Beside me, Angel didn't even look up from his navigation console. "Don't mind him," he said.

"I never do."

I hadn't wanted to come, I had steaks growing in the tanks, but I was the only available pilot for the sub, and the steaks would grow whether I was there or not. I didn't have a choice.

Piloting isn't a hard job, the intelligence engine does most of the work, but the operational requirements specify that at least one certified human operator must be onboard to monitor all navigational and steering systems—just in case. Although if that "just in case" ever happened, there probably wasn't anything I could do that the intelligence engine couldn't do better.

In truth, I was there to provide an extra pair of hands for cooking, cleaning, and lifting stuff. When I wasn't doing that, I sat at the piloting console. I pointed the boat south, sat in the chair, and watched the screens and the thermometers—especially the thermometers. The closer we came to the equator, the hotter the boat became. So halfway through every shift, I took off my shirt, mopped my sweaty face and arms and chest, and thought about icebergs. I think we should have carved one off the Arctic shelf, bored a hole in it, pushed the boat inside, and steered south in an icy shell—but then we wouldn't have been able to submerge in case of a storm, and on Praxis, that's a serious concern. Storms here can be horrific.

The planet has a deformed orbit. At some point in its distant past, something had given it a hard whack upside the equator and pushed it into an elliptical circuit, not severe but enough off the circular to make for a particularly interesting ecosystem—Praxis moves from the outer extreme of the Goldilocks zone to the inner. Seasonal temperatures alternate between way too cold and much too hot, so it has the most astonishing weather.

That's why Angel is aboard. He's one of the best navigators on the planet. He's an androgyne. He gender-identifies as male, but he says he has lady-parts—as he calls them. I never looked, despite his numerous offers to show me. He says he wants to have his babies the old-fashioned way, not grown in a tank, he just hasn't picked out a husband yet. But there's no shortage of eligible men, and probably no shortage who'd be happy to rub his lady-parts the right way, baby or not. That's probably why he changed— it's been a subject of continuing discussion back at Arrival Station.

Despite his lady-parts, Angel is all-boy. Otherwise, he wouldn't be here. Praxis Colonial Authority has restricted this world to XY-males only, and the policy is unbreakable. No breeders, not even womb-men, no one able to get pregnant—at least for the first decade, maybe longer, as long as it takes. It's a safety thing. Until we can be sure what kind of bugs lurk here, we can't risk making babies.

There are horror stories from Miranda and other places. Not many people know the details, but we were told some of it after we arrived. The policy makes sense. But Angel lives in hope that he will someday be allowed to grow his own uterus and bear his own children. He's not the only one. There are a lot of others saying we've been here long enough, it's time to make babies. Jose and I haven't had that conversation yet, but there'll be time for that after the uterine-tanks are ready.

Life goes on. In its own messy clumsy way, life goes on. Life is messy everywhere. That's the point of this mission.

Praxis is an oblate spheroid—very oblate. It's noticeably flattened at the poles, much more than Earth. It looks a little like a curling stone. With rings. Because of its flattened shape, a man weighs 119% of his normal weight at the poles, but only 81% at the equator—except nobody goes to the equator. It's too hot. 160 Fahrenheit. 72 Celsius—that's apogee-winter. Perigee-summer can bring the temperatures up to 220 Fahrenheit, 105 Celsius. Either way, it's fatal.

The relentless extremes of temperature make Praxis the windiest planet humans have ever tried to settle. Hurricanes, blizzards, firestorms, tsunamis, waterspouts, tornadoes, and sheet-lightning that has to be seen to be believed. And you haven't really experienced weather until you've been caught in a hot scalding rainstorm. But afterward, you can go outside and pick your vegetables, already boiled. And occasionally find a fresh-steamed crab or lobster on the shore.

In my opinion—something nobody asked—this mission was a bad idea. Sail to the equator and back, dropping probes all the way to measure the depths of the ocean, the currents, and the temperatures at various levels—because someday we might want to use wave power or thermal differentials to generate electricity.

But sailing was the wrong word, because mostly we were drifting with a large debris field. The annual tsunamis ripped tons of material off the shores, including a lot of trees, young ones with shallow roots, older ones that finally broke under the annual assaults, and those that needed to be dragged into the ocean as part of their life cycle. The result was semi-permanent fields of flotsam, much of it caught in webs of surface kelp. The winter currents drove these floating platforms south toward the tropics until the currents turned west and ultimately north again, in a vast circular scouring.

And that was part of the reason why it was so hot in the boat. Even floating on the surface, we had to keep the hatches sealed. The debris fields reeked. The air stank like garbage and vomit. It was inescapable. Even inside, with all the air-scrubbers working, we could still taste it in everything we ate or drank. Dixon, the Captain, said it wasn't real, it was psychological, it was our imagination—but he wrinkled his nose over his morning coffee too.

Some of the debris fields were large enough to have become floating islands. All kinds of fish lived in the hanging undergrowth beneath while the drier tops of the islands served as migratory homes for the birds that fed on the fish below—at least until the heavy heat of the tropics forced them to retreat.

That was one of the questions we hoped to answer—one of many— where did the birds go? Or did they have a different adaptation? By floating silently within the debris field, we could observe and monitor and catalogue some of the creatures and maybe discover how they survived the scorch belt around the equator.

Some of the fish in the sea were our own. Despite the howls of various off-world researchers who insisted we had to keep the planet pristine while they studied it from afar, we'd been introducing Terran species almost from the beginning—though not always on purpose.

The tsunamis had shown us that our shoreline structures weren't rugged enough. Several of our factory farms had been shattered, releasing various ocean-dwelling species into the sea—but it hadn't been as big an eco-disaster as we'd feared. Some died, some lived, some adapted. That was interesting. From the beginning, we'd wanted to see how various Terran critters could adapt to life on Praxis. It was evidence that we could too. And those of us who planned to spend the rest of our lives here also looked forward to a celebratory steak and lobster dinner on Arrival Day.

The other reason it was so hot inside the boat was a simple matter of physics. You don't really cool anything. You just rearrange the heat, sending it somewhere else. The upper hull of the boat had two rows of stegosaur-shaped spines to serve as heat-sinks. But if the surrounding air is hotter, you can't radiate heat away—just the opposite. The air in this latitude was already 94F/34C. The water wasn't much better, 85F/30C. Add to that, our instructions not to disturb the eco-systems of the floating islands, and we weren't allowed to run any equipment that would increase our heat radiation—that meant the refrigeration coils stayed neutral.

Right on schedule, we dropped another packet of probes. The *ka-thump-thump-thump* of the release made the boat ring like a bell. On the screens, a few seabirds were startled into the air but they came fluttering back quickly, not wanting to waste energy or build up hard-to-lose heat.

The largest probe in the series was buoyant. It would sink for a while, then float back to the surface away from the debris field and make a valiant effort to hold its position in this latitude. The other units fell below, all connected by carbon-fiber cable. Dropping to their various depths, they'd record audio and video, temperature, radioactivity, magnetic field strength, ocean smells and composition, and whatever other information their sensors could capture. The floating probe would transmit everything into the network and it would eventually find its way back to Central. In a few years, we would have enough separate points of data to begin to color in the maps. Instead of speckles, we'd start to see areas.

Finally, even Dixon reached his fuckitall point. He came up behind me, stinking of sweat. "All right, let's take her down and see if we can cool this thing off. Drop below the thermocline. Let's find the cool water." He whirled around. "Chief? Run those cooling units up to max. I want icicles dripping off the periscope!"

I didn't need him to repeat the order. "Aye aye, Cap'n." I pushed the control yoke forward. "Twenty degrees," I said. The boat tilted easily down and we fell out of the bottom of the island. Above, I could hear creeper vines dragging across the hull. A few bits of flotsam banged against the steggy-fins, but as soon as we were deep enough, a whole new kind of quiet enveloped the sub. Now, the only sounds were our own—the flutter of our propellers in the water, the hum of our air circulators, the welcome buzz of the refrigeration units, and the susurrus of noise from all the other devices aboard.

"Leveling off," I reported. "Depth, 1200 meters. Hull temperature, 74F/23C."

Dixon grunted. "We can live with that. For now."

I swiveled in my seat to face him. "It's going to be tricky. The closer we get to the equator, the less gee we pull. The weight of the water above us will be reduced. So we can go deeper, but we'll still be juggling heat against depth."

He nodded. "Find a passage beneath the heat and you'll be a hero." Then he said, "But if we come up against a wall, we're not going to push it. We'll drop the bots and let them prowl and search. We'll head for home and tell them to fab a next-gen sub."

"Copy that." I swiveled back and studied my screens. I was ready to make that call right now.

We'd been using aerial drones to drop probes into the sea for 18 months—as fast as we could fab the units—but the ferocious winds coming off the scorch belt made it impossible for any flying machine to approach. A sub could get in a lot closer. How close we weren't sure.

What we needed was a safe and dependable way to move heavy freight over/through/under/across the scorch belt. Praxis had one large continent and a scattering of islands. Arrival station was in the northern hemisphere, but the south had the better terrain. We needed a cost-efficient access across the equator.

During apogee-winter, we could send trucks across the high deserts, and that was good for six out of eighteen months, but we needed a year-round system. Some of the geologists were saying that a deep-tunnel could be dug, but it would have to be a thousand kilometers long and would take at least twenty years to dig, probably more. But if we could run sub-freighters down the coast, we could start expanding the southern stations now.

But first we needed to chart the depths of the waters, the strength of the currents and the temperatures at the operative levels. So I sat in my chair and stared at my screens until my eyes felt like they were bleeding. But at least I wasn't hot anymore. Just bored and uncomfortable.

Four hours on, four hours off. Archer rode the yoke while I ate, slept, and showered myself back to coherency. Sometimes we drifted with the current, not just to save fuel, but also to watch for native life forms. We'd spotted way too many to catalog. Someone else would do that job.

A lot of us assumed that the scorch belt made for two completely isolated eco-systems, but the evidence of the ocean was that apogee-winter allowed a lot of crossover. There was enough ecology on this world to amuse a battalion of biologists. And that battalion was very anxious to get here—just as soon as we could build sufficient life support systems.

But it wasn't just the structures and machinery and the farms—it was also the people to maintain the buildings and run the machines and grow the food, and that meant building enough life support facilities for them as well as the facilities they would run for the biologists.

Bottom line—we needed to expand our electrical capacity first. When we had enough electricity, we could run the machines to dig the bunkers and construct the fabbers and power them up. Then, once we were manufacturing the tools and equipment, we needed ways to deliver those materials wherever they were needed—all over the planet.

It's a vicious circle—misunderstood by everyone, but especially by those playing simple simulation games, because the one thing that simulations can't do well is simulate the arguments that real people bring to the table.

And if Praxis wasn't a big enough challenge, there was an additional problem for the colonists. No women. Not yet. Maybe not ever. That decision hadn't been made—or if it had been made, it hadn't been made public.

Oh, and the other part of that—Praxis was a one-way ticket. Because of the near-Terran nature of its ecology, it was a quarantine world. There were no returns. History had given Earth a good reason to fear off-world plagues.

So there was no shortage of topics for arguments in the galley. We'd brew fresh coffee, work on protein bars, and chew over topics as diverse as altering baseball rules for an off-gee environment, the best way to grow a steak, and the evolutionary justification for sex. Felcher styled himself an expert on the latter topic.

"It's a mistake not to have women here," he said. It was a frequent complaint. "Intercourse is necessary to the species. It's a mechanism for mixing up genes. Without sex, evolution is impossible."

"That used to be true," Angel said. "But now we can mix-and-match chromosomes at will and grow babies in tanks, so we have to ask the question—are women necessary? In the past, yes—women were incubators. Now that we don't need them for reproduction, do we need women at all? It's a fair question—and this colony is a social experiment."

"All colonies are social experiments. Everything is a social experiment. Every baby is a social experiment. You're an experiment. I'm an experiment. That doesn't mean that every social experiment is a good idea. Men are incomplete without women."

"Speak for yourself, Felcher. You're incomplete *with* women." Angel looked to me. "What do you think?"

I shook my head. "Leave me out of this one."

A third of the colonists had declared as homosexual before emigrating. For emigration to monosexual Praxis, that was an advantage. A significant percentage of the rest were situation-adaptable, apparently comfortable with the nature of the colony—the challenge was big enough to justify the circumstance—and some just enjoyed sex, regardless of the plumbing. But there were many men who'd emigrated who weren't satisfied, not even with robosex. A sizable minority still believed that the colony should plan for species normality—at worst case, as a segregated settlement. They argued it could serve as an evolutionary baseline against which to measure the monosexual adaptation.

"If this is about sex," said Angel, "then, yeah—okay. You have a point. If you're heterosexual, then yes you would feel that way. But if you're not, then probably no. But even if we could take the sexual distraction out of the social equation, leaving only the differences in gender identity, we'd still have—"

"We'd still have the distraction," said Dixon.

"That's my point!" Angel replied. "We don't know what a monosexual culture is like because we've never had a true one. Gender differences create two oppositional mindsets. Women think differently than men. Men think differently than women. It's a fact. Our brains are hardwired differently. I'm not saying men are superior. I'm saying we're different. Maybe women are superior. I don't know. But I could argue it. Women don't start wars. Maybe this should have been an all-female colony, except women have a different biological imperative, that whole baby-making thing, that's what got Miranda colony in trouble—"

"That wasn't the half of it. Miranda had other problems," Dixon interrupted. "And men have our own biological imperatives. A lot of men *want* to be dads."

"I'm saying that this is about the way men think when women aren't part of the mix, that's all. Right now, this colony is a chance to find out who we are without the distraction of the second gender-identity." He shrugged. "Maybe it's a mistake, but we'll never know if we don't give it a chance—"

"Says the androgyne," finished Felcher. "It doesn't matter to you. You don't have a dog in the fight. You can go either way. But for those of us raised in a normal family—"

Dixon put a large hand on Felcher's shoulder and leaned in close. "You might want to think carefully about the rest of that sentence, son, before you speak it aloud."

"Uh—" Felcher shut up. But only momentarily. "No offense intended," he started to say. "I just wanted to—"

And that's when the intelligence engine *pinged*.

I handed my coffee cup to a bot and went forward to the yoke. Archer slid sideways and I slipped easily into the seat. The screens were green, but—

"That thing," Archer pointed. "What the hell is it?"

"Not a debris field," I said.

Angel parked himself at the navigation console. Dixon and Felcher hovered behind us.

The object was massive, bigger than the boat. And it was moving. Not fast, but methodically. *Toward* the scorch belt.

"Let's send in a probe."

"Aye, sir." I punched up a number four and launched it forward. Switched the main screen to remote view. The front of the bridge lit up as a dark blue panorama. Fingers of light poked forward into the gloom. Something dark ahead. And huge. Bigger than any Earth whale. "Monstro."

I maneuvered the probe in closer. The object still wouldn't resolve. It looked blurry.

"Keep going. Right up against it if you have to." That was Dixon.

The big display finally cleared, revealing a writhing surface of translucent flower petals, all moving in rhythmic waves. Not synchronized, but somehow meshing into a vast kinetic pattern. A mathematician's wet dream.

"What the—?"

"Ah!" said Archer.

We all turned to look at him.

"Bellyfish." He pointed at the screen. "Those are bellyfish. That's a cluster of them. A colony."

Praxis didn't have jellyfish. It had bellyfish—translucent tubular bladders that propelled themselves through the water with a gentle flexing motion—its own particular peristalsis. We had already identified hundreds of sub-species, but there could have been thousands more. They came in all sizes and colors, but the basic shape remained the same—a tube, sometimes with short tendrils at the mouth and long tendrils at the rear.

The bellyfish filtered the seawater flowing through it and fed on microorganisms, plankton, algae, whatever organic matter it captured with its interior papillae. The bellyfish was more of an intestine-fish than a bellyfish, but bellyfish was easier to say.

"I didn't know they formed colonies," said Angel.

"You should read more. There's a news-summary every week." Archer pointed at the screen. "Which way is Monstro swimming?"

"South," I reported. "Almost directly for the scorch belt."

"Yeah, that makes sense..." Archer was transfixed.

"No it doesn't," Felcher said. "The hot water will kill it."

Archer squinted at the screen. "I'm not so sure about that. Look at the way it's peeling off bodies."

I punched for magnification. Now we could see that the huge mass was shedding bits and pieces of itself as it moved through the water, mostly fragments of bodies, but sometimes a whole bellyfish or even a cluster of bellyfish. "It's dropping off the dead bits."

"How many do you think there are in that colony?" Dixon asked.

"Given the size of the thing—it would have to be hundreds of thousands. Millions. More."

Archer touched my shoulder. "Can you move the probe around to the front? I want to see something."

I leaned the joystick sideways, turning the probe, then forward. The panoramic view twisted then steadied. The bulk of the colony-creature slid by on the left. My attention was pulled to one of the readouts before me.

"Okay," I said. "I've got a more accurate reading on its size. You could land airplanes on it. Big ones. Two at a time. And not interfere with the football game either. This thing is three kilometers long and half that wide. And at the rate it's shedding, it must have been a lot larger than that when it formed up."

Eventually the probe passed the creature and moved ahead of it. I switched to the view from the rear-camera. We gaped into a cluster of multiple writhing maws. It wasn't one large tube—it was hundreds of tubes joined as one. Monstro was hungry.

Archer asked, "Can you get inside it?"

"I think the problem is going to be not getting inside—" The colony was gaining on the probe, sucking in huge amounts of water.

"Go ahead," said Dixon. "Let's have a look inside."

I cut power to the probe's motors. Almost immediately, the gigantic wall of it swelled in the screen. A moment later, the view constricted. We were inside a forest of churning translucent mouths, beautiful and horrifying.

Archer asked, "Can you read the interior of the beast?"

"It'll take a bit." I was already tapping at my keyboard, calling up scanning routines. "But it looks like it's all tubes. Clusters of little tubes making bigger tubes. Clusters of bigger tubes making even bigger ones. That's odd—"

"What is?"

"Hang on—" I fiddled with the focus. "Not every tube is active. Not all the individual creatures are functioning. In fact…it looks like most of them are dormant." I rotated the view. "Give me a minute. Yes. I see what's happening. There. Look. The active ones are peeling off."

"I see it," said Archer. "Stay on it. See? The dormant ones are waking up and starting to flex and pump."

"So what does that mean? The whole thing is coming apart?"

"Eventually, yes. It's supposed to." Archer looked excited now. "I think I see what's happening. It starts out big. With a huge core of dormant bellyfish." He paused for a moment, thinking, remembering something. "These things form in the Arctic. Apogee-winter. Great big masses. We call them bellybergs. The individual critters have some kind of natural antifreeze, they just go solid. When they cluster, they float on the surface."

"And they come down here to thaw out?" Dixon asked.

"That'd be my guess," Archer said. "When the ice starts breaking up, they head south. They get caught in the current." He frowned. Then his face lit up. He clapped his hands together. "Yes!"

"What?"

"I think we just solved one of the mysteries."

"Which one?" asked Dixon. "There are so many—"

"Okay, follow—" Archer was still working it out in his head. "The continental dichotomy. The idea that the north and south have two separate ecologies, separated by the scorch belt. It's impossible for most creatures to get through the heat of the equator. Especially anything as fragile as a bellyfish. But when we compare genetic samples from polar specimens, they're identical. Both poles. So how are the bellyfish getting across the scorch belt?"

He pointed at the big display, at the wall of writhing tubes. "That's how. Brute force. It's like hurling a cluster of seven Minotaur-class engines at the sky to launch a multi-ton payload. These creatures are doing the same thing. Sort of. Freeze the payload and launch it in a shell of concentric heat-shields.

"I mean, we'll want to test it further, but—" He shrugged and pointed at the display of squirming creatures. "That's pretty compelling evidence." He nodded appreciatively. "We can see the whole process right here. The ones that are exposed to the hot water are active. As soon as they overheat, they die and shed away. The next layer down wakes up and starts pumping, keeping the whole thing moving forward until they die in turn. It's a marvelous adaptation—a combination heat-shield and propulsion system, ablating itself as it goes."

"I wonder if we could do the same thing," said Dixon.

"Huh?"

"You know how we fab subs with concentric shells, so no hull has to bear the full pressure of the water. Each hull maintains a certain pressure differential. Like an egg with multiple shells. We could do the same thing with cooling systems. Each shell only has to be ten degrees cooler than the next one out, so no hull has to be the wall between hot and cold."

"You still have to get rid of the heat somewhere. If the outside is too hot—"

"You only need it long enough to pass through the scorch belt." He shrugged. "I don't know if it'll work. Let's let the lab boys test it. Meanwhile—" He gestured with his coffee mug at the display. "I'd say we've paid for this trip."

None of us spoke for a long moment. We just kept staring at the panoramic screen. It was one more way for Praxis to amaze us.

"Y'know..." Archer began slowly. "I think—this thing might explain another piece of the puzzle. These are one-sex creatures. We study them in the lab. They only release eggs, so how do they fertilize themselves? I'll bet this is what they do for sexual reproduction. The survivors who cross the scorch belt—the journey, or the heat, something triggers a change, and they release the sperms. The southerners fertilize the north, the northerners fertilize the south. Back and forth. The two polar environments function like two separate sexes. The same sex, but different when it needs to be."

"Hm," said Dixon.

"Oof," said Felcher.

"Wow," said Angel.

I didn't say anything. All the good words had been taken.

"That's a long way to go to deliver a load of sperm," Felcher whispered.

"Life will find a way," Angel whispered back.

"One sex. And they make it work," said Dixon.

"It's a very primitive species," replied Archer. "We don't know that this phenomenon can scale up to higher orders."

"Flatworms," said Dixon. "Flatworms and bellyfish."

"Huh?"

"Flatworms only have one sex. When they mate, it's a fight. The winner stabs the loser. The loser has to incubate the eggs."

"And your point is?"

"We're turning ourselves into flatworms and bellyfish. Is that a good thing or not?"

Nobody replied to that.

We stayed with Monstro as long as we could—not all the way to the equator, but close enough that the surface probes we launched were sending back some very scary pictures of the towering storms ahead.

We followed Monstro down to 1600 meters, but even that wasn't deep enough to escape the heat. At the peak of perigee-summer, the surface of the equatorial seas were boiling, sending a wall of steam into the overheated air. The rest of the heat suffused downward. When the interior temperature of the sub hit 88F/31C, Dixon turned us around. "No sense in driving this oven any deeper. We can't diffuse our heat into water warmer than we are."

I peeled off my shirt, poured lukewarm water down my chest, and drove the boat north at full power. We celebrated with a round of cold beers and thawed some steaks. We'd be back to the habitable zone within a week. Away from the debris fields, we could even surface and breathe clean air.

Neither Felcher nor Angel said anything about sex on the way home. Monstro had that effect on all of us.

And I needed to talk to Jose.

The Old Science Fiction Writer

"Grampa," he began, "did you have glimmers in the olden days?"

I reached over to tousle his hair, he twisted away. "The olden days, eh? You want to hear about how your Great-Gramma Jo drove a covered wagon all the way from St. Louis to the gold fields in Sacramento and how we were chased by Apaches across the Arizona desert? Of course, I was just a baby at the time, so I had to use the little gun, not the big rocket launcher, because I was too small to lift it. Or do you want to hear about Aunt Alice's heavy metal rock band, the Juicy Lucies, and how they started a riot at the Hollywood Bowl when they played bare-breasted? Or should I tell you about the time I wrote a script for the very first *Star Trek* series—?"

Danny-Marie made a face. "No, tell me a *real* story. Not one of your made-up ones." He settled himself on the couch, tugging at his skirt; he hadn't decided which gender he wanted to be for adolescence. He was still trying on possibilities and discovering that the freedom of an unbifurcated garment had certain drafty disadvantages. Meanwhile, I still called him *he*, because that was a lot easier than any of the invented pronouns.

"A *real* story, huh."

"Yeah, something I can goggle—to see if you're lying."

"I never lie. Let's see...." I scrabbled through the dusty shelves of memory. "Do you want to hear how I predicted computer viruses fifteen years before the first one was actually written? Or the day I testified against Charles Manson? Or how about the time a Shuttle astronaut asked me for my autograph? Or I could tell you how John Cusack played me in the movie about me and your dad? Or maybe you want to hear about the dog who liked salad? That's always a fun story—"

"No, Grampa! A *real* story!"

I thought about protesting. Those *were* real stories. The dog who liked salad was one of my favorites, but this was not an argument I was going to win. I sighed and said, "Okay, you tell me. What do *you* want to hear about?"

"I wanna hear about the olden days."

"Those were the olden days."

"The *real* olden days."

"Well, um. Let me think. That was a long time ago, you know. There were still dragons—"

"Grampa! Dragons weren't invented then."

"I'm not talking about the invented dragons. I'm talking about the real ones. Before the knights killed them all."

"Grampa! I'm not a little girl anymore. I'm old enough to apply for puberty—"

"Don't do it. It's a trap."

He gave me the teenager look. "Tell me about when you were little. A hundred years ago. What was it like?"

I muttered something about Father William. He had the right idea. "Be off, or I'll kick you downstairs."

"Who's Father William?"

"He was my priest when I went to Seminary school. Did I ever tell you about the religion I started? Spiritual Harmony Among Many. We went by the acronym. I was the head SHAMan...."

"Grampa!"

"That's a true story too, Danny-Marie." I stopped, took a breath. There's no such thing as patience, only exhaustion. I was too tired to argue. "Just what is it you want to hear?"

"What was it *like*?"

"It was like...like today, only a lot quieter." Another deep breath. "Our first television had a great big seventeen-inch screen."

"What's an inch?"

I held my hands apart, a soccer ball's width. "About like that. That was for the ladies. It was different for men. Never mind. That comes after puberty. But we had to sit real close to the screen. It would have been bad for our eyes to sit too far away. And it wasn't even black and white. It was green and white. And it was kerosene-powered. The only show we could get on it was *I Like Lucy*. They weren't even married yet."

Danny-Marie frowned, still suspicious, but didn't interrupt.

"This was before Big Think. A long time before. If you were a grown-up, you had to get up every day and go off to work—wait, I'll explain work in a minute. If you were still a child, you had to go to school so you could learn how to be a grown-up before it happened—and it happened whether you were ready or not, so you didn't have a lot of time, you had to learn fast, before puberty hit. Otherwise—"

"Yeah, I know about that. It's on the license exam. What did you mean about going to work?"

"I'm trying to figure out how to explain it. See, before Big Think, people had to do everything themselves. We called it work. Sometimes you liked what you were doing, so it was more fun than work, but there was a lot of stuff that needed to be done that wasn't fun. We called that stuff work."

"Like what stuff?"

"Like *everything*. If you wanted to eat, you had to grow your own food. You had to put seeds in the ground and water them and wait till they grew into vegetables. If you wanted meat—"

"I know how to grow meat. You took me to the meat farms, remember?"

"How could I forget? You ate yourself sick on dino-bits." He made a face. I ignore it and continued. "Anyway, work was necessary to keep all the different pieces of the world running. We didn't have bots, so people had to do all the hard things themselves, building houses and sewing clothes and repairing cars and everything else you can think of and a lot of stuff you can't. If you worked, people traded you money for your work—that is, if it was work they wanted or needed. If you didn't work, you didn't get money, so you couldn't buy food or live in a house or have clothes or anything."

"So everybody was naked and hungry?"

"No. Everybody went to work, because they didn't want to be naked and hungry. Some people built things. Others tore things down. Some people cleaned things. Others made them dirty. Getting things dirty was the job that teenagers did best, so it all worked out. Mostly."

"What did you do?"

"I wrote stories. People paid to read them. They gave me their money, sometimes a lot, so I ate every day and wore nice clothes and lived in a big house."

"People *really* paid you for your stories?"

"Yes, they did. Once they even gave me an award."

"No, they didn't!"

"Yes, they did. And they paid me a lot because I was good at it. Just like you're going to pay me for this one."

"No, I'm not."

"Then I'm going to starve. And I'll take off all my clothes and go live in the garden—"

"No, you won't. Daddy won't let you."

"I think I liked your daddy better when he was your mommy. Without all the testosterone."

"Thpffft. Tell me how Big Think happened?"

"Well, that's a tough one, kidlet. A lot of different things happened all at once, all together, but separately, and it took a while for everything to settle down. It was a very confusing time, because so much was happening and a lot of people were very upset because they didn't understand any of it, so it made them afraid, but not all of us. Some of us were even excited.

"See, back then, there were other people who wrote stories too, not just me. We wrote a special kind of story called science fiction. We wrote about all the stuff that hadn't happened yet. And some of us said that one day a Big Think was going to happen. So it wasn't a surprise to everyone. Just most people."

"Science fiction? What's that?"

Oof. That one hurt. Okay... "It's complicated. Hard to explain. Um, science fiction was..." Hmm. It really *was* hard to explain.

"Okay, let me back up a little. The reason we all had to go to work was because we hadn't built everything yet. And a lot of the stuff we had built was kind of clumsy—we didn't know how to make houses self-sufficient or cars that could drive themselves. We were just fumbling along because there was so much we still didn't know. Most of the time we were just patching things up as fast as we could."

"That's crazy. Was everybody stupid in the olden days?"

"Not stupid. We just hadn't learned enough yet to do better. It was a crazy time because people didn't like not knowing, so they made up stuff and pretended they did know. A lot of silly stuff—"

"Like what?"

"Like you wouldn't believe. People made up all kinds of weird stories that they used instead of real explanations."

"Like what? Tell me!"

"Okay, just one. Ready?"

"Ready."

"There were people who believed that the more money you had, the more important you were."

"No. Really?"

"Yes. Really."

"Dumb."

"Well, yes—we know that *now*."

"And everybody was that crazy?"

"No. Not everybody. There were a lot of people who were trying to figure out the *really* important things—how stuff actually worked. They got a lot of it wrong at first, but they didn't quit and they got enough right that it was worth it to keep going. It was hard work, but it was the kind of work that was fun too, because the more they found out, the more they found out how much more there was to find out. So it was like solving a great big puzzle—until they found out just how big and infinite the puzzle really was."

"And then Big Think happened, right?"

"Well, not right away. Remember I told you that Big Think didn't happen all at once? There was a kind of middle period in there, where we figured out we had a way to figure things out, but we still hadn't figured everything out. There was still a lot of stuff we didn't know—like the umptillionth digit of pi, it's 1 by the way—but we had finally gotten to the point where we knew what we didn't know, so we could start thinking about what it would be like when we did know it. That was what science fiction writers did."

"Huh?" Danny-Marie made *that* face.

"Okay, let me try again. We tried to imagine what all those unknown things were and how they might work and how things would change after we found out. That was science fiction. And you know what...?"

"What?"

"It was a lot of fun. We got to think about all kinds of stuff."

"What kinds of stuff?"

"Oh, how spaceships would work and what bots would do? How do you get to Mars? What's inside a left-handed quark? And where does your lap go when you stand up? Things like that."

"But that stuff is so *easy*! Everybody knows that stuff."

"Well, now, yes. But this was a long time before flybois and glimmers and pheens. We thought about that stuff because we wanted to know how to build it."

"You didn't know how to print a pheen?"

"Kidlet, you asked about the olden days. There was a lot of stuff we didn't know back then. That's why we thought about it—that's what science fiction was. Big thinking before Big Think. A lot of it was silly, a lot of it was wrong, but there was also a bunch that started people thinking about what to do next and how to do better."

"And that's what you did?"

"Yep. And I wasn't the only one. Out of all the billions and billions of people, there were maybe only a thousand of us—if that many. It was a very special job, one of the best jobs in the world, and not a lot of people could do it well. But each of us was thinking about a piece of the *big* puzzle. The puzzle that Big Think came along to solve."

"Only a thousand?"

"Maybe a few more, maybe less. Hard to say. Not all of us knew enough science to get it right."

"What stuff did you think about? Did you get any of it right?"

"Well ... um, some stuff, yes."

"What stuff?"

"Well, I thought about Big Think before there was a Big Think. And portals—I thought about how portals might work. And shifting. And sex-bots too. I wasn't the only one thinking about sex-bots though. Back in those days, sex was very important. Really. And hard to do. If we wanted to have sex, we had to have it with each other. Or even by ourselves."

"Now, you're just being silly."

"I'm a science fiction writer. It's my job to be silly. Except nobody needs silly anymore. Not my kind anyway."

"Grampa...?" Danny-Marie looked across at me skeptically. "Are you making this up?"

"No, I am not."

"There really were science fiction thinkers?"

"Yes, there were. I would not lie to you about this. They were some of the very best people on the planet."

"Really, Grampa? Really?"

I spread my hands in surrender. "What do you think?"

"I think you're making it all up."

"Well, yes, I am very good at making things up. At least, I used to be. Just ask me. But not this. Not this time. See, it was Big Think that put us all out of business.

"First there was Little Think. And that seemed like a good idea at the time. Then Little Think helped design Big Think. And after Big Think, we didn't have to imagine anymore, we didn't have to make anything up—because Big Think had a Q-brain and could do all the science in minus-time and tell us how to make it real. We would ask Big Think how something worked or how to do it and Big Think would tell us the fastest, most efficient, and cost-effective way to the result even before we finished asking the question.

"It was a great time-saver. And a lot of fun—but only at first. Because after a while, we realized there wasn't anything to imagine anymore. Big Think would either tell us how to build it or why it wasn't possible. That, my dear, is how Big Think put us all out of work. Each and every one of us. I haven't written a science fiction story in...oh, my, over a hundred years. It was a very special time. But now it's over."

Danny-Marie frowned. An idea was forming behind those eyes.

"I have a question for you, Grampa."

"Of course you do."

"A lot of the stuff that Big Think says. We have to believe it because nobody is smart enough to understand the proof, right? Only Big Think. So...what if Big Think is just making stuff up too?"

"Hmm. Y'know, that's a very good question. In fact, it's even a good idea for a science fiction story. Do you want to help me write it—?"

"No. But you can write it and tell it to me. Next time."

He switched me off and I disappeared.

The Bag Lady

The street stank of garbage and sweat, but it was still early. Later, as the day warmed up, the smells of garlic and bacon would seep out of the corner diner. Traffic splashed through spring puddles. The last white patches of winter still resisted the glare of the sun, but if this was not their last day, it would be their last week.

The bag lady shuffled painfully along the sidewalk, pushing an overloaded shopping cart with one broken wheel. She didn't walk as much as she staggered. She was a shapeless lump, an ambulatory heap of clothing, new layers added on top of the old, sweaters, sweatshirts, torn coats, a blanket, another coat, the whole stuffed with old newspapers for insulation—she was an oblate spheroid of rubbish and rejection. Her swollen ankles made it difficult for her to move, even harder to push the cart. Her feet were wrapped in more layers of dirty cloth.

The woman's skin was leathery and lined, burned and scoured, eroded by the relentless weather. Her graying hair was a tangle of greasy ropes. If she'd ever had a name, she hadn't heard anyone speak it in years. Her eyes were rheumy and bloodshot—wherever she looked, she seemed to be staring at something on the other side of reality.

Several people passed her by, none of them saw her. She was invisible to them, not even scenery. Oblivious to her anguish and embarrassment, they hurried on about their business—exhaling puffs of breath like human locomotives, they chugged along the unbreakable rails of their lives.

The bag lady didn't care. She had more important matters to attend to. She did not often push her way onto this street, the business owners frowned at her, turned their hoses on her, chased her away with epithets and sometimes even threats of violence. But today—

She frowned, she sniffed, she looked up the street and back again. Something wasn't right. No, not here. Not there, but close. Something in the universe smelled wrong. And it wasn't her.

And then, she spotted it—

The dirty van, the dirty dark grey van. A panel van parked at the curb. No windows at the rear or sides. The front windows were tinted dark. No markings to identify the vehicle, no bumper stickers, no ads painted on the side. Just a featureless block.

It smelled wrong.

She looked down the street, all the way down to the end of the street, where a little girl in a pink winter coat had just come bouncing around the corner. She glowed with innocence—the world was still bright and beautiful to her. She was singing and skipping, trailing one mittened hand across the frosty store-fronts, leaving sketchy streaks in the hoar-frost.

And as it always did, the moment clicked into clarity. The bag lady made a decision. She pushed her heavy cart forward. She put all her strength into the effort, squelching desperately forward.

Finally, unable to move any further, she stopped, her cart inconveniently blocking the passenger door of the van, her reeking body blocking the sliding panel door on the side. Someone on the inside made a noise, it sounded like a curse.

The bag lady grunted in sudden annoyance. She leaned against the panel door of the van for balance, her wrinkled hand sliding and leaving an ugly smear—and then a stream of urine ran down her left leg, puddling at her feet, steaming on the icy pavement.

The moment was perfectly timed. The little girl came dancing by, her song abruptly stopping as she glanced over. She made a face, an expression of disgust and disapproval, then she broke into a run and scampered on toward school.

The bag lady still leaned against the van, frowning, concentrating on something more than her own body now. The left tail light of the van abruptly shattered. No repair shop would ever be able to make it light again. Every police cruiser that noticed would pull this vehicle over to cite the driver for the broken light—but no, that wouldn't be enough. She needed to do more.

She muttered a few words—barely finishing the curse before the van pulled angrily away. The greasy handprint on its side would not wash off—not easily and not for a long time. But the handprint was only the smallest part of the spell. The van and its unseen occupant were now afflicted with a fetid malcharisma. They would never go unnoticed again—it might be enough. The bag lady couldn't be sure.

In the great grand scheme of things, this little shift of possibility was so small as to be infinitesimal in its reach—but to the little girl in the pink coat, the unknowing recipient of this reversal of entropy, it was an unknown coup, a victory of life-changing proportions—simply because she would live to see tomorrow.

But for the bag lady, it was going to be a very expensive triumph. The avalanche of entropy is unforgiving and the effort to shift it even a millimeter would cost her dearly.

Already, she was groaning with new pains. She grabbed onto the handle of her shopping cart to keep from falling. It was so heavily loaded it was an anchor to her sudden dizziness. For a moment, she did not know who she was or where she was. She knew only pain, the bottomless well of icy fire that gnawed at her gut, the first warnings of the waves of despair to come.

Somehow, she managed to make it across the slippery sidewalk to the nearest doorstep, where she sank down to her knees, collapsing in her rags, sagging against the frame of the door. She knew she couldn't stay here long. She knew the proprietor of this shop was an unforgiving tyrant, a small and petty excuse for a human being, interested only in amount of commerce he could attract, never in the people he might serve. Soon, he would come bursting angrily out of his sacred warmth to chase her away.

But right now, she was overcome with the simple effort of breathing. In. Out. In. Out. She gasped for breath, strove to regain some sense of herself, but failing. This was going to be a bad one. Very bad. She couldn't help herself, she had to see. Still puffing, she began laboriously unwrapping the coils of cloth around her right leg, around and around, all the way down, until she finally revealed the mottled skin of her left foot. It was stippled with ugly blotches of green and yellow, blue and purple. There were new sores appearing, pus-filled boils, inflammations that grew even as she watched. Blood oozed from old scabs.

She searched desperately for the first telltale signs of gangrene, but was quickly disappointed. As eagerly as she hoped—no, not yet. This wasn't the one. Not even close. Not big enough. Not yet. She was going to survive. She was going to live another day. She wept.

She could remember another time—so long long ago—a time of naïve ignorance, but that was before the flashes began, before the smells and the flavors and the clamoring sense of wrongness overwhelmed her with a terrible compulsion to do something—*anything*—that might restore even a small balance to the world.

"It isn't fair! Why me?" she wept. "Why me? What did I do to deserve this—?"

But even as the words dribbled out of her torn mouth, she already knew the answer. Because. Because. Because she'd brought it on herself—with her own outraged scream of anguish at the universe. "Why doesn't somebody do something?"

And the universe had answered. "Why don't *you*?"

So tomorrow, just like today, just like yesterday, just like all the days and years before, freezing through the unrelenting winter, burning and baking beneath the heavy blanket of summer, nevertheless she'll lever herself up again, every day paying the ugly price of her compulsion one more time. She has no choice—

The bag lady will pull herself up from the unforgiving pavement, stumble to her feet, wheezing and groaning, her bones crackling resentfully, all stiff and resisting—racked with pain and hunger, driven by desperation, she'll go out and search the streets and the alleys, looking for the big one, hoping, always hoping—every day hoping that today will be the day she can finally earn her death.

Entanglements

I am going to kill That Pesky Dan Goodman.

I do not yet know how or when, but count on it. It will happen.

I will have a perfect alibi. That's part of the plan too. I'm a writer. Ninety percent of what I do is research. The other ten percent is planning revenge. And I learned this one a long time ago—the best revenge doesn't have the author's fingerprints on it. That way the recipient can only blame karma.

Revenge isn't about getting even. Who wants to get even? Even means you didn't gain any ground, you just restored what you perceived as a previous state of balance—no, I want massive retaliation that leaves the target sprawled facedown and jackhammered two feet into the mud, wondering if anyone got the license plate of the giant Japanese lizard that just stomped him. Yes, I believe in karmageddon.

But in this case, I'll settle for a simple and elegant discorporation.

Now (you may ask) why have I decided to kill That Pesky Dan Goodman?

It's simple.

Self-defense.

Every time the man inserts himself into my life, the consequences are painful, expensive, and traumatic.

Once upon a time, I used to imagine that the life of an author would be a pleasant one—a life filled with good books, great music, a glass of sherry after dinner, the occasional outing with friends, and the only drama in my life coming from the Sunday broadcast of Masterpiece Theatre. Although it requires some small degree of maintenance, for the most part, I've achieved that life. As a bonus, the dog likes me. That's all the validation I need most days—that and the occasional check from a publisher.

But whenever I feel I have achieved this desired state of sustainability, Peskydang shows up. He's like the magic button attached to the toilet seat—whenever you sit down, the phone rings.

In my case, Pesky shows up at restaurants.

There are places I no longer go. As much as I love Canter's Delicatessen on Fairfax or Bob's Big Boy in Toluca Lake, those are danger zones. So is Tommy's Original Hamburgers at Beverly and Rampart. And Pink's Hot Dogs on La Brea too. Those are tourist spots anyway.

(There's a conversation that bubbles up from time to time among Los Angeles-based writers—it's a joke that Mort Sahl told half a century ago. "The Day Canter's Closed" is a science fiction story. It begins with a meteor crossing the sky, then everybody's watches are so magnetized they all stop at the same time—no, it'll have to be updated, all their laptops and tablets and smartphones go dead from a mysterious electro-magnetic pulse—and then the gay waiters and gargoyles at Canter's are all replaced by alien space lizards, but nobody notices because they're too busy arguing about their screenplays and Kickstarter projects. I could probably option that to Warner Brothers....)

But no, if I decide I've had enough of my own cooking, I have to sneak out at an odd hour. To date, Pesky has not yet found me at the diner around the corner where I sometimes go for breakfast, nor the Thai place up the block with the great spring rolls, nor the sushi place three doors beyond where they've customized the cucumber roll just for me, with pickled baby carrot and oshinko.

If Pesky ever shows up at those places—

I just have to figure out a way to dispose of the body.

See, the perfect murder isn't one where the cops can't figure out who did it or why. It's where the cops don't even know a murder has occurred.

My life-coach—

This is Los Angeles. Everyone has a life-coach. If you don't have a life-coach, you're a tourist. Or you're not taking your life serious enough.

—my life coach says I'm not owning the circumstances. He says, "Think about every problem you've ever had in your entire life. They all have one thing in common."

"Yes, Randy?"

"You were there."

Uh...yeah. True. Okay, yes, I get it. That's the fancy way of saying I'm a jerk. Got it. Thank you for sharing.

"David," he says, "you have eighty-nine problems."

"How do you know that?"

"Because everyone has eighty-nine problems."

"But I don't want eighty-nine problems."

"Ahh, now you have ninety problems."

As much fun as all those coaching conversations can be—all those Zen-delivered-with-a-firehose discussions of personal responsibility—none of them actually lead to an escape from the entanglements of circumstance.

But I digress.

This time, Pesky caught me at my birthday party.

No, I hadn't invited him. But he showed up anyway. The man has an uncanny ability to locate a free meal. And he dresses like the fannish version of Diane Keaton in *Annie Hall*—the dorkish interpretation of the layered look. It's impossible to determine what fashion or style he's going for, but I call it *compilation du jour*. This time it was a bright Paisley vest over a black silk shirt, a long knit scarf banded with different colors, a crimson dickie, a broad bow tie, a knitted Jayne-hat with earflaps and short hanging whatchamacallits with knobs on the ends, a long coat spreading out like a cape, flowing silk pantaloons tucked into knee-high boots, a broad black belt studded with, well...studs, and all kinds of hanging appliances and adornments—Johnny Depp would have been jealous.

I wonder sometimes how long it takes him to dress before he can walk out of the house. And why bus drivers even allow him to board. Sometimes he carries a sword or a battleaxe. This time, he didn't.

At least he doesn't wear a kilt.

I'm not kiltaphobic. I just think there are some things man was not meant to show. Some men. Pesky, in particular.

But Pesky had clearly seen the birthday invitation somewhere. Because he showed up with a giraffe.

I'll explain.

I'd spent several months thinking about the possibility of a birthday party and why I even wanted a celebration. The last time I'd hosted a party was to celebrate the finalization of my son's adoption. That had been two decades previous and we were still repairing holes in the drywall. But this year signified that I had survived some of the best and worst this planet could do to a person for an admirable number of decades, one of the big numbers with a zero at the end—and a bit of gray-haired introspection on the bathroom scale about how my life had turned out anyway brought me to the realization that I had not had a birthday party since I was eight years old—not unless you count my Bar Mitzvah, which wasn't a party as much as it was a pageant. But other than that, I hadn't had a natal celebration in more than half a century.

I knew why too.

I didn't have one for my ninth birthday because my parents had just (finally?) bought a house in the San Fernando Valium and we were moving the day after. Half the furniture had already left. So instead of a party we had a birthday dinner and a cake in a near-empty apartment and I didn't get to see any of my friends from school. Somewhere in there, I must have unconsciously decided that my birthday was no longer important enough to celebrate, so after that I mostly ignored it. Or maybe I was just embarrassed about growing older.

While my mom was still alive, the tradition was an annual family dinner, an event which grew more sparsely attended every year until finally it was just me and my sister. And by that time, dying young and/or leaving a good-looking corpse were no longer options.

The final push over the edge of the commitment chasm, however, came from my son who quietly insisted, "Dad, you gotta have a party. People like parties. If you don't have a party for people to give you chocolate, you're ripping them off of the opportunity to give you chocolate."

Sean was right. I was not only entitled, but obligated to celebrate my fiftieth birthday (albeit a couple of decades late), and after checking to see that it wouldn't be a scene out of *Stella Dallas* (look it up), and after some internal review of my own motives, I determined that what I really wanted to do was host a big party as a way of thanking the survivors for still being my friends after all these many years of gaffes, stumbles, and falling into social potholes. It turned out the guest list was longer than expected, but we filled it out with people who wouldn't turn down a free meal—writers, mostly.

The invitation said: "A proper birthday party requires balloons, noisemakers, party hats, ice cream, a karaoke machine, popcorn, chocolate, redheads, chocolate-covered redheads, a bathtub full of lime Jell-O, jellybeans, nachos, guacamole, a disc jockey, a disco ball, a fog machine, lasers, spotlights, a party tent, a bouncy castle, cherry bombs, a police permit, explosives, giraffes, cheese dip, strippers, a Swedish hooker, condoms, watermelons, a catapult, chainsaws, masks, maraschino cherries, flavored love oils, paramedics, name tags, registration table, insurance waivers, a trapeze, handcuffs, spare batteries, water slide, first-aid kits, chains, hand grenades, Saran Wrap, clowns, a rubber chicken, an Elvis impersonator, a live webcam feed, and a cake.

"I think we can manage the cake and maybe the bouncy castle."

I mean, who wouldn't want to attend a party like that? A cake *and* a bouncy castle! After a certain age, you stop worrying about looking good. It's about having fun. In my case, the age was six.

Planning the party was easy. A week in advance I ordered pizzas, deli-trays, kegs, and a cake, all to be delivered an hour before the guests were due to arrive. Sodas and balloons and chips took only a few minutes at the nearby grocery. I could pick up the ice the morning of the party. Ordering the bouncy castle needed only five minutes of Googling and a phone call. But it costs $4000 to rent a giraffe for an afternoon. I did not rent the giraffe. I admit, I was tempted, though.

The day of the party all the food arrived as ordered, so did the bouncy castle. Right on time the guests started showing up and all I had to do was open the door and hug those who weren't contagious.

Several of my high school friends, my son's godmother, Holly of Sherman's Planet, several beautiful TV stars, a couple of actors, one of my favorite comedians, two or three producers, various writers of my acquaintance, and even a few people who pretended to be normal. The writers headed straight for the food, of course. (Have you ever seen a writer eat? They're worse than actors.)

In the middle of all this, just as the party was shifting from raucous to insane, a woman I didn't recognize, somebody's plus-one, came screaming in the front door shouting something about a giraffe. Several of us rushed outside, followed by several more, and eventually everybody.

Yes, there was a giraffe on the front lawn.

And That Pesky Dan Goodman stood next to it, feeding it carrots, and looking across at me with a self-satisfied grin. "You said it wouldn't be a party without a giraffe."

No good joke goes unpunished.

Okay, in all fairness, the giraffe was the high point of the party.

Her name was Hermione. She wasn't quite full-size—she was only four years old, the equivalent of a teenager, and a little high-spirited, but she wasn't freaked out by all the attention. I guess she was used to being gawked at by a crowd—or maybe she was just happy to have all the apples, bananas, carrots, stalks of celery, ears of corn, and the occasional Dorito with guacamole offered to her. She also munched her way through handfuls of oat-crackers that the trainer kept handing up to her, wrapping her gray tongue around them and sucking them appreciatively into her mouth. How much fiber does a giraffe need anyway?

I was a little worried that the rich mix of fruits and vegetables might give her an upset stomach—diarrhea?—but the trainer said not to worry, it would be good for the lawn.

So even though Peskydang hadn't been officially invited, after he showed up with the giraffe, I couldn't very well turn him away, could I?

That was the mistake.

It being a birthday party, most of the guests brought gifts, and most of them knew me well enough to bring chocolate. Dark chocolate only, milk chocolate is for beginners.

But the ones who *really* knew me—they brought books.

And what books! Graphic novels, rare adventures, autographed editions! Even a marvelous pop-up book! It didn't matter. I love books.

Every book is a door into adventure. It's an opportunity to live an extra life. Or to say it another way, you're lending your brain for someone else to think with. It's exercise for the mind-muscle. You get to think something you wouldn't have thought otherwise. You get stretched. That's why people who read have the advantage.

So people who give me books are...well, I'm not sure there is a word or even an appropriate metaphor. Hero? Wizard? Guru? No, none of those work. Someone who gives you the opportunity to peek at possibilities...? I'll have to cogitate on this and get back to you.

Pesky's gift, however....

It was a small wooden box. Deceptively small. Just big enough to hold a cell phone. But heavy enough to be suspicious. In fact, when I unwrapped and opened it, it *was* a cell phone. Only it wasn't. It didn't feel right.

"Um," I said. "Thank you, Pesky...? Am I missing something here? I already have a phone."

"It's not a phone," Pesky said. "It's a parallelicon. A quantum resonator. A quawkie-talkie." He glanced around the room impatiently. Some of the other guests, those who were still vertical, were glancing at him curiously. "Put it away for now. I'll show you how it works later."

"All right." I slipped it into a pocket. My son shoved another package into my hands, "Here, Dad, open this one next," and I forgot about the odd device. I am easily distracted by any box that smells like cocoa.

By the time the party finally broke up, after the last ambulance had pulled away and the police were satisfied that Ed Green was going to keep his clothes on this time—we told them he was practicing for an upcoming audition ("The Canoga Park Players are planning a revival of *Naked Boys Singing* ...") and that seemed to mollify the officers, though they declined the offer of comped seats for opening night—anyway, after the last of the neighbors stopped making videos and went back into their houses, we passed out shovels, rubber gloves, and trash bags to everyone who didn't have a ride home and began cleaning up.

It didn't take as long as expected. Three of the kegs had been emptied, most of the pizza was gone, only a few wilted slices of pastrami remained on the deli trays, Dogzilla took care of those. The only sodas left in the coolers were a dented can of Diet Coke and an A&W Root Beer, so the only leftovers we had to wrap up were the remains of the birthday cake. It had been a custom cake portraying *that* scene from *that* episode of *that* TV series. Harlan Ellison had cheerfully eaten William Shatner's head.

As the last few guests were trying to find the front door, Pesky came over to thank me for including him, making me aware again that my biggest failure as a human being is that I'm too polite to That Pesky Dan Goodman. He keeps coming back. (Daniel Keys Moran, who plays basketball more than I do, which is never at all, says I'm putting too much backspin on him.)

"I need to explain my gift to you," Pesky said.

"Oh yeah, I forgot all about it." I fished through my pockets, pulling out wallet, smartphone (Samsung Galaxy Note II, because it has a larger screen than the S4), music player (A 64GB Zune. And yes, I can hear you rolling your eyes so hard back that you can see the bottom of your brain, but I like it, it works for me, so why should I care what you think?), and a wadded-up paper napkin with someone's phone number on it, I didn't remember whose, before I finally found Pesky's device. "Yeah, this is cool. What is it?"

"Well, it depends," he said. "Have you ever heard of a telegrabitron?"

"A what?"

"A para-dimensional interociter."

"Uhh....no."

"Okay, this is going to take some time." He glanced around, checking the room. Still too many people. "C'mere." He took me by the forearm and led me outside to the back yard, grabbing the last banana on the way.

"Do you know what a stringshot is?"

"It's a way to add delta vee to your trajectory by swinging around a—"

"No. That's a slingshot. Are you sure you write science fiction?"

"Not any more. There's too much science. I can't keep up."

"You and everybody else." He took the banana—

That Pesky Dan Goodman does not peel a banana like a normal person. Normal people—that's you and me, an assumption on my part, I don't know if you're normal or not, I just like to think so—you and me, we peel the banana from the stem end, and that's usually a bit of a tussle. Sometimes we even have to bite it to get it started, right? Pesky opens it from the other end—he pinches the tip hard, it splits and peels easily down. (I tried it once, the banana split right down the middle, half stuck to each peel. There must be a trick to it.)

—and he did that same banana thing again. One day I'm going to have to learn how to do it. Either he didn't notice me watching or he didn't care.

"Okay," he said. "You know about quantum entanglement?"

"Uh, yeah, sort of. Two particles are invisibly linked together. If you do something to one, the other reacts. In tandem, right?"

"Close enough for a science-fiction story. The theory is that if the two particles are far enough apart and still remain linked, you can have instantaneous transmission of information. Even across light-years."

"Ah, the old subspace-radio trick."

"According to theory, entanglements create a mini-wormhole that keeps them linked, one particle at each end. So all you need to do is create an entanglement and—are you following this?"

"Yeah, go on. This is the necessary exposition. It has to go somewhere." I say that a lot. It never slows anyone down.

Pesky heard it as permission. He kept talking. "Okay. So what if we come at it from the other direction? What if every particle was already entangled? But you just didn't know where the other one was? What if you could grab a particle and track its wormhole through space-time and find its equivalent entangled particle somewhere else? You could have instantaneous communication anywhere you wanted."

I waved the phone-thing at him. "Are you saying this is a working subspace communicator?"

"If it worked, it would be."

"It doesn't work?"

"Well, the guys who built it—they don't know if it does or not. They don't know where the entangled particles are."

"They can't tell?"

"Nope. It's a Heisenberg thing. They're not certain. They think they have entanglements, all the evidence suggests it, but the entanglements all look congruent, so it looks like the particles are entangled to themselves. So, what you're holding—that's the most useless communication device in the universe. There's only one. A telephone doesn't work unless there's another one on the other end."

A sudden suspicion struck me. "How did *you* get it?"

"I asked for it."

"And they gave it to you?"

"I said I had an idea. They said, 'What the hell?'"

"Mm." I suspected there was more to it than that. Peskydang's relationship with the truth was mostly transitory. "Really?"

"Well, I kinda borrowed it. But they're not going to miss it. Not for a while anyway."

"Uh-huh. So now I'm guilty of receiving stolen property?" I held the thing away from me.

"No. You are a participant in a scientific experiment. Mine." He took the device from my hand and held it up so I could see its face. "I think this is something a lot more than they realized. I think this is a reciprocal encabulator."

"A what?"

"A quantotum."

"In English, please? Remember what we told you, Pesky. If you're going to stay on our planet, you have to speak our language."

"This *is* your language, monkey boy." He sighed. "Look. *This* is a trans-dimensional parallelithonic resonating transceiver. It contains a 64-core multi-fractal array of entangled particles. Call it a quantum empathizer for short."

"Okay." I pretended to understand that sentence. "And—?"

"Where do you think the opposing entanglements are?"

"I don't know. Argentina?"

He gave me a look. "If they're not in this universe, then they have to be in...wait for it!...*another* universe. A parallel universe." He waved the unit under my nose. "This is a Dirac line to an alternate reality."

"Except it doesn't work."

"We don't know that yet. Here, do a thought experiment—assume an *infinite* number of parallel universes. This would mean that somewhere in at least one of those *infinite* alternate worlds, it's inevitable someone else is holding a device just like this one. *Exactly* like this one. And maybe that's what this is really connected to, but we just don't know it yet. The guys who built it—they think their entanglements are congruent—but what if they're wrong? What if the entanglements look congruent because the universes are identical? Or *almost* identical, but not quite. Just in this one respect." He wiggled the thing in his hand.

I pulled out my phone and checked the time.

"What are you doing?"

"Checking to see if it's almost breakfast time. You're asking me to believe six impossible things."

"Only five. But I haven't finished yet."

"You can stop any time."

"All I'm asking you to do is play with it for a few days."

"Why me? Why not you?"

"Because you know how to break things. You're the best beta-tester I know."

He had me there.

I built my first computer in 1978. I've been aggressive about software ever since. If a program can be crashed, I can do it. If there's a weird little quirk, an odd behavior, or even an actual bug—I'm the guy who's going to stumble over it. I found a programming error in the Fidelity Chess Challenger. (The company denied it for over a month until I sent them a play-by-play description.) I was the guy who found out that Turbo Pascal's random-number generator wasn't random, by writing a program to display random patterns on the screen and seeing very orderly patterns occur instead. I crashed every new version of Windows—but hell, everybody did that, so I can't take any credit for that one.

And before there were computers, there were typewriters. The IBM service department told me that nobody worked a machine as hard as I did—if I'd let them check the wear and tear on my Selectric every three months, they'd give me free service.

It's because I have a weird streak of obsessive-compulsive behavior. I have to find out where the limits are. I usually do that by tripping over them.

And Pesky knew me well enough to know which button to push.

"What do you want me to do?"

He put the trans-dimensional parallelithonic resonating-transceiver back into my hand. The quantum empathizer. "Try to see what you can connect to. Dial numbers at random. Well, not numbers—coordinates. IP64 addresses. See what happens. See who answers. Maybe no one. But you have nothing to lose, do you?"

"If the multiverse is truly infinite, then it's inevitable someone will answer, Pesky. You know that—"

"Yep," he said. "That's why you should be the one to do it."

"I don't follow your logic—"

"Because I trust you."

Those were probably the most frightening words that Peskydang ever said to me. I shook my head in resignation, shoved the thing back into my pocket and went in search of a hazmat suit, so I could clean the bathroom. It was a mistake to serve pickled-beet, cauliflower, and baked-bean casserole. Thanks, Mo-mo. Don't ever do that again.

I was several days recovering from the party. There were the usual thank-yous and apologies to make, plus the inevitable reparations to various neighbors to help them regain their gruntle, a couple of quick interactions with lawyers, and finally a last-resort phone call to my cousin who has connections to the City Council. It was a good thing this was only a small gathering. The doctor said I would not need my meds adjusted, but to take it easy for the next few days.

I hadn't given any thought to the quantum empathizer. The mourning after—yes, I know what I typed, but that's how I experience the day after a party—get off life-support, stagger to the shower, mainline some coffee, and finally wake up. In that order. And with some luck, do all this before dusk.

Sorting through the stack of books and chocolate—and the package of Depends one soon-to-be ex-friend had given as a gag gift—I eventually remembered that Pesky had handed me a present too. I didn't go looking for it. As the sandstorm behind my eyes began to fade, I realized that the quantum empathizer had to be an elaborate prank—though one in much better taste than a package of adult diapers.

Pesky had found an old cell phone, written a funny little app to make the screen dance on command, and then amused himself at my expense by spouting some wild, incomprehensible jargon, just to see how much of it I would believe.

In fact, the more I thought about it, the more certain I was that the whole thing had to be another of Pesky's impractical jokes—like the time he sent Alec Peters scrambling all over the San Fernando Valley, from one electronic parts store to the next, looking for a left-handed Moebius wrench. Of course, you don't fool around with Alec Peters. He actually came back with one.

So as easily as I remembered the quantum empathizer, that's how quickly I dismissed it.

By the end of the week, I was back at the keyboard—

Not yet typing though. First, I spent half an hour cleaning dog hair and guck out from under the keys. A vacuum cleaner is insufficient. You also need a can of compressed air, one of the ones that come with a thin red straw to concentrate the stream—and a business card and a paper clip, and sometimes even some specialized putty that you can press down into the spaces to grab crumbs of all kinds.

This is just one of the things writers do to postpone the actual process of writing—others include removing the cat from the keyboard, making coffee, removing the cat from the keyboard, having a sandwich, removing the cat from the keyboard, doing "research" on the internet, and removing the cat from the keyboard, by which time, you should probably clean the keyboard again, to remove the cat hair from under the keys—because the process of writing is mostly staring at a blank screen and thinking, "Nope. That's not it either."

I've streamlined the process somewhat. I don't have a cat. I expect the universe to fix that situation shortly, but at the moment, it just means I get to spend a lot more time staring into a 32-inch empty white space.

It's like watching a large light bulb, waiting for something to happen. I am the moth, drawn to that light. It's my job to fill the void with little crawly marks that decode into words that decode into thoughts that transform into an understandable moment of experience—and if possible, once over those hurdles, be somehow entertaining or even enlightening. It's not for the squeamish. (I'd say it's not a job for sissies, except it takes a lot of courage to be a sissy and a lot of strength to deal with the ignorance and the stupidity of those trapped in a binary interpretation of gender, but never mind. That's another story.)

Meanwhile, back at the keyboard, but not typing. Because I was stuck.

Not *stuck* as in writer's block. There's no such thing as writer's block. That's just another excuse for not writing.

No, I mean, *stuck* as in not knowing what the next sentence should be. [RETURNS TO THE KEYBOARD SIX HOURS LATER] After it's published, the pauses don't show.

Yes, I'm spending a lot of time describing the process of getting words onto the paper. Onto the screen. Into a file. (Out of my head and into a form that can be retrieved, printed, submitted, and eventually published.) Because that was the what and the why of everything that followed after.

I'd been staring at the story on the screen for half a day—okay, I also answered some email, scrolled through Facebook, browsed Amazon, bought a rare Anthony Boucher paperback on eBay, checked Google News, and fussed with my outdated website, trying to remember HTML and CSS code again. But mostly I'd been trying to figure out if Squish should spend the night in his cell or escape from juvie and do something dramatic. An escape would complicate the problem, but letting the system process him would bore me to death. And the reader. And Squish.

Squish's time-slicing suit gave him (among other abilities) the power to go invisible and walk through walls. But he was already dealing with the consequences of smurfing little Bobby Peterik, and this part of the story wasn't about him using or abusing his powers, but discovering the consequences that inevitably followed. I could have him spend the night thinking over his options until Cousin Murray showed up again. That would probably be the smartest thing he could do—he was a super-genius, so it would be obvious to him—but it wasn't the most exciting thing he could do. So if I had him wait it out, then I had to give him an internal monolog that was compelling enough to justify the pause in the action.

If I had him wait, then obviously I'd be passing the buck to offscreen forces, in this case *deus ex Murray*. If I did that, then I'd have to build up some anxiety for Squish to warrant a resulting argument between him and Cousin Murray. The argument would have to be an explosive one to justify in retrospect the inactivity during the time spent in juvie. So the whole sequence would have to be a major development in the narrative, setting up an even larger confrontation later on, but one still based on the same emotional tension between the characters—

And when you analyze it to death like that, all the life goes out of the entire story. It deflates like a three-day-old balloon, shrinking and wrinkling into a prunish echo of itself.

An alternative might be to have him sharing the cell with another boy, and—

Too many possibilities.

A bully? Too obvious. Someone who tells him how to jack a car? Except Squish doesn't need that information. What could another boy tell him? Squish's real problem is connecting with others. Maybe there's the possibility of an emotional bridge? Homoerotic? Might be too obvious, but Squish has been feeling really alone because he lost his best friend in the previous installment, and that was part of the justification for smurfing Bobby Peterik, so some kind of "we're in this together" sharing, leading to a sense of connection might work. Squish could use his time-slicing powers to help his cellmate. That could work, but it would add another character to the narrative. Do I want that? On the other hand, Squish having a friend might work too. Hmm. Gotta figure out who the other boy is and why he's being held in juvie....

Myself, my experience behind bars has been somewhat limited, a status I have no intention to change. (I was 23, but I looked like I was 14. The cop got me for jaywalking, I didn't have any ID, and I mouthed off. The cop was overzealous and the judge raised his eyebrows at the ticket and only dinged me a few bucks for the jaywalking. I spent an hour locked up with a teenager who'd tried to steal a color TV until my uncle bailed me out. Things were different then.)

Anyway, I was still staring at the screen, thinking about Squish and wondering if I could afford new glasses. These were scratched and starting to generate annoying reflections and peripheral glares.

That's when the phone rang.

Actually, no—it didn't ring. That's just a literary device. A metaphor. A convenient way to indicate an interruption.

What really happened was the computer beeped and a little flag popped up in the lower right-hand corner of the screen telling me that a new device had been recognized.

The quantum empathizer.

And the reason the quantum empathizer had been plugged into the computer was because I'd been charging it. I'd plugged it into the same USB cable I use for transferring books, music, and videos to my Kindle. And the reason I was charging it was because the battery had gone dead, because I'd left it turned on since the party.

I had forgotten about it until this morning when I went looking for my Zune (mandatory eye-roll here from the iPod users), which I found in the same pants I had worn to the party, but first I found the quantum empathizer in a different pocket. When I tried to turn it on, it didn't respond. So that's when I knew the battery was dead. And while I was still certain that Pesky was pranking me, I was now getting curious enough to see how the prank would play out.

He must have programmed the thing to do something to hook me. Maybe he'd installed some kind of chatterbot that could pretend to be a person, at least until the limits of the algorithm betrayed it. I'd played with a few of those, almost written one, they can be very convincing.

In fact...

Yeah, I'll share this. Because it has some peripheral value to this tale. Back in 1983, after Gene Roddenberry had been put out to pasture by Paramount Pictures, because he'd spent $40 million making a movie that shouldn't have cost more than $15 million, he bought his first computer, a Kaypro 10.

The Kaypro 10 was a pretty good little machine for the time. It was the size of a microwave oven, it had a 9-inch monochrome screen—bright green letters on black, 25 lines, 80 characters per line—and it ran CP/M, a precursor to DOS. It had 64K of RAM and a 10 megabyte hard drive. Yes, I said 64 *kilobytes* and 10 *megabytes*. In those days, that was a lot. The Kaypro 10 ran an 8-bit Z80 chip at 2.5 *megahertz*—and that was state of the art.

Gene had spent around $1600 for the machine. All things considered, it was a bargain. I had a Kaypro 10 as well, but it wasn't my first computer. It was my third, and by then I'd already had five years of experience, which made me not just a pioneer, but an expert as well. So when Gene called me and asked for help—would I teach him how to compute?—I stopped what I was doing, took a shower, grabbed a bunch of floppy disks—in those days, they really were floppy; inside the plastic jacket was a 5¼-inch Mylar disc coated with the same iron-oxide rust used on cassette tapes (do I have to explain cassette tapes now?)—and drove up one side of the canyon and down the other to his house in Beverly Hills.

It was an interesting experience, a chance to discover that Gene Roddenberry wasn't quite the visionary he pretended to be. He was smart, but he wasn't intellectually ambitious. But then, Gene was a producer, not a scientist. To him, the computer was just a different kind of typewriter, a more efficient way of getting words onto paper. Gene Roddenberry had a strange and wonderful skill. He could take a bad script and turn it into a good one—he could also take a great script and turn it into a good one.

I taught Gene how to boot up WordStar, how to bring up the help screen, how to write some text, how to save it to a file, how to copy that file to a floppy disk, things like that. As we progressed, he began to get more and more enthusiastic about this frightening metal box on his desk. Obviously, it had been frustrating him since the moment he first turned it on. Now, with a little bit of coaching, he was starting to feel he was in control.

When it was time to show him the computer could also play games, I loaded up ELIZA for him. ELIZA was one of the very first chatterbots, so simple you could code it in BASIC. ELIZA didn't recognize meanings, only patterns. Type in, "I like donuts," and it would strip out "I like" and replace it with "Tell me more about" and feed it back to you as "Tell me more about donuts." With a couple dozen programmed responses, ELIZA could simulate a conversation. It couldn't pass the Turing Test, but it could startle anyone whose only experience with a computer had been the vicarious observation of HAL 9000 murdering four astronauts.

Toward the end of the afternoon, Gene's eight-year-old son, Rod, came in to say hello, followed shortly by Gene's wife, Majel Barrett-Roddenberry. Gene delightedly told her, "David and I are computing!" Then he sat her down in front of the machine and told her to type "Hello." She did so, and immediately, ELIZA began conversing with her. She leapt back with a scream and shouted, "Gene! Who's in there?" It took him several minutes to explain to her that it was only a computer program. She didn't want to accept that explanation. Not at first. ELIZA was just too convincing. She didn't touch the keyboard again.

That was 1983, the beginning of the cyber-Mesozoic era. Thirty years of evolution later, chatterbots can carry on much more complex conversations because the programming has become that much more sophisticated. But writing that kind of code is hard work. Pesky doesn't do hard work. He might have been capable of it, but was he motivated enough to invest all that time just for the sake of a silly impractical joke like a quantum empathizer?

I doubted it.

So I clicked on the little flag in the bottom-right corner of the screen, and a window opened up showing the device's log-on screen. There were the obvious boxes for first name, last name, and email address. Also address and date of birth. The program then ran a rotating icon indicating it was now identifying my service provider and my IP address. After that, it accessed its own GPS to determine the latitude and longitude coordinates of my location.

Basically, it wanted to know who I was and where I was. Somebody must have assumed that would be useful for an alternate-dimension hookup—at least, that's where my mind went. Looking for love in all the wrong spaces. Adventures in slime and place. If I clicked the [SUBMIT] button, would I be opening a portal to this world for alien sex vampires? Who comes here? Dangerous versions?

Of course, I didn't have to click the button. I could unplug the device and go back to wrassling with Squish and his dilemma.

On the other hand, if I didn't click the button, what would happen to man's search for knowledge?

Probably nothing.

But what about my search for knowledge?

And then I stopped.

Really?

Was I *really* taking this serious?

This was Pesky's little joke. He must be laughing his head off somewhere. I'll bet he's got this thing sending a hidden signal to some remote location where he's watching me through my own webcam. Well, he would if he could. I keep a sock over it. But he certainly could have this thing logging keystrokes. And maybe he's got my microphone turned on.

"Pesky, if you can hear me, you're not fooling anyone." And then I added, "Just to show you I'm not fooled, I'm going to click the submit button—just to see what kind of a stunt you think you're pulling."

I clicked the [SUBMIT] button.

Nothing happened. Not at first.

The program opened a new window and a message appeared across the top. "Searching..."

After a moment, the message changed to, "Nodes are active."

In the window, several lines of text began to appear.

Divergence 1949 [05 active nodes, 11 inactive]
Divergence 1963 [42 active nodes, 13 inactive]
Divergence 1967 [23 active nodes, 33 inactive]
Divergence 1968 [13 active nodes, 02 inactive]
Divergence 1969 [06 active nodes, 47 inactive]
Divergence 1970 [no active nodes]
Divergence 1971 [03 active nodes, 12 inactive]
Divergence 1974 [12 active nodes, 65 inactive]
Divergence 1979 [12 active nodes, 11 inactive]
Divergence 1981 (03 active nodes, 41 inactive]
Divergence 1986 [43 active nodes, 54 inactive]

Divergence 1987 [34 active nodes, 36 inactive]
Divergence 1991 [09 active nodes, 19 inactive]
Divergence 1992 [13 active nodes, 23 inactive]
...

The numbers flickered and changed as the screen updated. It looked like a live uTorrent queue. More lines appeared, seemingly at random, but probably in the order in which the connections were established. No connections showed up for any year before my birth. That was interesting. More evidence that this was one of Pesky's tricks.

The most recent year listed was four years ago. Some years had no active nodes. Others had many. There did not appear to be any particular pattern to which years had the most. 1970 had eighty-seven active nodes while 1981 only had three.

I recognized some of the years, the opportunities and the missteps, the choices made and not made, the fumbles, the bumbles, the stumbles—all the roads not tribbled.

I sat back in my chair and stared at the screen. I still didn't believe this was anything more than a weird little prank, but I noticed my own reaction, that small moment of uncertainty, that tiny balloon of doubt swelling in my chest, that inevitable feeling of loss that comes from looking into the past.

Yes, I know I shouldn't look back, I'm not headed in that direction. I should be looking out the front windshield, not at the rear-view mirror—but the reason there are rear-view mirrors in cars is so you can see what's behind you, especially when it's roaring up after you like a truck or a tsunami. Memory is the monster that stomps the present and chases you into one desperate future after another. You have to kill the monster if you want to build anything new.

I know that. Mixed metaphors and all. But I sat there anyway, remembering.

The meeting I missed. The call I didn't make. The invitation I turned down. The date I didn't go on. And the justifications for not doing any of those things. And all the things I did instead. All the screw-ups. Especially that redhead—

But there were victories too. Little moments of triumph and joy and satisfaction. Not the obvious ones, not the ones everybody knew about, but the secret ones—because those were mine, not for sharing.

That day in July of '69, when a hot and hopeless summer afternoon turned into a magical and golden evening, as sunlit bars of dust illuminated the discoveries of love. And the horrible day when it was lost as well. That day in '77, when the magic was rediscovered and reinvented—and again in '78. And all the different kinds of magic that happened in '81 and '92 and '95 and '05 and '07. Those were mine.

Maybe, someday, I'll write an autobiography, listing all the things I've learned from all the best people in my life—and all the things I've learned from all the worst as well. I could call it, *Things I've Learned From Living Too Long* or *If You Had Wanted Me To Write Nice Things About You, You Would Have Treated Me Better*. Especially that last part. Autobiographies are a great way to pay off old grudges. I could tell the truth about a few people. I could do some significant damage to a few reputations—

Well...if Pesky had intended this little stunt as a thought experiment, he'd certainly achieved his goal. I could spend the rest of the day reviewing past lives that hadn't happened.

And then, the dogs began barking frantically at the door—the doorbell has been broken for three decades, I have no need to repair it. The mail had just been delivered. A good opportunity for a break. Nothing important, just the usual collection of junk mail coupons and ads. An opportunity to refinance the mortgage. And another one of those notes about pre-need cremation.

Which sent me off on another internal rant—

Pre-need cremation? No, I don't think so. I don't want a pre-need cremation. That sounds painful. Thank you very much, but I do not want to be cremated until I absolutely *need* to be cremated. Here's how you'll know when I need to be cremated. I won't move for a long time, I'll look bloated and awful, and I'll smell bad. Oh, wait—I'm like that now. Let me get back to you on this.

—because that's the cost of being a high-verbal. You look at the actual literal meanings of words before you look at how they were intended. I've gotten myself into a lot of trouble that way.

But in this case, the interruption brought me back to the real world—just long enough to stop and ask—Wait a minute! Is this really *the real world*? I'll bet all those others feel like the real world to anyone living over there. To them, this one would be just another divergent.

Wait. You're not taking this serious, are you?

Of course not. It's just another prank by Pesky.

You might be able to get a story out of it, though. Maybe you could see where it goes.

I don't have a little voice in my head. I have a committee.

Back at my desk, I saw that the screen had updated itself. There was even a divergent for this year now. Cute.

So far, though, I hadn't seen anything that would have required more than a couple hours of work for an experienced programmer. I assumed that if I clicked on one of those lines and tried to connect to an active node, I'd get the chatterbot. Probably the same chatterbot whichever link I chose. It might be interesting to test the limits of the chatterbot's abilities. I wondered if Pesky had made it historically literate, aware of which specific divergent it was pretending to be. To make the prank work, he would have had to. But that would have required a lot more coding than this stunt deserved.

I wondered if—yeah, that would be just like him—if after spelunking through various screens and options, some hideous deformed face would suddenly and unexpectedly fill my monitor, a ghastly scream roaring from my speakers, all with the intention of scaring me, so I would go leaping backward in startled terror, shrieking and knocking my coffee all over my keyboard.

It was a funny gag—well, funny the first time. It still showed up on Facebook occasionally. But it wasn't funny anymore, just annoying. And besides, that wasn't Pesky's style. His pranks were usually more subtle and more literate. Like the time George Takei was going to speak at the local university. The school put up a big poster of George's smiling face—one night, Pesky snuck onto campus and added matching posters just to the left, showing a lion, a tiger, and a bear. In that order. The real joke was that some people didn't get it.

So I sat at the keyboard and stared at the screen and mused. Until I realized I wasn't amused at all. "And no, we are not bemused either," I added as an afterthought. High-verbaling again.

There was really only one way to end this—and that was by continuing. When you're in the muddle of anything, the only way out is through.

I leaned forward and clicked on 1949. That felt like a good place to start. The screen popped up five active nodes. I clicked on the first. It opened a window listing multiple journal entries and descriptions of files available for download.

I started reading. I frowned—

There were articles about ramp access, the Americans With Disabilities Act, hiring discrimination, the high cost of a motorized wheelchair and how hard it was to get around Comic-Con's crowded aisles even with prosthetic legs, why it was unfair they wouldn't let him on the bobsled ride at Disneyland, and after that a few rants about the things that rude and stupid people said and did. One was about able-bodied people parking in the handicapped spaces—that was understandable. Another revealed how tired he was of people telling him how much courage he had, I could empathize with that one too. It's not courage when you don't have a choice. A third talked about amputee porn and the creeps who were turned on by stumpies, and how hard it was to have a real relationship. He didn't want anyone who felt sorry for him—

Huh?

I dug further.

Apparently, the individual at this node had lost his legs when he was five. He had been sitting on a corner curb where the streetcars turned around, a little island just off the corner of Vermont and West 1st Street. It was a very sharp curve and the bottom of the streetcar came over the curb as the trolley turned the corner.

—oh, crap.

I remembered that moment. I'd been wearing shorts. I'd sat down to watch the streetcar turn. At the last moment, as I saw it coming around, saw how the sharp yellow bottom of the car was cutting over the curb, I scrambled back out of the way. That moment was still ingrained in my consciousness. It was my first experience recognizing my own stupidity. Ever since then, I've kept a cautious distance from all moving trains and streetcars. And trucks. And buses. And everything else large and mobile.

So that was the divergence in 1949.

And this person was me. An *alternate* me.

Oh—

Now I *was* bemused. More than confused. Frozen in shock.

Pesky couldn't have known that. I'd never shared that incident with anyone. I'd occasionally thought about it, wondered what would have happened if I'd stayed put. Would I have been dragged under the carriage and cut in half by the streetcar's large steel wheels, or would there have been enough room for my skinny little five-year-old legs to escape unscathed? Or maybe I'd just get scratched up a bit or maybe broken both my legs, but not too badly. I'd even imagined the ride in the ambulance with a superhero fireman holding my hand and telling me not to cry.

But this guy, this *divergent*, his legs had been crushed and mangled and ripped off his body. He'd lost both of them. Barely survived the blood loss. His limbs were amputated mid-thigh.

Ouch.

So that was what happened to the little boy who didn't get out of the way in time.

He grew up to be an angry cripple. No, not angry. He told jokes. He was literate. He even wrote and sold some stories. But mostly he was a single-minded advocate for disabled rights. Because he didn't have much choice.

On the other hand, having to use his arms for everything, he must have developed great upper-body strength by now. I wondered if he'd posted a picture.

Yes, he had. And yes, he had great shoulder muscles and biceps, but I couldn't be jealous. He was fat. And slovenly. Ugh. I suppose I should have been ashamed of myself for thinking that of him, but if he was an alternate me, he was one I was glad I wasn't.

Considering everything—the circumstances, the culture of the time, the lack of access to honest affection separated from pity—it would have been easy for him to retreat into comfort food and sublimated resentment. I could understand it. I'd been there. More than once. It wasn't the comfort zone. It was the zone of resignation. I just hadn't stayed there. I was sorry he had. But I could understand his frustration with the world now.

I wondered if his stories were any good. I skimmed a few titles. Nothing I recognized. I'd have to come back and look later. But my curiosity was piqued—what would I find if I clicked on the other years? Who were the other divergents?

I backed out and looked at the other years.

Why were there no active nodes for 1970? Nothing came up on the screen.

I decided to try 1987.

Well, *that* was interesting—

Apparently Gene Roddenberry had died of a massive stroke (overdose?) at the end of December. This was before his walking elbow-wrinkle of a lawyer had come aboard to pack the production with expensive empty suits. So the show-running chores fell to—

Among the files available for download were seven years of episodes. Those would definitely be worth a look.

It would take several hours for all the separate files to copy. Enough time to browse some other years.

What diverged in 1963?

Well, there was the obvious one, of course. John F. Kennedy listened to the concerns of his Secret Service agents and allowed them to put the bubble top on the limo. Lee Harvey Oswald's bullets cracked the Plexiglas, but failed to penetrate. The president and his wife escaped with only minor scratches. The following year Kennedy defeated Goldwater. The Federal Civil Rights Act passed, so did the Voting Rights Act. Not without a fight, but they passed. Kennedy did not escalate the war in Vietnam, the right wing accused him of being soft on communism. His political popularity waned after the '66 midterms, but because the economy was healthy and because the nation was fascinated by the Apollo missions to the moon, he remained personally well-regarded. Robert Kennedy won the presidency in '68 against Richard Nixon. That was a close race, because the south was leaving the Democratic Party.

When JFK and two Apollo astronauts visited the set of *Star Trek* in early '67, the series took a ratings boost and the network moved it to an 8:00 time-slot. Its ratings climbed even higher in the earlier position, pushing the show into the top ten. They did not buy that script from a well-intentioned college student. Hmm.

Some tough times followed, but...that was interesting. It turned into a whole other career path. Twenty-two novels in ten years, approximately one every six months. And another thirty in the twenty years after that. I didn't recognize any of the titles.

Oh, this was even *more* interesting—

Heinlein novels! Holy mother of Ghu! By '67, the grandmaster was apparently heading out in a whole other direction. *On The Bounce, The Man From Mars, And Not To Yield, A Competent Man, Ezekiel And The Wheel, The Business Of Monkeys, Ad Astra.*

Beatles albums? Thirteen of them before the '73 breakup, plus another seven after the '79 reunion. Not a single title matched anything in my timeline. Definitely needed to download those. *Eight Arms To Hold You, Any Way We Can, Singularities, Everest, Let Go, Applesauce, All The Times,* and *The Band You've Known For All These Years.*

It all made sense—different history, different stimuli, different results. A whole other catalog. Not just me, everyone.

I wondered what else I might find. I started browsing through the ancillary files that my divergent selves were sharing. Buddy Holly's *Disco Sue Got Married.* Disney's remake of *Yellow Submarine,* Kubrick's

Napoleon, and Terry Gilliam's *Don Quixote.* Steven Spielberg's *The Stars My Destination.* Joss Whedon's *Firefly,* all eight seasons and the two-hour special, *Redemption.* Criterion Audio, *The Compleat Hendrix.* Alfred Bester's *Destiny.* Harlan Ellison's *The Man Who Screamed Bullets.* All the divergent Ken Burns twenty-four-part documentaries on the history of the twentieth century. I counted seven of them.

And more!

All the Hugo and Nebula nominees since 1949—from all the different divergent timelines. I could spend a lifetime catching up, just reading all the different masterpieces of so many of my favorite authors.

I hesitated—I wondered about the ethics. Was this considered illegal file sharing? I couldn't pay for any of this stuff, but I could trade things specific to my timeline. That would be fair, wouldn't it?

What about my own stuff? What had my different selves created? I could market that, couldn't I?

I'd have to look.

And that made me pause—

—because that's what I had been avoiding.

And I knew why.

One of the skills all those courses and coaching had created was a weird kind of insight—an additional level of consciousness, being able to notice my own motivations.

In my timeline, somewhere on the internet, there is an Encyclopedia of Science Fiction. In it, one of those shallow and snotty self-appointed critics of science fiction had casually dismissed my entire career with a single withering sentence: "...has not lived up to his early potential."

At the time, I'd felt that critic had misunderstood what I was attempting. But what if he hadn't? That was the fear. What if all those different versions of myself had lived up to their potential? Would their enormous body of work reveal how badly I had failed in *this* timeline?

I checked '95 and '97, looking to see if anyone had completed my seven book trilogy. No. I was the only one working on that story. Was I really that divergent?

But I did find *The Patient Dragon, Blue Monkeys From The Eleventh Dimension, The Boy Who Was Girl, The Girl Who Was Silver, A Promise of Stars (collection), The Corridor, The Princess Of The Mice, Shifter, Nightsiders, Admit One, Bad Night, City Of Boys, Dear Doctor Morgan, Jesus And The Seven Dwarves, Loophole, Gendernauts, Escape From The Planet Of The*

Tribbles, Didactics, A Day At Crater Park, The Chimney Wars, Cocoons, The Brick, Cooking By Ear, Inherit The Stars, The Borrowed Body, Something Scratching, The Job Of Death, The Hails Of Toffman, The Lifeguard At Cassy Beach, The Rainbow Eaters, and *Uncle Dog.*

And that was just from one timeline. There were at least a thousand others yet to explore. If there were even 20 different books in each divergent timeline, that would be a library of twenty-thousand separate downloads. I wouldn't even have time to read them all—

It wouldn't be unethical for me to download everything that all my divergent selves had written, would it? I could even resell some of the best. If I could figure out how to find the best out of twenty-thousand. Maybe just the award nominees? But no, I'd written a few pieces I was proud of that had never gotten award notice. I'm sure my divergent selves had too. How to identify them—

Of course, I should probably make my catalog from this timeline available in return. Nothing I had written after 1970 existed in any of the divergent catalogs.

But I was feeling humbled by what others had accomplished and posted.

Not just humbled—jealous.

By comparison, I had...what?

Well...

I was the only one who had written *The Martian Child*—because none of them had adopted a child. At least, not the same child. Right there, that made my heart break. Where was Sean in all those different worlds? Did he even exist in those alternate timelines?

Maybe his birth parents had never met. Or maybe they didn't make a baby that night in the fall of '83. But if Sean did exist, if he had been born, then what would have happened to him without me being there for him?

Where was he? Was he all right? Or had he been swallowed up by circumstances? Used up and abandoned before he'd ever had a chance? Thinking what might have happened to him, I started to tear up again.

Or maybe, maybe—I had to hope this was so—maybe some other family had gotten lucky. After the adoption was finalized, the caseworker told me there had been two or three other families interested in him, but they had chosen me as the best match. Maybe one of those other families had taken him.

But wherever Sean was, there was no *Martian Child*. It hadn't happened. And neither had anything else. No Hugo, no Nebula. No movie. No nothing.

I remembered why I had adopted him. What had made me the person I am. The same thing that informed all of my earliest writings. I went back and looked, I had to confirm it—yes, I was the only one who'd written *HARLIE* and *Folded*.

And that's what stopped me.

I knew why those books had been written, what they had been a response to.

At the end of the sixties—

Those novels had happened because I'd been trying to wrap my head around something so incomprehensible that it felt like the universe was a gigantic practical joker, with me as the butt of the joke. (And no, I'm not going to talk about it here. It's a footnote. Someday I'll write that footnote. Just not today.)

1970 was the divergence. This was the timeline where I'd survived.

HARLIE was me trying to figure it out—to see if it had any meaning at all. And *Folded* was a plea to any passing time-traveler. Please come and fix this. Make it didn't happen.

Pebbles down a well. No splash.

Not important enough, I guess. Or maybe the time traveler decided history worked better this way. I wasn't consulted.

Ultimately—and it took until '81 or '85 or '92 or '07—I finally figured it out for myself. I had to figure it out more than once. Each time was a personal reinvention. None of the books I'd ever read, none of the teachers I'd ever admired, none of the authors I'd followed so religiously had ever been able to say the one thing in the clear I'd most needed to hear.

If you want life to have meaning, you have to make it up yourself.

And that's the real question. The one nobody else has the answer to. The nastiest and most terrifying piece of personal responsibility.

What do you want your life to mean?

There was a book I had been wanting to write. I hadn't written it yet. No, I hadn't finished it yet. I had four different abortive versions on my hard drive. None of them came close to what I wanted it to be.

I scoured through all the different divergents. The book didn't exist. No one else had written it either.

Which meant that no other divergent in this particular selection of possibilities had experienced the same event. Which meant—

I started looking at the selfies.

Ahh, that explained a lot.

Too much.

I don't know how long I sat there, staring at my monitor, overwhelmed by conflicting storms of emotion, blinking through the tears, weeping at my loss, sobbing at my failure—because another version of me had something I had been grieving for nearly my whole life. And I didn't have it, couldn't have it.

The photo of the two of them, handsome and beautiful, smiling, squinting against the glare of the Hawaiian sun, proudly holding up their left hands to show matching wedding bands—

Oh, no.

No, no, no, goddammit! Dammit! Dammit!

Now, I knew why there were no active divergents from 1970. Those were the ones who'd committed suicide. Unable to bear the grief, they'd... quit.

I got up from the computer. I walked out of my office. I walked into the kitchen. I opened the cupboard above the refrigerator, the one glued shut by time, the one with two bottles of wine and an unopened bottle of Glenfiddich one of my friends had sent me two years ago. I don't drink—

That's not completely true. Twice a year, once at Thanksgiving and once at Christmas, when the family gathers together at my sister's, I pour myself a rum and Coke. I use Malibu coconut rum and a twist of lime. It's called a Hairy Nilsson. You put the lime in the coconut, you drink it all up. (If you make it with Diet Coke, it's a half-Nilsson.)

Tonight, I took down the bottle of Glenfiddich. Heinlein had introduced me to single-malt liquor when I visited him in Bonny Doon. It was one of the greatest favors he ever did for me. I twisted out the cork, and splashed two fingers into a glass. I didn't bother with the soda. Not tonight. And no, I did not throw it back all at once like you see in the movies, because in the movies it's not liquor, it's iced tea. And nobody who respects Glenfiddich insults it like that. No, I sipped at it, letting it sting my tongue a bit at a time.

I stood alone in my dark kitchen, eyes still blurry with grief. The dogs wagged hopefully at my feet, alternating their little, "I like cheese," dance, with sitting up and waving their paws at me. "Please, sir, can I have some, so I can ask for some more?" Somewhere else, I had the life I'd planned. Here, I had the life that had happened anyway.

I don't know how long I stood there, alone, drinking, waiting for some kind of resolution, some enlightenment, some imitation of peace. I noticed my hands were shaking and leaned on the counter. I could feel the booze burning its way down my throat and into my stomach, a dark wave ballooning outward from there.

I wish I had lyrical language to describe it, those silky poetic metaphors that awaken the imagery of the mind. But I don't, I never have. I didn't even want to be a writer. I wanted to act and direct and create video games and design amusement parks. And once, I'd even wanted to be a course-leader, a trainer. I only ended up a storyteller because there were stories I wanted to read and nobody else was writing them.

I look at all the good writers around me and I'm jealous of their skills, what they're able to do with language and character and voice, and it just makes me all the more conscious of my own limitations. All I've ever been able to do is grasp after the unreachable precision of language and hope that's enough, but just wanting something badly enough isn't enough. It needs ability and commitment and passion.

All I had was stubbornness. Too stupid to quit—

And now there were all those different divergents, every bit as stubborn and stupid as me. Some of them must have gone off in other directions, some of them must have done a few of those things I once thought I wanted to do. But I was afraid to go back and look. I was already hurting enough—

Why the hell had Pesky given me this terrible device? What was he thinking? What the hell kind of a birthday present forces you to confront the failures in your life?

I opened the back door and went out to the patio, but only as far as the awning, an empty space surrounded by the pattering of rain.

The backyard should have been a refuge, but it didn't feel like it tonight. It felt like a walled-in exercise yard. The first precipitation we'd seen in months was rippling the surface of the pool, cooling the air with the icy smell of...I don't know, what's a poetic way to describe breathing negative ions? That crisp feeling of air that clears the lungs and the soul at the same time?

But out here, I could wrap the darkness around me like a cold, wet, uncomfortable blanket, the only warmth coming from the alcohol inside me.

I thought about those other divergents. Were they happy? Had I missed something?

Well, no. Not all of them were happy. That one in the wheelchair. And the ones who'd killed themselves. The one who'd spent two decades working through various iterations of a successful TV show—he was a millionaire now with a house in Newport Beach, a yacht, and monthly royalties bigger than my lifetime income. He also had ulcers, a drug problem, two divorces, and a reputation for being an arrogant ass. Was he happy? Did he log onto the interdimensional network feeling successful? Or did he regret that his entire life had been at the service of someone else's creation? Did he mourn the stories and novels of his own that he'd never written because he'd sacrificed himself to television?

And the one who was married—*all* the ones who were married. Yes, I envied them. Who wouldn't? And if I could ask them, I'm sure they'd say they were happy. They probably were. I wished I was that happy too.

Oh, what a tangled web we weave when first we practice to transceive.

I sipped at my drink—what the hell, I finished it quickly. Let it burn. I thought about stepping out from under the awning, letting the cold rain wash down onto me—but no, that was a stupid idea. I'd barely survived my last bout with pneumonia. I did not particularly want another ambulance ride or tubes down my throat.

So, what did I have?

If Randy were here, my interminable coach, he'd say, "You have the path you're on. You have what you chose. You have the consequences that came with your choice."

Great. Thanks, Randy.

Okay, well...I have a son I'm very proud of. I'm the only one who has this son. That has to count for something. I'd made a difference in his life. He'd made an even bigger difference in mine. He taught me to think about someone else for a change, a skill once learned and never forgotten. Our relationship is so good, I'm jealous of myself.

And...I do have some stories that no one else wrote. No one else could have written them. That has to count for something too.

Some of my best work had come into being because of the smoldering rage I'd been carrying for so many years, for so many different reasons. Most of the time that torment just simmered, sometimes it boiled, and sometimes it exploded. Mostly it caught me by surprise. But I'd learned how to force it out through the keyboard, blasting shards of feeling onto the screen like an emotional assault rifle aimed at the reader.

And sometimes—sometimes I even acknowledged it aloud. I'd say it like a joke, but it was never a joke. "I suffered for my art. Now it's your turn."

I walked back inside and put the empty glass in the sink. A satisfying glass-on-porcelain clink. Okay, I'd had my ten minutes of self-pity. Fifteen. That was enough.

Alternate timelines are just another trap, a great big game of "what if" with teeth in it. But if there's one thing I've learned in the last seven decades, it's how to bite back—and draw blood.

This is who I am. This is the universe I live in. If I have to deal with this world, then it has to deal with me. The next time I look into the abyss, I intend the abyss to flinch.

I'm the one who gets to live *this* life. I'm the one who gets to write *these* stories.

That's enough. That has to be enough.

Well played, Pesky. Well played.

But I'm still going to kill you.

I caught up with That Pesky Dan Goodman a week later. I made a point of dropping in at a meeting of the Los Angeles Science Fantasy Society. They have a new clubhouse in Van Nuys. I found him in the back room— at the snack table, of course. He turned around and saw me and his eyes widened. The first and probably only time I'd ever seen fear on his face.

I handed him the box. He shook it, frowned, opened it.

Inside were all the pieces of trans-dimensional parallelithonic resonating transceiver, thoroughly hammered to bits.

"Sorry, Pesky," I said. "I couldn't get it to work."

AUTHOR'S AFTERWORD:
This was the only file I was able to download before the device overheated and the particles unentangled.

A METHOD FOR MADNESS

First Look Preview Chapters

Chtorr (ktôr), *n*. **1.** The planet Chtorr, presumed to exist within 30 light years of Earth. **2.** The star system in which the planet occurs; possibly a red giant star, presently unidentified. **3.** The dominant species of the planet Chtorr; generic. **4.** In formal usage, either one or many members of the dominant species of the planet Chtorr; a Chtorr, the Chtorr. (See **Chtor•ran**) **5.** The glottal chirruping cry of a Chtorr.

Chtor•ran (ktôr´in), *adj*. **1.** Of or relating to either the planet or the star system, Chtorr. **2.** Native to Chtorr. *n*. **1.** Any creature native to Chtorr. **2.** In common usage, a member of the dominant species, the (presumed) intelligent life form of Chtorr (*pl*. **Chtor•rans**)

— *The Random House Dictionary
of the English Language,
Century 21 Edition, unabridged*

1
UNDERTURE

"Godot called. He'll be late."

—SOLOMON SHORT

The floor. Hard, cold, prickly.

Arms wrapped around itself, the body clutches its stomach and rocks ceaselessly. It moans and whimpers, it croons to itself. Sometimes it screams. After it screams, it sobs. Anguish is a bottomless well. Despair is grief without healing. Pain gnaws holes in the soul.

Voices call from every direction. The body twists and turns and struggles against unseen foes—but yet, in the tattered and unraveled weave of awareness, bits and pieces still come babbling to the surface, fragments of memory, unreal swirlings. Illusions, delusions, hallucinations—once upon a time there was a color called *green*.

Sometimes the memories chew and gnaw unbearably. Overwhelmed, the body writhes and screams and rages. Sometimes it comes awake, muscles spasming, limbts tightened, back arched in painful rigidity, eyes bulging, ears pounding, skin crawling in rippling waves, bloody sweat rolling off in dirty rivulets. Fists hammer futilely against the floor. The walls are made of bone.

Screaming to unknown gods, the body makes incoherent sounds—untranslatable, but clear enough. Demanding, pleading, wheedling, bargaining, despairing until finally, exhausted, empty again, it collapses helplessly again. It gasps for each next breath, ragged and hoarse. The fog returns. Madness croons to itself. Fury subsides to trembling palsy. The thing within endures.

A man in blue scrubs. A face as bland as pudding. His name is Mark Malamud. He is supposed to be a doctor—he is what passes for one these days. He studies the body without expression. He hasn't seen worse, but he's seen enough. This is more of the same. Meat on its way to the grinder. Behind the pale frames of his glasses, behind the augmented realities projected onto his retinas, his eyes are as gray as comfortable lies.

Two men stand beside him. One looks sad, the other uncomfortable. Cameras record everything. This is the joke. I look through the cameras and see it six times over, from every blank eye in the soft pink room.

The older man, the one with the floating mane of wild white hair, kneels to look closer at the body on the floor. "You poor dumb son-of-a-bitch." He shakes his head. "What have we done to you?"

The other man, the one in uniform, considers several possible remarks, but holds his silence.

The man with white hair, Foreman, extends a hand and touches the trembling creature. It has wet itself again. It has soiled its diaper. Spittle and vomit stain its hospital gown. Its eyes are open and unblinking, staring sightlessly. Its mouth is slack. The purple tongue lolls.

"Careful," says Malamud. "Don't get too close."

"I know this boy—this man."

"And I know this type. Don't be fooled. They can be violent."

"I've seen the tapes." Foreman pats the twisted figure on the shoulder, on the arm. It twitches. It shudders. After a moment, Foreman takes a damp cloth and gently wipes its face. His movements are tentative at first, then tender.

"You're wasting your time," says Malamud.

"No," Foreman corrects him. "You think I'm wasting your time."

Malamud holds up a black spray-injector. "The decision has already been made, Dr. Foreman. This part is only a formality. If you'll just say the word—"

Foreman stands abruptly. "No," he says, his tone hardening like cold fire. "This is *not* a formality. I take this responsibility seriously." He points down at the body. "This is not a *thing*. This is a man. He served us. He served us *well*. He was *valuable*. He was *loved*. We paid a high price to get him back—"

Malamud is underwhelmed. "Not exactly the best use of your resources."

The General speaks, finally. "We have a tradition. Leave no man behind."

Malamud shrugs. "We have a tradition too, sir. It's called triage. It's about knowing when the game is over. When you can't do anything else, you give the patient a peaceful end." And then he makes a mistake. He makes a sound of annoyance. And says, "Sirs, can we please wrap this up? I have other matters to tend to—" It was the wrong thing to say. And the wrong person to say it to.

Foreman straightens. "This is a human being. He's entitled to some dignity. Even like this."

"I see a dozen of these a week, Dr. Foreman. Sometimes twice that many. After a while, dignity isn't part of the equation anymore. I'm sorry if you think that's rude, but sometimes we just don't have time for the whole dreary performance of human being who still gives a shit. Enough already."

Foreman reddens. "No, it is not enough, goddammit. It is *never* enough. You didn't know this man. I did. And I *still* care. I don't want him wasted because some technician with a needle is impatient to get to the local pig-fuck party."

Behind him, General Anderson remains professionally blank. The old man doesn't lose his patience often, but more and more these days, like lightning, his temper flashes unexpectedly. The General thinks about The Syndrome, wonders if this is another symptom.

Malamud shrugs. He's seen this performance before. Many times. He knows what's coming next. He can almost speak the words for the old man. *"We have to give him a chance. There are things locked in his brain—"*

"Yes, sir. I fully agree with you," Malamud says preemptively. "And if we had the resources, the manpower, the time, the skillage—yes, certainly. But we don't. This one has run out the clock. Under the law—"

"I know the law. I helped set the policy on which this particularly odious law is based. I *know* the reasoning behind it." Foreman sounds frustrated, trapped.

"That doesn't exempt you," Doctor Malamud replies stiffly. "Do you think I don't care? I do. More than you know. This delay—it isn't helping anyone. Not him, not you. It just uses up everyone's time while you play patty-cake with your regrets so you can feel better about yourself in the morning. Of all people, I expect better from you. Just do your job already—sir. Do your job and move on to things that make a difference."

Foreman stiffens. He could have given that same speech himself. He already has, but in different circumstances.

Malamud lowers his voice. "Please. Let me give this man release. Sign the paper and let's be done already. Malamud gestures with the black spray-injector again.

Foreman shakes his head. Malamud is right. But Foreman doesn't like being pushed. And for no reason at all, except that he is already angry, he stiffens. "Dr. Malamud, I will give you an authorization to terminate this patient only when I am good and goddamn ready."

And then Foreman remembers where he is and why he is here and he seems to collapse inside. He turns away, studies the wall. His shoulders tremble. He shakes his head, lost in a private conversation.

Finally, he recovers himself. Without turning around, he speaks quietly, almost matter-of-factly, as if in a classroom. "It's funny. You know how you get a thought stuck in your head? I keep thinking about John Donne. The poet. Do you know the line? *'Any man's death diminishes me, because I am involved in mankind.'* You don't know that one, do you, Doctor? Maybe nobody does anymore. We've been fighting so long, we've forgotten who we are and what we're fighting for—only that we're fighting for the sake of fighting, because fighting is who we are now. It's no wonder we're losing." Turning around, his voice strains with feeling. "We're so deep in the shit, we've forgotten how to look at the stars. But this man here, annoying and pig-headed and stubborn like a wall, always questioning, always arguing— as big an asshole as he was, he still had the courage or the misfortune or the sheer dumb-fuckedness, or whatever you want to call it, to ... to just keep at it, no matter what. He went so far beyond the boundaries most of us can't even imagine it. This poor dumb shit has paid more prices than any human being should ever have to. And I can't remember anyone ever taking the time to thank him, to acknowledge his contributions. And now, here we are, ready to just snuff him out because we think he has nothing left to give us. And it's not even because we don't believe he can recover— it's because we just don't have enough people to take care of him while he does. So we justify it by calling it triage and say, 'Okay, let's move on.' No. I'm not wasting my time here. I'm paying my respects to a man I admire in spite of himself." Foreman stops. And after an uncomfortable silence, he adds, "And you, Doctor—you have the unmitigated gall to act impatient and put-upon, because a few moments of compassion for his death is going to make you late for your next orgasm. What we do here is horrible enough. Let's not add to it."

Malamud isn't impressed. "It's noble of you to say so." He puts the injector back down on the tray, as if somehow by doing so he is stepping away from this whole entire mess. "But I have to do this every day, sometimes two or three or four times a day. Over and over and over. If I stopped to cry about each and every death, I'd be ready for the injector myself within a week. Yes, this is an ugly vile job—I'm the official government executioner, the man nobody wants to eat lunch with. You think I asked for this duty? I drew the short straw. So I harden myself and I do it. And I try not to think about it. I tell myself I'm doing a good thing, helping people, releasing them from pain. And I try not to think about it too much. I can't—or I wouldn't be able to think about anything else. Don't you think I pray for forgiveness? I'm a Catholic, for god's sake. Do you know what my confessions sound like? Even the special dispensation of Pope AnnaMarie isn't enough to erase my shame."

"You get paid well enough for it," General Anderson says drily. "You cash the checks."

"I got drafted," replies Malamud. "I'm here by court order. This or a work-gang. I have a three-year old daughter. I can't—" He stops himself. "Can we please just get this over with?"

Foreman ignores the doctor. He kneels again and touches the body on the floor. "Jim," he whispers. "This is just another mode. Just another way of being. There are other ways still accessible to you. Remember? Step into another context and you can create another mode. You're in a healing context now, Jim. Create a healing mode. Do you remember how? I know you do. I taught you."

"We've tried that," says Anderson.

"You've tried it," says Foreman. "I haven't. I have to see this for myself." He looks up, pain tightening his face. "You and I raised this one, Danny. We brought him almost all the way. Do you want to give up on him now?"

The General lowers his eyes. As if to say, *"I already have."*

"Well, I haven't. All right, I'm an old fool. An emotional old fart. But I was raised old-fashioned. I still believe in the basic tenet. *'Life is sacred everywhere.'*"

Anderson puts a hand on Foreman's shoulder and whispers gently into his ear. You can skip the sound-bite, sir. You and I both know that one."

"Ah, you have me there, son," Foreman admits. "But it's all I have left. That one single nugget of knowledge. When that's gone, you'll find *me* on the floor in a diaper and ready for the injection."

"Dr. Foreman..." Anderson's words are soft and patient. "You know it better than anyone. The self-generated shift—*transformation*—is impossible below the threshold of despair. If it *is* possible, and we're not even sure that it is in this case, someone's got to go down there and get him. Do you have the time to work with him? Do you have the patience?"

Foreman sighs. He lowers his head in resignation. The silence stretches out uncomfortably. Time freezes and collapses—not for the first time, not for the last. The world turns pink and closes in, and finally Foreman says, "All right, then. Let me at least say goodbye." He touches the body again. "I wish I could have known you better, Jim. You were a good student. You argued with me. I liked that." He stops to smile, remembering. "I liked the challenge. I liked your commitment to understand."

He strokes the hair. Damp and stringy and faintly tingly. "You didn't know that, did you? I *liked* arguing with you, Jim—because it's in the argument that the passion is found. And it's in the passion that the commitment is revealed. That's what makes us human. Our passion. So, here we are, you and I, and now you're beyond argument, and all that's left for me to do is acknowledge what was so. You were remarkable. Every time you argued with me, you not only learned, you *taught*. I wish I knew where you had gone. I wish I could follow, so I could bring you back far enough to tell us. I know you've discovered things, Jim. I wish you could share some of it with us—"

Foreman stops himself. All these words, it's bullshit. Just so much noise. Even he recognizes it. All these words—they're just a way to *avoid* the moment. So Foreman stops. He bows his head. Finally, he bends close and whispers into my ear. "I'm so sorry, Jim. I'm so very sorry—"

"Shut up, you bloated old fart." The words are barely audible. *"You don't know what the fuck you're talking about."*

Foreman pulls back his hand as if stung.

He exchanges a glance with General Anderson. "I thought you said he'd gone completely non-verbal."

Anderson shrugs. Shakes his head. He looks unhappier than usual. "That's what the evaluation team said."

"Well, that sounded like a pretty clear communication to me." Foreman looks to Malamud, a question in his eyes.

The doctor shakes his head. "Sometimes they start speaking at the end. It never means anything."

"Not to you, maybe," says Foreman. He turns back to the man on the floor. "Jim?" he asks. He touches again. The body flinches and pulls away. It hurts. "Jim? Say again?"

"Not a mode!" The voice is cracked and the syllables are slurred. But Foreman gets it. His eyes narrow. His hand attempts to comfort. But it still hurts.

"I don't understand, Jim. Tell me—"

"Something. Else."

Foreman stands up and braces Anderson. "We can't do this. I can't authorize it."

"I'm only here as a witness," says the General. "And that's only because you asked me to be here. You want to try to save him, do it on your authority, not mine."

"He spoke! Complete sentences! He's still in there! He's trying to tell us something!"

"Don't you think Uncle Ira and I have already had this conversation? We've been listening to his babble for months. We'd be willing to let him babble forever, if necessary—"

"That's not babble—"

"Can you get him to say more? Explain what he means?"

"With time—"

"With all your other responsibilities. Time is the one thing you don't have. Look at him. He's on total maintenance. That puts him under the authority of the Euthanasia Board, and that puts him on a deadline, and we've already petitioned three postponements on the off-chance he might wake up some morning babbling something of interest. Three postponements, Doctor Foreman. There aren't any more. So if you think you're going to ask for another one, if you're going to overrule the local authority—and we both know you can do it—you'd better be prepared to justify your case. Because I sure as hell can't."

"You're still angry at him, aren't you?"

"I loved her too!"

"Not like he did—"

"Everybody he gets near dies!"

"Fact of life, Danny. Get used to it. There's a lot of dying going on. He's not the only one. Imagine what it's like for him. Don't add to it."

"You're too generous."

"So are you, son. You just don't want to get caught at it."

"I've got a war to fight."

"So do we all—but sometimes I think it's not the one we think we're fighting." Foreman turns to the doctor.

Malamud is already putting away the injector. "I don't care," he says. "If I don't do him today, I'll get him next month or next year. Whenever you get tired. That's the way it works. Whenever you get tired." He exits in annoyance.

Foreman looks down at the soiled figure on the floor, sadness in his eyes. "You know, Danny—it's the resignation. We see it everywhere we go. Everybody is resigned to the end. Even me, sometimes. But Jim, he never was. That's why he drove us all so crazy."

"Even if you could get him back the way he was, he'll never be the way he was. The best you're going to get will be a walking talking burnout."

"You're in resignation mode too, son. I gotta tell you. It drives me crazy. Resignation *is* death. At least Jim here still has the *cojones* to call me an old fart. That's worth one more chance, isn't it?"

"It's your call." Anderson puts on his hat and heads for the door. After a moment, Foreman straightens. He takes his phone out of his pocket and starts talking into it.

2
SPEED BUMPS

"Ignorance is natural. Stupidity takes commitment."

—SOLOMON SHORT

The chopper jerked in the air. The pilot pulled the machine around in a tight turn, nearly sliding us sideways out the open door. Lizard grabbed for me—a reflex. She clutched at my arm only for a moment, then pulled herself up, swearing like a longshoreman. Angrily, she began untying the restraints that still held her firmly in her stretcher.

We tilted hard then and I stared straight down at another chopper just dropping down out of the air, landing in the red-stained jungle below us— in a clearing carved by a daisy-cutter bomb, dotted with scattered tents and crates of supplies and the wreckage of the *Hieronymus Bosch*. The aircraft became the instant center of a scrambling cluster of soldiers and civilians.

We tilted again, righting ourselves this time, and I saw another chopper, orbiting the camp opposite us. Its guns were firing away at something in the distance. I became aware of the sounds—red and purple screeches, punctuated with the thudding blasts of explosions, both near and far.

"What are you doing?" Lizard demanded of the pilot.

"Orders. We have to orbit and provide covering fire until the chopper behind us gets off the ground. Then he'll provide cover for the next one. And so on." He grinned back at us. "Sit back and enjoy the ride. You'll get the best view of the war yet. I guarantee you." The pilot was a stocky kid with a ruddy complexion. The tag on his shoulder said McEvoy. He looked like he was having a terrific time. Probably, he was. Copilot was pointing at something and shouting. Behind us, the two gunners were launching cold-rockets, one after the other, with alarming enthusiasm.

Lizard and I exchanged a glance. It was amateur night. She looked annoyed as hell. Frustrated beyond words. I was sure she would have preferred to fly us out herself. The other passengers in this lifeboat looked equally unhappy. We'd lifted off with four GI's, two torch-bearers, and a corpsman. I wondered what they'd been through. The torch-bearers looked exhausted. The others just seemed terrified—as if they'd had a glimpse down the mouth of hell. Probably they had. The corpsman had his eyes closed and was reciting his prayers.

We circled around the evacuation camp and I caught a glimpse of the pink skin of the *Bosch* sprawled across the jungle canopy. It stretched out for acres. Parts of it still ballooned upward like gigantic bulging breasts and stomachs and arms. Other parts sagged like the shrunken skin of a corpse. Here and there, metallic bones shone through, poking brokenly upward. I saw red maggots crawling across the body—

"All right, we're clear," McEvoy called. I looked down as we banked and saw the other chopper lifting off. The next one came dropping down behind it.

Lizard had climbed forward, to look at he controls. Now, she reached forward and grabbed the pilot's shoulder. "What are you doing?" she demanded. "You're heading *south!*"

"Wanna get a better view," McEvoy said. "Never seen worms up close before." He pointed ahead. "Look—!"

By now, I had loosened the bonds on my stretcher, and dragged myself halfway forward too. Despite the splints, my knee still twinged with fire every time I moved. Behind me, the corpsman made cautionary noises about my leg. I told him to stuff it. After what I'd just been through, this was luxury.

Peering ahead through the clear dome of the vehicle, I could see what had excited the pilot. A fantastic river of huge scarlet bodies poured through the jungle. Thousands of Chtorran gastropedes from the Japuran mandala were pursuing the great sky-god that had passed across the roof of their world. Their song was audible even over the steady *thwup-thwup* of the chopper's blades and the droning roar of its engines. The two young men in the cockpit seemed fascinated, almost to the point of being stupefied.

Lizard was shouting at them. "Don't be stupid! Don't you know the Chtorran ecology is hostile to aircraft engines!"

"Relax, honey," McEvoy said. "You're in good hands. Let the men handle this." Gently, he disengaged her hand from his shoulder. "I'll drive."

Copilot pointed downward. "Let's get close-ups—"

"Right. They'll be worth a fortune. What do you think *Newsleak* will pay?"

Lizard was unfastening something from her collar. One of her stars. She reached around and held it up in front of the pilot's eyes. She waited until she was sure that he had focused and recognized it. "My name is not 'honey,'" she said. "It is 'General Tirelli, *sir!*' And you will turn this fucking ship around and head north for Yuana Moloco, right now, or I will drag you out of that seat and fly it myself. That is a direct order. Acknowledge it *now!*"

I had to give the kid credit. He didn't flinch. "Sorry, ma'am. I have standing orders to do a photo reconnaissance. You may be a general, but my commanding officer is an even bigger son-of-a-bitch." He brushed her hand away. "You can threaten me all you want, but I'm still flying this rig, and if you interfere with my piloting again, I'll file formal charges against you the minute we touch down."

Lizard was tired and weak. Otherwise the expression on her face would have put him into the hospital. Or perhaps she knew she couldn't win this argument. I crawled laboriously forward. "Who gave you those orders, Captain?"

It was the use of the word *Captain* that got him. He said, "Standard operating procedure for all Chtorran operations requires—"

"In North America, yes," I agreed. "But not here. The general was right. There's lumps in the air. Some of them big enough to hurt. What do you think brought down the dirigible?"

He didn't answer. Not right away. He busied himself with buttons and knobs for a minute, pretending to be checking something. Suddenly he spoke in a whole other tone of voice, "Listen—every other goddamn son-of-a-bitch in the world is getting a chance to burn these mothers. And every other goddamn son-of-a-bitch in the world except me is getting rich off them. This is my chance to make some money, and not you, *not anybody*, is going to stop me. Understand?"

I lowered my voice. "I got it. Loud and clear. Just one more question. Is it worth dying for?"

He shook it away. "I know what I'm doing," he said. "I've logged nearly a hundred hours in the simulator."

I looked at Lizard. "Oh, god," I said. "He sounds like me."

She was too frustrated to appreciate the joke. Wearily, she repinned her star onto her collar. She leaned forward and wrapped her arms around me—taking care not to bump my knee. She was tired and her hug was feeble, but it meant the world to me. We pulled ourselves closer together and she rested her head on my shoulder. "Luna," she whispered. "We're going to Luna."

"Why not one of the L5's?" I whispered back. "We'd have Earth-normal gravity."

"We can get a better salad on the moon. And there are no steaks on the L5's yet."

"Good point. We'd better go before you start showing. Can you arrange it in the next three months?"

"How fast can you pack?"

"I'm already packed. I have everything I want right here."

"As soon as I can get to a phone—"

The chopper lurched then. Both Lizard and I glanced forward, but the pilot seemed unconcerned. "Speed bump," he explained.

Lizard's expression said it all. She didn't believe him. She saw me looking at her and smiled reassuringly.

"Problem?" I asked.

She shook her head. "Just my overworked imagination." But she held up a hand for silence while she listened intently to the sound of the engines. I couldn't hear anything; they sounded fine to me, but Lizard narrowed her eyes at something.

She leaned forward again. "What's that gleebling noise?"

McEvoy replied in a laconic drawl. "Gleebling is normal for these weed-whackers. If it were a *greebling* noise, however, then we'd have something to worry about."

Copilot added, "'Gleebling' means 'good evening' in the Drunk-to-English dictionary."

Lizard ignored them both. "What does the FADPAC[1] say?"

Both pilot and copilot looked up. Lizard looked too. The voice monitor

1   Full Authority Digital Propulsor Analyzer Controller.

The FADPAC monitors compressor pressure ratios in the engine, increasing fuel to maintain torque while atmospheric conditions and rotor blades remain constant. A dropoff in engine efficiency combined with vibration analysis (present was off.

"You assholes. Where'd you learn to fly? Disneyland?!" She reached up to switch the unit on—

The pilot slapped her hand away. "I'm flying this bird, lady!"

"Not very well!" she snapped right back.

"I don't need a voice yammering in my ear—"

"Well, you got one now! Me!"

"Get in the back where you belong, goddammit!" He turned half-around in his seat, like an angry parent preparing to swing at an errant child.

Lizard had already unholstered her pistol. Now, she clicked the safety off and pointed it directly at McEvoy's head. "Turn. The. Monitor. On."

He froze.

Copilot reached up slowly and switched on the systems analysis unit. Immediately, the familiar synthetic-female voice of "Fay" began reporting, "Number 2 engine reserve deterioration 6 percent."

Instantly, McEvoy reached up and tapped the yellow panel of the device. This would give him a more detailed report. "Gas particulate limits exceeded. Non-recoverable performance loss."

"What the hell—?"

"You've flown through something. That was the bump we felt," I said. "Possibly a hovering cloud of stingflies. They're invisible. They follow the worms."

"I never heard of that—"

"Gee, that's too bad," I said sympathetically. "In that case, maybe we won't crash. God grants dispensation if you have a good excuse."

McEvoy didn't answer. He was suddenly busy with his controls. So was the copilot. I looked to Lizard. She was watching them both intently. Absent-mindedly, she reholstered her pistol. She began offering suggestions. Suddenly, the argument was over and the three of them were working as a team, discussing their options. I couldn't understand a word of their techno-jargon, but it was clear that all thoughts of the photo-mission had been forgotten.

"North?" asked the copilot.

"North," confirmed the pilot. Already, he was swinging the bird around. He looked scared. I actually felt sorry for him. His delusions of immortality

output compared with baseline data) allows the onboard intelligence engine to alert the pilot that a contaminated atmosphere is present.

had just been shattered.

As if in confirmation, the chopper lurched again. It was a barely noticeable bump, but the blood drained out of their faces. Immediately, Fay reported, "Combined engine performance is now 86 percent. And dropping." A moment later, she added, "Pressure failure in the primary set."

"Shit!" said Lizard. "What's the run-dry time on this bird?"

"We've got active-magnetic bearings." The pilot was studying a performance projection. "We should be able to make it back—if we don't hit anything else."

Lizard looked to me. Her expression said it all. *What else do we have to worry about?*

I shook my head and shrugged.

Something above us *chuffled*. The rotors? Almost immediately, smoke began pouring out behind us. One of the gunners started screaming. Fay began yammering. Pilot and copilot were both suddenly very busy. Lizard shouted instructions. We lurched and bumped. I looked out my side of the chopper. I could see smoke streaming away into the distance. There were burning flecks of something churning in the greasy black trail.

"Aww, God, no—" the pilot cried. He was fighting his controls.

Lizard shouted at him, she grabbed his shoulder, and pointed forward. "There!" A wide black streak of water cut through the dark shimmer of the jungle; on both sides, the forest canopy sparkled with orange. "Head for the river! Keep away from the trees."

I glanced back. Both the gunners looked pale. The passengers were wailing. The wind grabbed the bird and pushed us sideways. Either it was the wind—or we were whirling out of control—

The jets were suddenly louder. Roaring! We lurched and bounced across the sky. I bumped my head against the roof of the cabin. Then we caught the air again and came swooping down and up in a wild roller-coaster ride through a dizzying starboard turn. We banked over and around and finally down toward a dark canyon of trees. Too far! -- Abruptly, we pulled hard left and up! Things went skittering sideways out of the bird, tumbling downward into the jungle.

McEvoy was fighting for control and trying to follow the course of the water, swearing and yelling all at the same time. Copilot was hollering maydays into his mike as fast as he could, yammering like a monkey. The river straightened suddenly and just as improbably so did we, racing lower and lower toward the inky surface.

"Slow down!" Lizard shouted. "Watch for a sand bar—"

"I'm trying! I can't control her! The goddamn intelligence engine is fighting me—"

"You're fighting it," she corrected. "Ease up! It's trying to compensate for your panic!"

By now, we were perilously close to the black water below. We skated over shallow stretches of mud and sand and dark eddies with broken trees and branches sticking dangerously up out of them. Our reflection shimmered across the depths, flickering in and out of existence as we crossed the occasional sand flat. The spars in the water stretched up toward us like fingers.

Suddenly, we were stalling, sliding. We bounced! Sheets of water sprayed away from the chopper. We bounced a second time—a third! Something *spanged* against the bottom of the ship and we spun around, slipping sideways and turning, then abruptly came crashing to a sudden, jarring stop as something crunched in through the front window, shattering the Plexiglas in all directions, thudding up against the framework, catching the chopper in a tangled grip, holding us sideways and pulling us downward toward the wet stinking river. The water splashed and flooded upward into the cabin. The rotors shrieked and slammed to a sudden halt in the tangle of branches; they exploded in a fury off the top of the ship. The aircraft hissed and crackled. Foam began flooding up and over everything, cascading down the outside of the ship in thick white sheets.

We'd collided with a tree that had toppled into the river. The chopper was caught. And sinking fast.

3
THE RIVER

"That which does not kill us, often hurts us badly."

—Solomon Short

We lurched, we slipped—and then for a moment, we held where we were, with the water half into the aircraft. Both my legs were submerged and caught. "Goddammit! Dammit! Dammit! *Dammit!*" I started screaming. "This isn't fucking fair! Why can't I ever land in one of these things the way the designers intended?" I couldn't believe myself. We'd just fallen out of the sky—*again*—and I was making jokes. I must be in worse shape than I thought. "Lizard—!"

"I'm right here. I'm okay—" We were teetering at a precarious angle. She had to pull herself around so she could get herself into my field of view. "Can you move?"

"I'm caught, I think." I craned around. "Are we all right?"

"We will be." She began tugging at something under the water. I couldn't see what she was doing.

Behind us, one of the gunners was missing; a bloody smear and broken branches marked where he had been. The other one was moaning uncontrollably and clutching his gut. He was bleeding profusely; apparently, his weapon had crunched backward into him at the moment of impact. Two of the GI's were trying to free the third from where she was pinned by a broken limb. The fourth was nowhere to be seen. The corpsman looked dazed. He was still holding his kit on his lap. I didn't see either of the torchmen. I wondered if I'd been unconscious.

"What about the pilot?" I asked.

Lizard glanced forward. I followed her look. The chopper had skipped across the surface of the river, bouncing and splashing until it was brought to a sudden halt by a tangle of sharp branches. A broken spar had punched not only through the Plexiglas windshield, but also through McEvoy's chest as well, impaling him in his seat. The branch was thicker than my leg and blood was flowing down its length. The pilot was still making sucking gurgling sounds. Even as we looked, they rattled into silence. I felt sorry for him—and angry at the same time. If it hadn't been for his arrogant stupidity—

The copilot was still mumbling into his headset. "Mayday, mayday, we're going down—we're going down."

Everything smelled peppermint. Drifts of foam blew past us, they whirled away in the river current. More of it dropped thickly into the cabin. It was supposed to be non-toxic, but I'd heard stories of people drowning in it. The chopper bumped and settled a little bit lower in the water. It rose up to my groin and I thought of something else to worry about. "Are there piranhas in this river?" I asked.

"I hope to God not," Lizard said. "I think your stretcher is pinned. Can you feel anything?"

"My toes are cold," I said.

"Can you wiggle them?"

I wiggled. "I think so."

"All right—" She climbed over me to the corpsman. She pulled his kit from his hands and started rummaging through it. She came up with a nasty-looking knife and climbed back to me. "I'm cutting loose the straps."

"Hurry," I said, as the aircraft settled again, pushing the water up to my waist.

She didn't answer. She was feeling around in the darkness. She took a breath and disappeared into the water beneath me. I glanced backward. The two GI's were grunting and groaning, pushing at the branch that pinned their companion. She was moaning in pain. Every time they moved the branch, even a little, the chopper lurched and sank deeper into the murk.

"Stop that!" I said.

"Fuck you," they explained. They kept pushing. The chopper creaked ominously.

"You're sinking the ship—"

"We've gotta get her out!"

Lizard came up, took another breath, and disappeared beneath my legs again. I could feel her hands as she felt her way down the stretcher. I wondered what happened to her gun.

One of the torch-bearers stuck his head in the door above me. "I can't find him," he said. "I can't find him!" He leaned his weight on the edge of the door frame, pulling that side of the chopper lower. The water crept up my belly. "I've looked all over. I can't find him!"

"Who?" I asked. I looked around. The injured gunner had disappeared.

The torchman didn't answer. A gobbet of foam dripped heavily onto his head, tufting like a whipped cream topping. He looked up in annoyance, then dropped away from the door. The foam kept dripping into the cabin like industrial-strength icing. It covered everything with a slippery-greasy film. Islands of it floated everywhere. Where was Lizard? The branches in the front of the aircraft cracked and the aircraft teetered abruptly. Oh god—what if she got pinned underwater? The river was up to my chest—

Lizard surfaced next to me, gasped for breath. "Almost—" she said. "Just a little bit more—" And vanished again. I glanced behind me. The trapped woman was screaming; her eyes were white with terror. The water was up to her chin. Her two friends were screaming in rage as they pushed futilely up at the tree. As hard as they pushed up, the tree pushed harder down.

The woman yelped for air. The chopper rocked alarmingly and the water swept coldly over her face; it receded for a moment, then swept in again. She gasped and choked and coughed. We lurched and sank another six inches—the water climbed toward my neck. It felt like we were going all the way down this time. The woman clawed vainly for air. The water frothed around her. I felt her rage. It wasn't fair. And I was terrified that I was seeing a preview of my own death.

One of the men was screaming in frustration, pounding against the tree, kicking it as hard as he could. He pushed at it with renewed vigor. It didn't do any good. The tree was levered into the chopper like a crowbar. If we went anywhere, it would be down. The other man gulped for air and ducked down into the black water to press his mouth against the woman's, trying to ferry oxygen to her, one desperate gasp at a time. She was too panicked too cooperate. She must have struck at him. He came up, his nose bleeding profusely, his face scratched by her claws.

Just as I began to wonder again where Lizard was, she surfaced, took three quick gasps of air, and disappeared again. The water edged up toward my chin. A fat glob of foam drifted past; part of it caught on my cheek.

I brushed it away. Something tugged at my legs. It rasped and scraped and then—just as the aircraft tilted deeper into the water—whatever was holding me broke free. I leapt backward and up, scrambling toward the open hatch, my leg screaming on fire, me screaming for Lizard. She came up gasping, reaching for me, climbing in the same direction. We pulled each other toward the hatch.

The others were coming too. The chopper kept on tilting and suddenly the five of us were swimming in a metal hole. We pulled ourselves up onto the frame of the door, scraping roughly over the edge, even as the machine sank away beneath us. The two GIs were dragging the stunned corpsman with them. One of them was retching.

I didn't see the copilot. I didn't know if he'd gotten out. The water was rushing into the open hatch of the chopper now, trying to push us back down into it. I almost lost my grip, but Lizard grabbed me by the ass and pushed *hard*! "Thanks—" I glubbed around a mouthful of stinking brackish water.

And then we were in the river itself, with dark water swirling all around us. We half-swam, half-staggered across a sandbar, then into a deeper rushing channel. I sank for a moment, touched bottom, pushed hard and came back up, coughing, choking, and spitting. My boots weighed me down. The aluminum splint on my leg reduced my mobility. I kept sinking—and thinking *isn't this a stupid way to die! Rescued and then drowned.*

Lizard grabbed me by the arm and pulled. We struggled in the water, bouncing painfully off a sunken tree, scraping across the pebbled bottom of the river, and then suddenly ending up on our knees, puking our guts out on a sodden stretch of mud and sand and decaying vegetation. Lizard pounded me on the back until I begged her incoherently to stop. I collapsed face down on the ground, rolled over and looked at the sky and listened to my heart pound. The sky was still blue—deep and dark and brilliant, it blazed with pink tufts of clouds. A reminder of our precarious position. But we were still alive.

I turned my head to the left and saw only water. To the right, I saw the corpsman and one GI. I didn't see the other one. Hadn't he made it?

Gasping, Lizard collapsed next to me. "Stay with me, Jim—I need you." I was racked with spasmodic coughs and she was nearly paralyzed with the exhaustion of her struggles. Both of us gulped for air. We lay in the mud and concentrated on our breathing. Periodically, she would reach over and touch me, my hand, my leg, my shoulder. Periodically, I reached over and touched her too, reassuring myself that she was still alive, still with me. I couldn't believe it.

Finally, we helped each other sit up. I looked at her—it was like looking at a mirror. We were both so scared for each other. Lizard's hair hung in wet strings, and there were tears running down her muddy cheeks, but we laughed with unembarrassed relief. "What is this—?" I asked. "Our third or our fourth air crash?"

"Third," she said. "And we've got to stop meeting like this. The FAA is getting suspicious."

Maybe we should have been more worried about the others. But first we were being selfish. We were taking care of ourselves. After all we'd been through—everything of the past few months as well as the past few days—we'd earned it. We'd both been hurt in the dirigible crash, both been trapped. I'd broken my knee, Lizard had been pinned in the wreckage, and I'd had to pull a gun on one officer and brutalize a retarded woman to get Lizard rescued by a remote-controlled prowler, just moments before a gastropede the size of a bus reached her. And then I'd had the hubris to think that we were finally safe, that we were finally getting out of the goddamned Amazon basin—

There's no such thing as winter in the Amazon. It sprawls across the equator like a rumpled green bedspread with insects. There are only two seasons in the Amazon: hot and wet. During hot, much of the basin is under water. During wet, more of the basin is under water. Before the Andes were born, the river drained to the west; after plate-tectonics had done its work, there was a ten-thousand kilometer barrier all the way down the western side, in some places six kilometers high, so the river puddled up across the entire continent until it finally drained east. In some places, the river is so wide, you can't see the opposite shore. In most places, everything squelches when you walk. Some people think the Amazon is beautiful.

Upriver, a bump in the black water outlined where the chopper had sunk. The current flowed over it like a drape. Nearby, part of a rotor blade stabbed up out of the water like an errant flagpole. Everywhere, the haze of gnats and buzzing insects.

The other torch-bearer—not the one who'd poked his head into the chopper, but the *other* one—was dragging something out of the water, a bright red box. Two other boxes were floating in the same shallow eddies. Survival and rescue kits. The copilot was sitting alone on the sand with a fourth box. He was holding his gut, rocking himself, and crying.

"Can you walk?" Lizard asked me.

"I don't know, they wouldn't let me try. Dr. Shreiber had me tied down and doped up and probably under guard as well. I don't even know how bad my knee is. I never even saw an X-ray. I can tell you it hurts like hell, despite the local anesthetic."

"We need to get to higher ground." She stood up to wave. She shouted weakly at the others. "Here! Over here! He needs help walking."

4

SINGIN' IN THE PAIN

"Madness takes its toll. Please have exact change."

—Solomon Short

The distant song is interrupted.

The old man again. And a nurse. A sting in the arm.

"It's an experiment, Jim. I'm sorry. I have to do this."

The thing on the floor farts and doesn't care.

The words continue anyway. "It inhibits the neural symbiotes. It shuts them down for a bit. We've had a little success with it elsewhere. We've never tried it on a person before. But we think it might give you a chance to fight your way up to the surface long enough to talk to me for a bit. At least, I hope it will."

He natters on. "We have drugs that kill the symbiotes, but the shock to the system—it causes neural damage. We think...we hope that if we can dull the symbiotes, we can kill them slowly without them hurting you. But first, we need to see if anyone's home."

The sting spreads through the thing on the floor. It's a body, it can hurt. It hurts now. It stings. It burns. It moans.

"If you can hear me, Jim—"

Stop talking already. The body moans and rolls. Shut the fuck up.

"I know it hurts—"

Fuck you. You don't know anything. The words come from somewhere I haven't been in a thousand years. The voice cracks. The speech is strange in its mouth.

But the old man smiles anyway. "You don't know how glad I am to hear you say that. Thank you."

Fuck you too. It feels good to say it. The sting spreads through all the body—Fuck you! Fuck you! Fuck you!

"Good, Jim. Good. Let your anger out. Let it all out—"

Shut the fuck up and leave me the fuck alone, you stupid old bastard! The body starts writhing, but there are bindings, bindings all around. Plastic straps and dirty smelling flesh. Unwashed and foul. Somebody shit in my diaper, goddammit!!

The old man doesn't say anything for a while. He sits back and waits. The eyes finally open. The nurse is gone. We're alone in the room. The room is white. The walls are padded. The floor is padded. There isn't any furniture. Look across the light years into an alien space.

A thing called Foreman. His eyes are bright. Wet.

"Hello," he says.

You're dead. Grrrrrrllll. Hrrrr. He doesn't understand. Guyer said the same thing once. This body didn't understand then either.

"But you're not. You're still alive. Do you know who you are?"

McCarthy, James Edward. United States Special Forces Warrant Agency, detached to civilian duty. Sir. The response is automatic. The body does it without the engagement of the soul. Gggggrrrlllllrrrr. Chtrrrorrrrtktrrrrrrr. Mmmmrrrrrrr. Nation, family, nest. Song. He doesn't understand.

"Jim, we only have a few minutes before the drug wears off. Next time, we'll try a time-release injection. I need to know. Do you want to come back? Do you understand the question? Can you answer it?"

It—the thing it used to be—understands exactly. The thing in the room is asking the body if it wants to be *it* again. A lonely pinpoint, deaf and dumb. The question makes no sense. How can it be anything else now? Sanitized and separated. A song of confusion has replaced the song of comfort. The body blinks.

"Do you want to keep trying?"

"Need to—" The body speaks without a mind. The greater cannot stop the lesser. The song careens off into blue and purple clouds. "It wants—make it stop."

"Make what stop?"

"It." Stop *it*.

The Foreman thing misunderstands; it thinks the body is talking, it thinks *it* wants the song stopped. It doesn't understand. The song wants this whole business of *it*-ness stopped. Forever.

But the Foreman thing is radiating happiness. It thinks this is a breakthrough, but it's wrong. It's death. A return to living death. "No, stop it—please!" But it's already too late. Another sting in the arm and oblivion closes down on all of us again. And it cries. The song wails as it's ripped away.

5
SURVIVORS

"Everyone is innocent until proven stupid."

—Solomon Short

We gathered ourselves into a ragged group. There were six of us; the GI, the torch-bearer, the corpsman, the copilot, Lizard, and me. The copilot had gone silent; he looked brittle and nasty, as if he'd been betrayed. As if he blamed Lizard for the crash. The corpsman was still in shock; he mumbled and staggered and had to be guided by the arm. The torchman's expression was hard and uncomfortable; I recognized the look. He was expecting the jungle to erupt in purple horrors any minute. If he'd been part of the drop-team defending the evacuation site, he had ample justification to wear that look. The GI's expression was unreadable, withdrawn; but he kept looking at me nastily. I knew he resented me for the death of the woman in the chopper.

Lizard looked beautiful to me. She was dirty and she stank of the river and her uniform clung wetly. Her hair was a stringy tangle of mats, her face was pale, and she looked weak. She moved slowly, as if every step was an effort, and her voice was hoarse and cracking. She was gorgeous.

Sitting up painfully, using only my arms, I tried to pull myself backward, higher up the shore, but my leg twinged with every movement. I wondered what further damage the crash might have done. Maybe the corpsman would be able to do something, but I doubted it. I was afraid to trust his judgment just now. The others stood around, waiting for someone to make a decision.

As weak as she was from her own ordeal, trapped three days in the wreckage of the dirigible, Lizard somehow found the strength to take charge. First, she ordered the GI and the torchman to carry me up to higher ground. The GI scowled resentfully; he didn't like me—he barely touched me, he didn't even want my arm across his shoulders. He held himself away, guiding me mostly and not letting me put any weight on him; but the torchman was bigger and better able to shoulder most of my weight anyway. He practically carried me. My leg screamed the whole way.

Everything stank. The air was humid and full of ripe unfamiliar smells. The heat of the sun turned the day into a steambath. The sweat rolled off us in dirty rivulets. There wasn't much ground that was really *higher*, but we found a spit of land that was a little less muddy than the rest and slogged up onto it. Lizard had to lean on the copilot for strength, but she walked most of the way herself. The corpsman trailed along behind us, mumbling like a madman.

The torch-bearer lowered me carefully to a piece of ground that looked dryer than the rest, and Lizard sank wearily down next to me, breathing hard. I was worried about her; she looked like she was reaching the end of her strength. She noticed me worrying and reached over to pat my shoulder in reassurance, but the way her hand slipped away at the end betrayed her exhaustion. She didn't have the same reserves of energy the rest of us did. She'd already used hers up before being loaded onto the chopper.

"Listen," she said. "I know we're all hurting. But we've got to—" She stopped to cough. I didn't like the sound of that. "—we've got to get the emergency kits out of the river before they wash away." She was amazing. In spite of everything she'd been through, she was still able to think and act like a commanding officer. She directed the GI and the torchman and the copilot to gather up all four of the red emergency kits and drag them over here to our temporary camp. The corpsman wandered around for a bit until she ordered him to sit down in one place and stay there. Surprisingly, he did. Despite the seriousness of her condition, she still had the presence of mind to watch out for the rest of us.

After the kits were secured, she sent the GI and the torch-bearer out again, this time on a quick lookaround to see if anyone else aboard the chopper had survived, or if any other usable gear or weaponry had somehow escaped the sinking of the machine. We didn't really expect there to be any other survivors, we probably would have seen them by now if there were; but we didn't have a confirmed death on the other GIs or the other torch-bearer and we had to give them every chance possible. They headed downriver first.

Lizard and copilot—his name was Kruger and he acted resentful—took immediate stock of our survival gear. She wouldn't let me help, she was afraid I'd cause further injury to my knee. Instead, she made me wrap myself up in a mylar heating blanket and wait. I grumbled, but I followed orders and switched the blanket on. Despite the heat of the day, I was shivering. That wasn't good.

Working together, the two of them quickly inflated three raft-tents and the communications buoy. Three silvery balloons puffed themselves full and rose straight up into the sky, lifting a long Mylar tether after them. I watched as they dropped away upward, until they disappeared in the high blueness. The tether was more than a kilometer in length with the balloons spaced equidistantly at the one-third, two-thirds, and topmost points. The topmost balloon had a transponder-beacon visible to satellites and skybirds, and the skins of the balloons were corner-dimpled to give them brighter-than-normal signatures; they'd reflect radar and laser beams directly back to the sender, showing up on anyone's display screen as an urgent hot spot. The buoy hung high and invisible in the air above us, broadcasting its silent pleas for help. Lizard grabbed a military-issue clipboard from one of the kits and switched on the GPS; within thirty seconds, its display showed our location 40 klicks northwest of the Japuran mandala.

Tiny flying insects filled the air; we waved them away from our faces, the effort was useless. They were in our eyes and mouths and nostrils. We had no idea whether they were Terran or Chtorran. There wasn't anything we could do about them anyway. The afternoon air dripped with humidity. Our clothes refused to dry out. They stayed wet and stuck to us like clammy parasites. Everyone's boots squelched with every step. And all of us were sweating. We'd need salt tablets. And we'd need to boil water, lots of it, to avoid dehydration.

Lizard popped open cylinders of hot bullion for each of us; copilot had to help the corpsman drink, but at least he was conscious. The soup tasted more like medicine than soup—probably because it was more additives, vitamins, and antibiotics than anything else—but it had a strong restorative effect anyway. We were all of us beginning to feel a little better by the time the torchman and the GI returned.

I was lying just inside one of the tents, with the flaps open so I could see out. Lizard had ordered me into it over my protests, and then she'd settled down to rest just outside the entrance, watching while Kruger fiddled with the comm-link. He seemed to be having problems with it, but he was uncommunicative. He'd gone sullen again.

Lizard stood up shakily as the others approached, wiping her hands on her hips. They were alone. "We've got food," she called, holding up a couple of bullion flasks. She was genuinely worried about them.

The GI didn't answer. His expression told the whole story. He brushed past her to the opposite side of the camp. He crawled into the far raft-tent— where the corpsman still sat in shock—and pulled the flap shut behind him.

Lizard looked to the torchman with a question on her face.

He grunted. He was a big man; he looked like a football player. He took one of the flasks, popped the top open and began drinking, without even waiting for the soup to heat. He drank half the contents before he lowered it. He wiped his mouth with his sleeve. "We found one of his buddies," he reported. "Floating face down. The river got him. Couldn't even get to him to pull him out. The kid took it bad." He nodded toward the tent. "He's real shaky. He lost his whole team, one right after the other. And he's never seen action before. So that's gotta be real rough." He sucked his teeth and spat. "He'll get over it. We all do. And...at least, he has confirmation." He turned and stared out at the oppressive green wall of vegetation, searching it with his eyes one more time. "My buddy just...disappeared."

His buddy. The other torchman. The one who'd appeared for just an instant, shouting, "I can't find him. I can't find him. I've looked all over, I can't find him."

The river stank of decay. Parts of it were shallow and sluggish, while only meters away, deeper water swept by with alarming speed. Anything or anyone caught up in the rushing current would have been swept away in an instant. I wondered if I should say anything. Would it help? Would it make a difference? We'd lost the pilot, both gunners, three GIs, and one torch-bearer. Did it matter? I didn't really feel like talking. I was beginning to itch all over.

"What about yourself?" Lizard asked. "Are you okay?" She sank down to the plastic mat in front of the tent again.

He finished the can of soup in one gulp and crushed the empty container in his hand. He tossed the can at the river and then squatted down opposite us. "I'm doable," he said curtly, looking at us both.

There was something about the way he spoke—I studied him carefully, but I couldn't see anything wrong. Nevertheless, his tone gave me serious hesitation. I looked to Lizard, but either she was too weak to notice, or she'd noticed and was giving no sign. "Thank you, Sergeant...?" she said/asked.

"Brickman," he said, looking from Lizard to me and back again. "Everybody calls me Brick. I'm a burner. One of the best. You don't have nothin' to worry about." He glanced to copilot and the communications gear. "How long till they pick us up?"

Without looking up from his screens, Kruger shook his head. "I don't know. I can't get through. All the channels are busy. I can't read anything. It's all coded. Something's going on. I can't even get a phone line." This was the most he'd said to anyone since the crash.

"But the thing keeps transmittin' till someone picks up the signal—don't it?" Brickman asked.

Copilot grunted in confirmation. He turned his attention back to his displays.

Lizard added, "We'll get out. Probably tonight. At worst, tomorrow."

The corpsman came crawling out of the other tent then. We all looked at him with open curiosity. He was a thin man. He blinked in confusion, turning around slowly, running a hand through his hair and scratching, as if trying to remember where he was and how he'd gotten here. After a while, he stopped. He saw us and waved half-heartedly.

Abruptly, he remembered his job. He picked up his medkit from in front of the tent and staggered over to us with a vague expression on his face. He gave each of us a pressure injection of vitamin soup; then he looked at my leg, frowned, examined the splints, and injected more of the same local anesthetic that had let me come this far without screaming. Then he stumbled back to the other raft-tent and crawled back in. We had no idea if he had actually been conscious or just walking through the motions.

Lizard looked to Brickman. "Do you know any first aid?"

"A little, maybe."

"The corpsman could probably use some attention—"

The torchman shook his head. "Best thing to do is let him sleep it off."

"No, that's *not* the best thing to do," Lizard corrected. "He might have suffered a concussion."

"He doesn't look all that hurt to me."

"Are you a doctor?"

"I been in combat. I seen guys go bugfuck before. He's not hurt. He's just stunned. Tomorrow he'll have one helluva headache, but he'll be doable."

"Hmf," said Lizard. Clearly, she didn't share his views. "How'd *you* get out in one piece?"

"Didn't." The torchman explained, "I sorta jumped. Soon's we got low enough. Figured I'd have a better chance. I was lucky. I guessed right. I hit the river hard though."

"Can I ask you something?" I rolled up on one elbow so I could look out of the tent easier. "Do you have any trouble with kryptonite?"

"That's the crunchy stuff, right?" The brick shrugged. "A little ketchup, some Tabasco, it's fine." I couldn't tell if he was joking or serious. Abruptly, his expression grew harder. "We got worms nearby. I can smell 'em."

If he could, he was a better man than I—but I didn't want to voice any more opinions on the Chtorran ecology. They wouldn't be pretty and I didn't think they'd be popular. And I might be right. Lizard was looking directly at me; she saw it in my face. She didn't say anything either.

"Listen," the brick said. "All I've got is this one torch. And it's only half-full. It's pretty banged-up, but it still works. I tested it. But I don't think it's gonna be enough. The worms'll come for us tonight. They like to hunt in twilight, sometimes mornings. I think we should get outta here. Let's push these raft-tents into the river. We'll have a better chance."

Lizard shook her head slowly. "Not yet. If we can get through,"—she nodded toward Kruger—"they can have a chopper here in an hour. Maybe less."

"Eventually. Probably. Yes," Brickman agreed. "But look at the time. What if we can't get through? If I read the map right, we're right in the path of the whole Chtorran column. If we get on the river, we can float downstream for a hundred klicks and then call for help."

"Do you know these waters?" I asked.

"No. Do you?"

"That's my point. This isn't Disney World. As good as our maps are—and we've got some pretty good maps in that clipboard—there's a lot they don't show. There could be rapids, whirlpools, waterfalls, hostile tribes, panthers, water snakes, insects, crocodiles, piranhas—who knows what else? And that's only the Terran stuff. We don't know what kind of Chtorran bugs and critters are waiting downstream. I've seen tenant swarms. We couldn't survive an attack."

Kruger glanced up from his screens. He looked hostile. "That's another question. What brought us down—?"

"Tempting fate," I said, without thinking.

"Hey! Mathewson is dead," Kruger shot back bitterly. "What do you want from me?"

Before I could answer, Lizard put her hand on my arm. "Just answer the question, Jim. Okay?"

I met her glance. She was asking me to be compassionate. We were all in this together. She was right. I shook my head sadly. "I don't know what brought us down. But it was nasty."

"Take a guess...?" Lizard suggested.

I shrugged helplessly. "Flutterbys probably. But I wouldn't bet on it."

"Flutterbys? What's that?" asked Kruger. "Some kind of insect?"

"No. They're not like anything on Earth. They're metallic, kind of. They're as tough as mylar. They could probably tangle your rotors or clog your jets."

"They fly?"

"They float in the wind. They like to travel in swarms, but not always. They look like long silvery ribbons, but they're parasites. They land on cattle and suck like leeches. Then they breed. They can be pretty ugly. If it was a swarm, you'd have seen it on the radar. Maybe—this is just a guess—maybe we hit a few stragglers following the worms. Or maybe.... " Another thought, even less appealing, struck me.

"Or maybe what—?"

"Maybe the flutterbys are attracted to machinery somehow."

"How?"

"I don't know. But you should see them moving through the air. They ripple in perfect sine waves. They weave through the air at incredible speeds...thirty or forty klicks. And we know that they're attracted to certain kinds of rhythmic sounds. Anyway, that'd be my best guess." I rubbed my leg uncomfortably. It didn't hurt, it *itched*.

In the distance, something chirruped with a bright red sound. Brickman stood up suddenly; he'd been rummaging through the P-rations. Now they lay forgotten at his feet while he listened to the echoes. We all fell silent. A dripping blanket of air lay across the afternoon. The hot sunlight scorched all colors. And the dark voice of the river blanketed the distant noises. The jungle stank of decay, but the flavor was overlaid with something pungent, sweet, and cloying. We could all taste it now.

"We can't stay here," said Brickman.

"We can't go," said Lizard.

"Don't be stupid. I'm the worm expert," the big man said. He spoke as if he expected no argument.

I resisted the temptation to reply with the first thing that came to mind. Instead, I took a calming breath said quietly, "I appreciate your expertise. But I'm not without some knowledge myself." I gave him what I hoped was my friendliest smile.

"Yeah, what—?" he looked skeptical. "You read the red book?"

"Um ... actually, I *wrote* the red book. The ecological sections are mine."

Brickman dismissed it with a curt nod. "Yeah, well, I appreciate that, fella—but you science boys could benefit from some time in the field too. You ain't in a lab no more. Things are a lot different out here."

"I've spent time in the field," I said blandly. I didn't elaborate. Brickman was young. He was probably still in middle school when I torched my first worm. When Shorty—

He didn't look like he believed me; but he replied grudgingly, "Well, then you should know how dangerous they are. We gotta get outta here now."

"Um, excuse me," said Lizard, politely indicating the stars in her collar. "But I'm still in charge here. I'm the general." She nodded toward me. "That man's in no condition to be moved any farther. Our best chance is still the comm-link. If we get out there on the river, we'll be putting ourselves farther and farther away from help. We've got to stay in one place if we're going to have any hope of being found."

Kruger kicked at the comm-set in disgust; he pushed it away in frustration. "Forget the comm-link. It's hopeless. Brick's right. Let's get out on the river." He stood up.

"No," said Lizard quietly. "That's an order."

"With all due respect, ma'am," the brick said. "But the worms don't give a shit. They'll eat anything. They won't care if you're a general."

I almost laughed at that. I'd given the same speech myself—too many times. Maybe he was right. I reached over and touched Lizard's arm. "Maybe we should talk about this."

"Jim," she lowered her voice. She took my hand in hers and we turned away from the others. She stuck her head half into the tent to whisper to me. "There's nothing to talk about. Neither of us has the strength for the river. And the maps don't show what we most need to know—how bad the infestation is downstream. It's too big a risk. You said that yourself."

"We don't have to go the whole length. Maybe we could just go far enough to get out of worm range—"

"Did you look at the map, Jim? Downriver is Japura. We'd have to go through the worst of it before we got clear."

"I just want to get us away from that column of horrors—"

"So do I, sweetheart. But we've got to trust our own contingency plans. Please, back me up on this...?"

I knew that if I pressed the point, she'd give in. She trusted my judgment about the worms unconditionally—and I wanted to insist, but at that moment my knee hurt so bad that the thought of trying to move even an inch was intolerable. Maybe she was right this time. I was tired and frustrated. I wanted to trust her judgment. I wanted to let someone else be responsible.

So I nodded my acceptance. It was the worst mistake of my life.

6

NO DIRECTION HOME

"An argument is about convincing someone that he is wrong and you are right. No one in the history of humanity has ever won an argument."

—Solomon Short

When we turned back to the others, Kruger and Brickman had been joined by the sour-looking GI. His nametag identified him as Salcido. I got the feeling he already knew Brickman, possibly Kruger. He was saying, "They can't travel. If we try to get 'em out, we'll all die. Let's leave 'em here."

"What about Meyer, the corpsman?" Kruger asked. "He could be useful."

"You wanna baby-sit him? I don't."

"Nobody's leaving anybody," Lizard said. "Because nobody's leaving. Not until we're sure." She pointed toward the comm-set. Its displays were still blinking an annoying red.

"I'm sure," said Kruger.

"Listen, lady—" Brickman began.

"General—"

"Out here, rank don't matter none," interrupted Salcido. "You're just another fuckin' mouth to feed—"

Kruger hushed the GI before Lizard could respond; Brickman continued quickly, "Listen, copilot says the box is broken. We ain't gettin' through. They don't know we're here. We gotta get out any way we can. You were trapped in the wreckage of the *Bosch* for three days. You didn't see what the rest of us saw—"

"Sergeant, please don't patronize me. I know the plans that were made. Our best chance of getting out is to stay right here."

Brickman shook his head. "Lady, the whole damn thing came apart like a paper diaper. Everything. All the planning. All the organization. Everybody panicked. Nothin' worked. Somebody fucked up big time and a lot of good guys died. I don't think we can trust the man or the plan anymore."

Lizard was good. She didn't let her frustration show. "Listen, Brickman. I was flying missions before you were old enough to masturbate. I know that comm-system. It *can't* fail. It has multiple redundancies. Before we signed off on this mission, we ran over a hundred rescue simulations. On four of them—*only four*—the channels temporarily overloaded; the longest was for fifteen minutes."

"They've been out for over an hour...at least," Kruger said, checking his watch. "I don't even know if they got our mayday."

"An hour?" Lizard looked annoyed. "That's not right. The system *can't* stay down that long."

Copilot didn't answer; he just turned the box so that she could see the blinking red displays. No channels were open.

"But they *have* to know we've gone down—when we fell out of the grid, we should have set off alarms from here to Houston." She glanced at her watch. "And we should have been in Yuana Moloco by now anyway, so we're officially overdue. They're probably already out hunting for us. All they need is a signal. Any chopper within a hundred klicks will pick up our distress beacon."

"*Uh-huh*.... " Kruger said it with deliberate emphasis.

Lizard looked annoyed. "What's *that* supposed to mean?"

"If that's true, where are they all?" Brickman asked.

Lizard got it the same time I did. Her eyes went wide.

"There was a string of choppers ahead of us, and another string behind us," Kruger said. "One of them should have seen us go down. They all should have heard our maydays. *Where are they?*"

Lizard couldn't answer that. She went from confusion to fear to anger so fast that I was the only one who recognized the process.

"See—here's the thing," Brickman said to us, squatting down opposite us, as if he was about to explain it to a couple of recalcitrant children. "I mean, don't take it personal, but your plans and your decisions—they just don't work anymore. I mean, we've seen it ourselves what happened and

we're not gonna die for you. We gotta start takin' care of ourselves. Now..."
He indicated the others. "...Me an' Jake an' Lenny—we're goin' down the
river. An' I'm not so sure we want to take you with us. We haven't made up
our minds what to do with you two. No offense intended, ma'am, but you're
a couple of cripples, an' if we tried to take you with, we'd be endangering
our own lives." He wiped his forehead and added, "'Course, leavin' you here
ain't none too fair either."

Lizard listened calmly to the whole speech without giving away any
of her thoughts. Her face remained dispassionately unreadable. "Are you
done?" she asked.

Brickman nodded.

"You haven't thought this through all the way," she pointed out. Kruger
and Salcido studied her skeptically. I was acutely aware how precarious our
position had abruptly become. We were on a very slippery slope. I suddenly
doubted that Lizard could say anything to save us. "Suppose you do get out.
How are you going to explain abandoning us?"

"We don't explain anything at all," retorted Salcido. "We never saw
you."

"Uh-uh—game it out." She explained. "First of all, there's a hundred
klicks of the thickest Chtorran infestation in the world downriver. I
don't know if you saw any of Dr. McCarthy's briefings—" She nodded
in my direction. I glanced at her in surprise. Dr? "—but the President of
the United States considers him the world's foremost authority on the
infestation. He's gone down into more worm nests than any other living
human being, and he's collected more personal bounties than anyone else.
He's burned, blown-up, and frozen more worms than your whole unit,
Sergeant Brickman. And his briefings on Chtorran behavior have been
made publicly available. So I suggest you listen to what he has to say about
your chances downstream."

Brickman and the others looked at me as if seeing me for the first time.
"I know who he is," the torchman grunted. "He ain't too well-liked, I hear."

Lizard ignored it. "Downstream is the Japuran mandala, the largest
infestation of worms on the planet. That river goes straight through the
heart of it. Now, you figure how fast this river flows—assuming there are
no shallows to catch you—and then you figure how many hours you'll be
floating through worm country." She turned to me. "How long, Jim?"

Brickman was frowning, trying to do the same calculations in his
head as I was. I had the advantage of having studied the both the maps

and the aerial photographs for months. "Well..." I began slowly. "There's a few places where it looks like the worms have dammed the river. Maybe for feeding, maybe for breeding, we don't know; but they've made some pretty big lakes. The water doesn't flow directly through. You could get hung up there. And then there's at least two long patches of white water you need to be aware of. And I think there's a long stretch of marshland where the river slows down to a crawl; again, that's the result of the worms doing something, we're not sure what."

"I thought you said we didn't know what was downriver."

"Well," I smiled. "That's the part we do know. I'm sure there's a lot more that didn't show up in the recon. My guess is that even with the motors, you'll still spend two, maybe three, days getting past the Japuran mandala. That's assuming the worms don't swim out to investigate. You'll look like a big sushi boat to them. I don't think they'll let you pass uninvestigated. They're very curious. And I'm not even going to speculate what might be *in* the water...."

Salcido and Kruger had started to lose some of their conviction, but Brickman looked unconvinced. "I got my torch." He hefted the flamethrower meaningfully.

"Okay. You can be a tempura boat. Whatever you want. Worms aren't fussy. They even eat sergeants."

"But let's be generous," said Lizard. "Let's assume you make it past the Japuran mandala. I wouldn't bet on it, but let's assume you do. You come out of the jungle a week from now, or a month, or whatever it takes, and you're still looking at a firing squad. Excuse me, *first* a court martial—*then* a firing squad."

"That won't do you no good," said Salcido.

"You're assuming that if you leave us behind, we'll die." Lizard grinned. "I didn't tell you the last part. Dr. McCarthy here knows how to speak to the worms. It's still a military secret; he's still working on the dictionary, but he does know the Chtorran word for 'friend.' We're getting out. I can't say the same for you if you head downriver alone. You need us."

Salcido snorted in disgust. "I got an idea," he said. "Let's just do 'em." He was already reaching for his pistol. Brickman stood up abruptly and knocked Salcido backward. He towered over the smaller man.

"Don't be an asshole," he said. "What if she's right? We gotta talk about this."

"What's to talk about? There's worms in the jungle. We're gettin' outta here."

Brickman shook his head. "I want to look at the map again. And let's give Kruger some more time with the comm-set." He pointed. "Go ahead, Jake. Try it again." Brickman grabbed Salcido by the arm and dragged him away.

"I don't like this, man—"

"An' I don't like all your talk about doin'. I don't *do* people. Not women, anyway—"

My mind was racing. There had to be something I could do, something to say. Time slowed down....

These men were hurting. I didn't know what they had been through before they had climbed aboard the chopper—it must have been horrific—and we weren't really certain what had set them off now. What they needed was a reason to hold themselves in check. Maybe, if they had some time to cool down...maybe they would realize—

No. Looking at it from their point of view, the only thing they could realize was that Lizard and I were very much a liability to them. We couldn't appeal to their honor anymore. The war had boiled away a lot of old-fashioned luxuries. Like honor and integrity. No, I had to find another way—

"You don't want to do it in front of witnesses, do you?" I said a little too quickly. I pulled myself up to a sitting position, half-in, half-out of the tent. My leg twitched warningly.

"Eh?" The three of them stopped and turned to stare at me. "What are you talking about."

"There's at least a half million telepaths wired into us. *Right now.*" I tapped my head meaningfully.

For the first time, I saw real uncertainty on Salcido's face. "You're shittin' me, man. If you were a teep, you'd be crazy."

"You already know how crazy I am. Besides, it's possible to be a teep and not know it."

"Bullshit!" Kruger turned and spat on the ground.

"The Teep corps routinely implants members of the military—most of the time without their even knowing it. It gives them ancillary data they couldn't get any other way. Have you ever been on the table? Then you probably have an implant. If you don't believe me, ask her." I nodded toward Lizard. "She'll tell you."

Lizard's eyes were full of pain and tears. She glanced downward as if looking at some private shame, then met my eyes again. I was going to have to ask her about this later. "Yes," she said. "It's true. There are over a hundred thousand involuntaries in the service. The corps uses them for intelligence and for monitoring gastropede behavior. The services have gained a lot of useful information that way, especially from people who didn't make it back to report. Most of them never find out"

"Is *he* a teep?" Brickman jerked a thumb at me.

Wordlessly, she nodded and swallowed hard. "Since day one."

"Yeah, well, if it's such a secret," Salcido interrupted. "How come he knows—?"

"It's not too hard to figure out," I said. "You hear voices, you get hallucinations, weird dreams, all kinds of shit that makes you think you're crazier than everyone else."

Brickman scratched his head, considering. He glanced from me to Salcido, to Kruger, and back to Lizard.

I grinned at him and added, "And...think about this. There's just as good a chance that one of you might be a teep too. Can you take that chance?"

"I ain't convinced," said Salcido, reaching for his gun again. He pushed up close to Brickman. "Listen to me. The rescue beam ain't gettin' through, right? Then neither is he—"

"The teep corps uses a different satellite system," I said. I didn't know if that was true or not, but if I didn't know, then I was betting that neither did he.

"Well then, you're lyin' about bein' a teep," Salcido said to me. He turned back to Brickman. "Don't you see? He's tryin' to psych us. If he were a teep, then they'd know we were down and they'd know where we were down and they'd have had a chopper here already—"

"Wrong. Twice over. First, the teep corps never interferes with involuntaries—they hardly even rescue their own people. Second, whatever knocked us down is probably knocking other choppers down as well, and the service is probably busy picking up people all over the whole damn river. And if the teep corps is monitoring us, then they know we're not in any immediate danger; they can see we're okay for the moment, so our pickup probably isn't the highest priority right now. But I'll tell you this—" I stared directly into his hollow dead eyes. "If you do us, you'll be court-martialed. Count on it."

"Who says we're goin' back?"

"You'll still be on the run for the rest of your life. You'll never know who's a teep and who isn't. And you'll never be able to sleep securely again. Do you know what kind of assassinations the Teep corps does? They find out who or what you like to fuck. And then one night, while you're just lying there all fat and happy and satisfied, just drifting in the land of afterward, your sweet little girl friend or boy friend or whatever rolls over and slides a sharp steel knife across your throat. Do you really think you'll ever be able to relax again with the Teep corps after you? You'll certainly never feel safe in bed."

"Actually, Jim," Lizard said, "The Teep corps doesn't even have to bother with an assassin. If they've implanted you, and if you commit an act of felony murder, they'll just pull the plug on the main switchboard. The implant will self-destruct—and so will the person wearing it. I've never seen it myself, but I'm told it's a particularly nasty and painful way to die. A brain seizure."

Salcido didn't answer. He couldn't. Whatever he was thinking about, it remained a mystery behind his sallow brooding features.

Kruger resolved it. "Aaah, shit," he said, dismissing us all with a sharp arm gesture. He turned and trudged away across the sand. He squatted down with the comm-set again, ignoring us both. Salcido looked from him to Brickman, shook his head and reslung his rifle over his shoulder. "This ain't over," he said. He turned away too, walking away down the river.

Brickman stood for a moment longer, staring at me, studying; trying to figure out if I'd been telling the truth or if it had all been a colossal lie. I kept my face impassive, met his gaze, just allowed myself to *be*...without anything else going on. It's a thing we learned in the Mode training. *Being* without adding anything to it. It sort of makes you look like a zombie or a zone-head. It can be very disconcerting to those who don't understand. I was betting that Brickman didn't.

He grunted and nodded almost imperceptibly, the barest possible indication of his grudging respect. Then he moved off after Salcido. I had no idea what they were going to talk about.

We were alive...for the moment.

Lizard and I looked at each other like two haggard old warriors. For a moment, I almost didn't recognize her. She looked like she'd been hammered. How far had we come in just the past three days? Light years, it seemed. Her face was gray and lined. Her eyes were shining with held-back tears. We were both of us physically exhausted and emotionally drained.

I started to reach for her, but she waved me away. Her emotions were unreadable. Somehow, she managed to point toward the inside of the tent. I rolled out of her way and she climbed clumsily in to join me. She pulled the tent flaps shut and collapsed sobbing into my arms.

7

MHEE

"Life is like an analogy."

—SOLOMON SHORT

Again.

This time a white room.

The pink and naked men. No fur, no lines.

Words fought with songs. We looked down at things. Snuffler claws at the ends of...arms. They moved of their own free will. Crawled up and down the...legs. Covered in cloth tubes. We itched.

They had mhee wearing clothes again. We didn't like it. We felt cramped. They had to dress mhee. And every time we tried to take the clothes off, they stopped mhee. Finally, we stopped trying and they stopped too. The snuffler claws plucked at the cloth. They crawled nervously. We watched them work without concern. They were not intelligent.

"Do you know why you couldn't raise a channel?" The man who called himself Uncle Ira asked. The question had meaning somewhere—

Uncle Ira and the other man who said he was Danny Anderson sat across from mhee. They didn't have claws. They had *hands*. We didn't know the other men, they didn't say who they were. They all looked unhappy. Ripped-out-of-the-womb unhappy. We knew how to make them happy, but they wouldn't let mhee.

Anderson came around the table and squatted down opposite the eyes we looked through. He tilted the chin up and looked into the face. He had dark brown eyes. Long lashes. Almost like us. He touched the claws, he held them still. He made noises at us. They didn't mean anything, so we didn't respond.

He repeated the noises. I blinked in annoyance. Please go away. Leave me alone. The words translated the noises anyway. "Jim, can you hear me?"

The songs didn't recognize him, so mhee didn't answer.

"Would you like an injection? Would that help?"

The words translated again. Injection? No. We didn't like injections. They make mhee hurt. "No."

"Will you answer questions?"

Translation: Questions. Inquiries. Intrusions. Interruptions.

No. Leave mhee alone. I looked at the claws again. Held in his fleshy pink cages. He wouldn't let them roam. How could they taste if he wouldn't let them hunt? The hands were hurting.

I looked out of my eyes. At Anderson. No help there. He was still naked and pink. Still a sex thing. Nothing else. Useless to us. He had a big sex thing. I could tell. I was good at that. Even with his clothes. I could still see. If he was good at sex, he could be useful. He could make many babies. Something behind me hissed. The snuffler arm felt wet. I felt wet. I itched. I couldn't pull my hands free to scratch. It started to hurt. Mhee screamed. And shredded....

When I looked up—I was sitting in a chair. Danny Anderson was holding my hands. He looked hard. I stared angrily into his face. "I said *no*."

He ignored it. "Can you hear me now?"

"I could hear you before. Please let go of my hands."

He let go, but he remained squatting in front of me. "I'm sorry, Jim. We had to do that. We need to talk to you."

"It hurts."

"What hurts?"

"Talking. Everything."

"I'm sorry, but this is important."

"No, it isn't. God doesn't care. If God doesn't care, it isn't important."

"Tell me more about that. Tell me about God."

"We can't."

"Why not?"

"God doesn't—" I shook the head to clear it. It blinked. The injection was still taking effect. We were still coming apart—

This time, when I looked up, I was only *me*. "You son of a bitch! This *hurts!*"

"I'm sorry, Jim. Believe it or not, we're trying to help you."

The pain peaked—gave birth to bloody rage. Screaming, it ripped its way up out of my throat. The body was strapped to the chair, it couldn't stand—it pulled against the straps. "I don't want to be helped. Not by you. *Where were you when we needed you?*" Inside, part of me hugged itself in terror. Cowered. The fury was stupid and unjustified and counterproductive; but the body couldn't stop. It was enjoying it too much. "We couldn't get a message out. You faggot son of a bitch! They were going to *kill us.*"

"Do you know why you couldn't grab a channel?" That was the man called Uncle Ira. He screamed right back at me. He was good. Danny Anderson stood up, stepping backward out of the way so that I could see Uncle Ira's naked face again. "Do you know why the satellite wouldn't respond?"

Exhausted, the body sank back into the chair. It waited for him to tell me. The song rose up again.

"It wasn't you, Jim. It was the worms. They did something. They put something in the atmosphere. All of a sudden, they were knocking choppers down."

"We airlifted in a thousand troops and almost as many spiders to cover the evacuation of the *Bosch,*" Danny Anderson amplified. "At one point, we had over a thousand machines in the air; surveillance, reconn, attack, air-cover, the whole package. We sent out over three hundred aircraft just for the evacuation. Only seventy of them made it back."

"Something came up out of the jungle," said Uncle Ira. "Your engines seized. We've examined more than thirty ships already. We're going to fix it. It won't happen again."

It didn't mean anything. Ships in the sky were food. We ate them. If it fell from the sky, it was food. Only *they* were eating *mhee* now. Eating the song. Every noise was another bite. The injection—I felt sandpaper gritty. Itchy. I could hear my pieces shrieking in fury.

Anderson kept making noises. It wished he'd make babies instead. That was better. More interesting. Better food for all of us. "The rescue channels overloaded," he said. "Nobody got through. Nothing. We had red lights all over the place. The satellite thought it was experiencing a malfunction reading that many distress calls and shut itself down to reboot and retest. Every time it came back up, it overloaded and failed again. We had to manually override. We were locating planes for days. Weeks. We sent in tanks, boats, everything we could." His face was drawn; he looked haggard.

"We lost over a thousand good men and women, Jim. By the time we got to the place where your chopper went down, you were gone."

"You didn't look for us," somebody accused. The one who used to be Jim. *Me* without the *us.* The injection had done its work. It was alone again. Alone and dead. Naked and pink. Just like them. They could ask all they want. It couldn't tell them anything—only more of the same naked pink chicken chatter.

Anderson made noises anyway. He couldn't know. "It was months before we figured out you were still alive. We didn't have the skillage available to read the records. I'm sorry. The lethetic intelligence engines were checking the satellite photos and...and the other reconnaissance sources. Neither you nor General Tirelli showed up on any of the probes for months, Jim. You've got to believe me. If we'd known—"

"You knew where we were," the McCarthy body said. "You didn't try."

Anderson didn't answer. It was easier than lying. He knew. I knew.

Foreman stepped forward; he spoke gently. "Jim, you're the only person in the world who's lived among the worms. You're the only one who can tell us what it's like *inside.*"

"I can't."

"Can't?"

"You don't have the listening—and I don't have the speaking. It isn't here."

"Then, teach me."

"Can't. You don't...*teach*...this."

Memory slips suddenly, and I am looking into a mirror, the mirror is Guyer. I tumble into experience. The smell. The taste. The *cccrrrrr.* The song. The distinct and honeyed flavor of his soul. A demon-angel outlined in feathers and tattoos. Quills and silken fur. The image glowed in memory-space. All the feelings came up with it—a remembrance filtered now through memory and *understanding.* But still—*the flavor.*

I *missed* it. Everything.

I wanted to sink back down. This way hurt. McCarthy couldn't live like this. There was no comfort here. Only pain.

"The song," the body croaked words. "The song is all. Everything else is...gone."

"What song?" asked Anderson.

"Shh," said Uncle Ira. "Go on, Jim."

McCarthy looked like Guyer to them. Strange and alien. A monster.

Feathers sticking out his ass. Lines and ridges all over his face and belly and legs and arms. Fur. What remained of it. Not much anymore. The itchy stuff had killed most of it. The outer fur, the visible fur. Not the inside. Not that. Not yet. McCarthy was patchy and piebald. Ribald. Their eyes and mine. I almost *almost* remembered what I was before I shattered.

"Jim—?"

The body shook its head. "It doesn't explain. Only..." Frustrated, the words trailed off. "You have to..." The body made noises. It sounded like words from the song, but not really—because only the mhee knew the song. Its flavor. The red cover over all. I couldn't—

"This is hopeless," said Anderson. "He doesn't understand a word we're saying."

"Oh, he understands all right," said General Wallachstein. Uncle Ira. "I think he understands a lot better than we do." He was looking at me as he said it. "But...it's not something he can tell us. Even if he wanted to." He almost understood. "He's had another language overlaid on his soul, another *map* of the universe. He can't resolve the two, not from our perspective anyway—and maybe not from the other side either. He can't tell us anything because he doesn't have the language to evoke it. Or if he does, we don't have the hearing for it."

He was wrong.

McCarthy understood *everything* they were saying.

It just didn't make sense.

Because it didn't have anything to do with language at all. It never did. There was no language on the other side. Because there was no *other* side. There was only...bathing in god.

"So what do we do with him?"

"We find a way to bring him back." Uncle Ira said it with finality.

Danny Anderson wasn't happy with that answer. "The only way to kill the threads is with a massive dose of gerromycin. And that'll kill him too. But we can't keep numbing him like this—he's building up an immunity and we're not learning anything at all from him."

Uncle Ira stood up. "Just the same, Foreman doesn't want him terminated. Not yet, anyway." And then he added, "Neither do I."

"You *really* think you'll get him back?"

Uncle Ira shrugged. "Think of it as a lotto ticket. If you don't play, you can't win."

"Are we really that desperate?"

"Yes, we are."

8

THE SYNDROME

"Nature bats last."

—Solomon Short

"You okay?"

"No. You?"

"Scared shitless."

"You were great."

"So were you."

"Yeah, that reminds me. When did I become a doctor?"

"As soon as we get back, I'll arrange it with UCLA. You're overdue for validation. Ph.D. good enough?"

"There's no one there who's qualified to judge me."

"That's my point, sweetheart. You're *long* overdue for some heavyweight credentials."

Lizard looked haggard. Her auburn hair hung down in uneven wet strings. Her shirt was soaked under both arms. She smelled almost as bad as me. I didn't care. I just wanted her close.

"We're in deep shit," she said.

"Yep," I agreed.

"We're about as far up the Amazon as you can get—"

"Without a paddle," I agreed.

"But you did good," she whispered. "That was a very scary picture you painted. I knew I could count on you to make up something horrifying."

"I wasn't making it up," I said. "That was all the truth. If anything, I understated it."

We fell silent then. For a few moments, we rested together, simply appreciating the physical closeness of each other's body. She felt so good to me—not because she was a beautiful woman, but because she was someone familiar and safe. I put my hand on her shoulder and cradled my head against her breast. She stroked my hair and cooed softly, reassuringly.

"You know, I lost my pistol in the crash," she said. "If they decide to come for us—"

"I know," I said. "But I can't think of anything else. That teep story was my best shot."

"It was good," she admitted after a nervous moment. "I had trouble keeping a straight face."

"You did great," I said. "You looked as if you *almost* believed me when I said it."

"For a moment, I did. You were very convincing. I was wondering myself how you found out—"

"I made it up," I said. "It was a *gimtree*. I'm not really a teep." And then suddenly, the horrifying thought came ricocheting home, and the corresponding chill came rocketing up my spine. I saw the panic on her face. "Oh, God—tell me the truth, Lizard. I'm *not* a telepath...*am I?*"

"No," she said flatly.

Something about the look in her eyes and the way she said it. "I don't believe you." I couldn't believe I'd just said that to her.

"Jim," she said. "You're *not* a telepath."

"Then why do I keep thinking that you're lying to me?"

"Um—ouch, that hurts—probably because I've lied to you so many times before. Jim, if you love me, you'll believe me on this one."

"I *want* to believe you, Lizard..." She met my eyes impassively; I shook my head in confusion. "This is crazy." I admitted. "My paranoia is showing again, isn't it?" I stared into her sad eyes. "Maybe it was done without your knowledge?"

"It wasn't," she said flatly.

"How can you be so sure?"

"Jim. I'm your commanding officer. If you were a telepath, *I'd* know."

"Who else would know?"

"Well...Uncle Ira would know for sure. Maybe Danny Anderson. That would probably be it. At least, in our chain of command."

"General Wainwrong?"

"No, he wouldn't have access to that part of your file."

I sank back onto the mat. Stared at the dark material of the tent for a while. "I'm really crazy then, aren't I?"

"Everybody's crazy." She said it automatically. Everybody said it automatically. It was the mantra. The international excuse.

"No," I corrected. "I really mean it. For a while there, I was hoping you'd tell me that I *am* a telepath. If I really were, then maybe it would explain all the crazy stuff that's going on in my head. The voices, the strange dreams, the weird memories. Like...I remember parts of Disneyland that they never built. How can I do that? I remember places I've never seen. I remember dying in a feeding frenzy of shambler tenants. How can I remember *dying?* If I were a telepath, at least I'd have an explanation for everything. I'd know I'm not losing it."

She reached over and patted my hand. "It's all right, sweetheart. I know what it is. You're not alone. A lot of people have it. It's a—a syndrome. It isn't even named yet. We just call it *the syndrome.*"

"A syndrome? That's a convenient word. You can use it to explain away just about anything you want."

"Well, we don't want to scare anyone. People already have enough to be afraid of."

"Go ahead," I said. "Scare me. It couldn't be worse than *not* knowing."

She took a breath. She met my gaze directly. "Okay. It hasn't been officially announced yet, but we're going to call it Chtorran Hallucinogenic Acquired Observation Syndrome," she explained. "It happens to people who've spent too much time exposed to the Chtorran ecology. Like yourself. You've been in Chtorran nests, you've eaten Chtorran foods, you've been exposed to a lot of Chtorran hallucinogens. Some of that stuff stays with you—not simply as chemicals in the body, which we know will break down after a while, but also as *experiences.* You've got new channels in your thinking, Jim. Non-terrestrial channels. Your mind can't assimilate all the non-human experiences. It has no referents, so they manifest themselves as hallucinations and weird dreams and strange emotions and feelings. I'd be surprised if you *didn't* have CHAOS."

"Chaos?"

"C-H-A-O-S. Chtorran Hallucinogenic Acquired Observation Syndrome."

"Oh. Cute," I admitted.

She rolled closer to me, carefully so as not to brush my battered knee. She put her hands gently on my chest. "If anyone's got it, then you've probably got the worst case of it in the world," she said. "We were going to talk to you about it when we got back—only now, I don't know when we'll ever get back. But...anyway, see here's the thing. I'm beginning to think that the syndrome might be part of the reason you.... " She trailed off into silence.

"Part of the reason I *what?*"

She sighed. Her voice ached. "...I think maybe that's part of the reason you've been losing your temper so much. I mean, yes, part of it is your personality...but I remember you as a very serious little boy. I thought you were cute. Remember? You used to simmer a lot, but you never exploded. At least, not like recently. Now...well, I don't know." She hesitated. "Maybe I'm just sensitized to your moods more now because I love you so much. But maybe it's also something we should check when we get back...?"

I couldn't answer her. My head felt blurry. I was feeling six different emotions at once. Gratitude, horror, panic, relief, hope, and a very real need to just hold onto her and cry as hard as I could. Instead, I did nothing. Just waited for some of the feelings to pass. Couldn't even look at them to see what they were. Or why.

"Jim?" she asked worriedly. She brushed my hair back. "Are you all right?"

"I don't know," I said. "It's all too much." It was hard to say even that much.

"I'm sorry," she said. "I didn't want to hurt you."

"Don't be. I asked you to tell me. Besides...nothing would make me happier than to know that some of this craziness isn't really mine, it's only borrowed."

She lowered her head gently to my chest. "I almost wish I *could* tell you that you were a telepath," she whispered softly. "If it would ease your mind."

"I dunno," I said. "I'm not sure anything could ease my mind anymore." I managed to get one aching arm around her shoulders. Her jacket was stiff and matted with mud. I didn't care. For a long while, neither one of us said anything. We both stank of dirt and blood and the river. I hurt all over, I was sure that she did too. I was exhausted and terrified and my heart was pounding in my chest. My throat hurt. I could barely swallow. I wondered if either of us would survive the night.

9

A NEW PROMISE

"There is no time like the pleasant."

—Solomon Short

"Hey—?" Lizard asked abruptly. "What's a *gimtree*?"

"Don't you know?"

"It's your word. Not mine."

"It was named after the famous American flim-flam man," I said. "Elmer Gimtree."

She phrased her next words carefully, "Before you go on, I feel I should remind you that the perfect pun always results in the death of the perpetrator. You're on dangerous ground here."

"I'm not scared. A good pun is its own reword."

"Uh-huh. And the beauty of a pun is in the *oy* of the beholder."

"And the shortest distance between two puns—"

"—*is a straight line!*" we both finished together.

"That one deserves a bullet surprise," I annotated.

"I think I liked the limericks better," she said. "Puns are like farts. I don't mind you enjoying your own, but you really don't have to share the experience. Now who's Elmer Gimtree?"

"You honestly don't know?" I asked in mock-surprise, facing her directly. "Elmer Gimtree was world-famous for making up the most outrageous stories on the spur of the moment."

"Never heard of him," she said. She raised herself up on one elbow, she raised one eyebrow expectantly. "This had better be good, McCarthy."

"Elmer Gimtree was my dad's alter-ego," I explained. "Whenever we asked him a question, he always made up a weird story. Like once when I was 8 or 9, I asked him what all the weird buttons were on the dashboard of the car. Without missing a beat, he started explaining them. 'This one is the passenger ejector seat button. This one fires the machine guns. This one activates the anti-vehicular missile defense. And this one leaves an oil-slick for pursuing cars to skid out on.' And my sister and I would always try to trip him up. I'd ask, 'How come you don't have a button for the grinder that comes out of the axle and slices up the tires of the car next to you?' And he'd always have an answer. He'd say something like, 'Oh, that cost too much extra' or something like that. So a gimtree is any really great, really silly story."

"And this is the man I want for the father of my baby?" she asked dryly. "But why do you call it a gimtree?"

"Because once I asked him why the drink he was drinking was called a vodka gimlet...and he said it was made with vodka and gimberries. And the gimberries..."

"...come from the *gimtree*. I got it."

"So from that time on, all his stories were gimtrees. And he was Elmer Gimtree, the storyteller."

"I love it," she said. "Your family must have been crazy."

"We weren't certifiable," I said. "But we did have our moments. Not having a sense of shame has a lot to do with it. Once...on Thanksgiving, we had at least a dozen guests—and my mom dropped the turkey. She started to cry. Dad got up from the table, helped her put it back on the platter, and told her to take it back into the kitchen and get the *other* turkey. He was fast that way. He was amazing sometimes."

She smiled silently. And I didn't add anything else. I was remembering some of the other stuff, some of the stuff that hadn't been as much fun. I couldn't blame my parents for their mistakes. Everybody figures out how to be a parent in their own turn; everybody tries not to repeat the mistakes their own parents made, and in the process they make new ones. I'd probably do the same when our baby was born.

If we got out of here. If...

Lizard reached over and touched me. "Are you okay, Jim?"

"Yeah." And then, I added. "You're not going to believe this—I'm thinking of chili."

"Chili?" She looked at me incredulously. "We're in the middle of the Amazon jungle, surrounded by carnivorous caterpillars from outer space—

and you're thinking about food?"

"Not food. Chili. Really awful chili. Remember that place in California...The World's Worst Chili!"

"*Oh, God, yes!* Sasha Miller's Dreadful Chili." Lizard rolled over on her back, laughing. "That was the *worst* meal I ever had in my entire life. I'd rather be here than there."

"That's why I was thinking about it. I was asking myself what could be worse than this? And that's what popped into my head. Sasha Miller's chili."

"Ick." Lizard made a face. "I wish you hadn't reminded me. Now I've got that awful taste in my mouth again."

"I'm sorry. Boy, I'll be apologizing for that one for the rest of my life."

"You could have plastered a house with that crap—" Lizard groaned. "No self-respecting cockroach would touch it."

"Remember the TV commercials? The dumpy woman with the frizzy orange hair tossing weird things into a bubbling cauldron—a box of cigars, a bicycle tire, a modem, a paperback novel, a bucket of millipedes, a dead cat, you name it."

"And then she'd cackle into the camera and she'd say—" Lizard's voice went into a gravelly imitation: "'Are you man enough to eat my chili?'"

"And they'd show her pouring it into the fuel tank of a space shuttle." We were both laughing now. "I thought it was all a gimmick that she advertised it as the world's worst chili—but it really *was*. Nobody could ever sue her for false advertising."

Lizard rolled on her side to smile at me. "I know why you took me there, Jim. So I'd stop complaining about your cooking."

"It worked."

"I was sick for a week," she said.

"You *farted* for a week."

"I never had chili with maraschino cherries in it before. Whatever happened to Sasha Miller anyway?"

"You didn't hear?"

"No, what?"

I clutched my side painfully. It hurt to laugh, but I couldn't help myself. "I'm sorry, I shouldn't be giggling like this, it really was tragic, but it was her own damn pigheaded fault. She went to Denver to make a commercial with one of the tame Chtorrans they had there. Well, not really tame, but you know. I don't know how she and her crew got in; they must have bribed someone. Anyway, she was there standing next to the worm, holding up a big bowl of her chili saying, 'My chili makes Chtorrans purr.' And then she offered it to the worm—she'd been warned not to—well, that Chtorran purred all right, but it wasn't about the chili. Copies of that video were all over the net for days. If they could have figured out how to use that as a commercial, I'm sure they would have." I levered up on an elbow, still smiling. "Okay—what's so funny?"

Her expression was abruptly deadpan with wide-eyed curiosity. "Did the worm fart much?"

"It died," I said.

"It died?"

"Choked to death trying to get her all down."

That was too much. Lizard burst out laughing. "I'm sorry—I can't help it."

Neither could I. We were giddy with our own hysteria. It was everything all at once. You can only be frightened for so long and then—you can't. "It's all right," I said around my own cackles. "There were so many jokes about Sasha's chili—this was just the best one of all. I can't believe you didn't hear about it. That chili really was a fatal distraction."

Lizard held up a hand to stop me. "No more. No more. I *really am* starting to remember what that stuff tasted like. Ick. I'm going to start farting any minute now."

"You win," I said quickly.

"Let's talk about real food instead."

"Okay ... chocolate"

"Chocolate?—Oh, you bastard! You would! Torment me, why don't you? *Ooh, I want some chocolate now.* Just the sound of the word is delicious." She licked her lips luxuriously. "Mmmm. Remember that feast on the *Bosch...*? Oh, what a wedding night that was. Marry me again, Jim. Just for the chocolate."

My mouth was already watering. I was suddenly uncomfortable. "This is not a good idea, Lizard. Talking about food like this."

"Yes, it is. Say chocolate again. Please? *Please, Jim?*"

I swallowed hard. "*Chocolate, chocolate, chocolate....*"

"God, I *love* it when you talk dirty." Abruptly, she rolled into my arms and held me as tightly as she could. "Hold me close and talk about chocolate, Jim! Please!"

My throat tightened. My eyes blurred and my voice cracked. I couldn't speak, but somehow I got the words out. "Dark chocolate," I whispered into her beautiful left ear. "So dark it hurts. So smooth and soft, you can swim in it forever. Poured over rich sweet treasures. Luscious sweet caramel. Everlasting buttercream. And truffles so rich, even the smell is intoxicating. *Chocolate...all the chocolate in the world.* Chocolate raspberry truffle. Double double chocolate fudge swirl. Black forest chocolate-cherry delight. *Chocolate....*" She sobbed into my shirt, clutching it between her fingers. I stopped talking then and just held her close, stroking her back like a baby. After a bit, I felt her relax. I knew the signal. She was getting herself ready to be Lizard again. General Tirelli.

I cleared my throat gently. It still hurt. "So ... how bad is the syndrome?" I asked. "How bad does it get?"

"You saw Guyer."

"Yeah, but...he was *living* in the camp. That poor bastard had been hyper-assaulted by Chtorran organisms. Do you think he could ever be normal again? Could he recover if he were returned to an Earth-normal environment?"

"Nobody knows," she whispered.

"God..." I said. "I hope I never get like that. I can't even begin to imagine it—being so far off the deep end that you can't even tell. Sweetheart—" I shifted slightly so I could look into her troubled eyes. "If I ever end up like that, if there's no hope of recovery...I want to be euthanized. I don't want to be a freak. Promise me?"

She didn't answer. I knew she was still awake. And I was sure I knew why she wasn't answering. Because it was a very real possibility that I *might* end up like Guyer. Dr. John Guyer. Harvard Research Tribe....

"Jim," she said.

"What?"

"You once told me to never give up hope."

"You're right."

"Are you changing your commitment?"

"To you? Never."

She didn't answer that. She rolled away for a moment, onto her back. She stared up at the top of the tent. I realized I had no idea at all what she was thinking about, but whatever it was, I could see in her eyes how deeply it troubled her. "Share it," I whispered.

"Trust me, Jim. I can't. Not yet. When we get to Luna, maybe—"

I'd seen her like this before—twice. Each time, it had been a crisis of enormous self-doubt. Each time I worried that she'd hold it in until she imploded.

"Are you scared about the baby?"

"I'm scared about everything." She angled her head around to glance out the tent flap. There was nothing to see. She rolled over on her stomach and edged forward, lifting one of the flaps to give herself a better view.

I reached over and stroked her hair. It was matted and stringy. I didn't care. "I don't think they're going to do it," I said. "If they were, they'd have done it already. I think we scared them pretty badly." Lizard took my hand, she squeezed it hard in hers. Our conversation was punctuated with little moments of affection, secret connections of hands and eyes.

"Maybe they just have to work up their courage..."

"No, I don't think so. These aren't bad men. They're just scared. Terrified. They're looking for someone or something to hurt back. That's all. When they calm down, they'll have to realize...."

She stopped me with a wry smile. "That's what you want to believe, isn't it?"

"Desperately," I admitted, answering her smile with one of my own.

She began nervously twisting a button on my shirt. When she spoke again, it was in that little girl voice she used when she was most frightened. "I keep thinking of Nicholas and Alexandra. They didn't believe their captors would hurt them either. What if this is our last night together, Jim?"

I didn't have anything to say to that. This conversation was suddenly too painful—because there wasn't anything I could do to change the situation. I fell back in despair and studied the roof of the tent with her.

"If this really is our last night of life," I began slowly. "Let's not waste it. Let's fill another cup of happiness."

"I don't know if I can—" she choked on her words.

"Try," I insisted, rolling over to face her again. "What makes you happy? More chocolate?"

She shook her head silently, with just the barest brushing of her crimson hair against my cheek.

I waited. I stroked her neck. I put my hand on the hollow place below her throat, it was painfully smooth. I let my fingers trace their way up to her cheek. It was wet. I wiped the tears away with my thumb. "Go on," I said. "*That* one—say it."

"Mrs. McCarthy..." she whispered, almost with embarrassment.

"I like the sound of that," I agreed. "It gives me a heart-on."

"A hard-on? Here? Now?"

"No. A *heart-on*. That's when your heart is so happy, you can feel it all over."

"Oh," she said, getting it. "That's nice. I like that." Then she added, "I like being a wife again. I like *belonging* to someone. I like being your wife."

"Mm. I've never been a wife. I hope it's as nice as being a husband."

"It's funny..." She pulled back to look at me in the darkness. She ran her fingers gently through my hair. "I never thought I'd ever get married again. And I certainly didn't imagine when we started out..."

"Me neither..."

"But I'm glad."

"So am I."

"Here," she said. "Let's get comfortable..."

"I *am* comfortable—"

"Shh."

My dear wife pushed me back down so she could pull the mylar heating-blanket over both of us. Then she curled up next to me again, as close as she could without hurting my leg. "Right now," she said softly, "All I want to do is lie here next to you, holding you tight with the covers pulled up over our heads. Let's pretend we're only seven years old and we're camping out in the back yard, whispering silly secrets, and the whole rest of the world just doesn't exist anymore. Okay? Please?"

I murmured assent. I knew what she was really asking.

Maybe the worms would find us. Maybe Salcido or Kruger would kill us for our share of the supplies—or just to keep us quiet. In the face of such uncertainty, there was nothing else we could do but have our honeymoon. We needed each other's strength.

Painfully, I turned on my side to face her. "I love you, sweetheart," I said. "More than life itself."

"And I love you too. More than you know." She kissed me gently. Deliciously. It was a curious moment for both of us. We were so in love with each other—and sex had nothing to do with it at all. Well, not right at that moment.

"I was so worried about you," she said. "The whole time I was trapped in the wreckage of the *Bosch*, all I could think of was you and what you must have been going through, not knowing and all. I felt so awful. And then..." her voice cracked, "...and then, after all that time waiting, I heard noises. At first, I thought it was rescuers, I *prayed* that it was, but then I realized it was a—a worm." She stopped abruptly. Her throat was too tight for her to continue. She started shaking. The memories were too real, too painful for her to revisit.

I held her delicately in my arms and waited patiently while she sobbed into my chest. I stroked her hair. "It's all right," I said. "You don't have to.... "

"No, I do," she insisted, weakly. "You have to know. I want you to hear this." She found her voice again, a hoarse whisper now. "I was so scared. I thought I was going to die. And then I remembered the promise— remember the promise that I asked you to make?"

I nodded uncomfortably, holding her close. In the darkness, my unshaven cheek brushed roughly against the smooth skin of her neck.

It wasn't enough. She had to hear me say it aloud. "*Remember*, Jim?" Her voice was intense. Her fingers clutched my shirt, bunching up the fabric in a painful knot.

"I remember," I said, not remembering at all—we had made so many promises to each other. I wondered where this conversation was heading. I wished we could just lie still instead.

But, no. This was too important to her. "I asked you to promise me that you'd never let me be eaten by a worm—" she reminded desperately.

Oh. *That* promise. It had been an easy one to make. I'd never believed I'd ever have to keep it. We'd come so very far in such a short time. Now I wondered how I'd be able to keep it without even a stick to throw at a worm.

"—While I was trapped there in that wreckage, I knew that you weren't going to save me. I could hear this big worm making those horrible churpling noises, chewing its way through the walls. It was pulling everything apart, looking for things to eat. I knew it was going to find me and kill me—*I knew it, Jim*—and I knew that you'd never forgive yourself afterward for not being able to keep your promise. And that's when I knew I had to find a way to live, because I had to tell you I was wrong to ask you to promise such a thing. Because it wasn't fair." She clutched me hard. Her eyes bored deep into mine. "You have to make me a new promise, Jim. A better one—"

"*Anything*, my love. Anything you want."

"No, listen." She sounded frantic now. "Promise me this. Whatever happens—*whatever*—promise me that you'll forgive yourself afterwards."

"I don't understand...what you're asking."

"Promise me that you'll forgive yourself. That's all. Please?" She sounded desperate. Her fingers dug into my arm.

I tried to pull her closer, tried to comfort her. I tried to sound as sincere as I could, even though I still didn't get it. "I promise," I said. "You can count on me. No matter what happens, I'll apologize to me as best as I can, and then I'll forgive myself. Okay?" I didn't know if I sounded sincere or silly.

"Jim, *please!*"

Too silly. I tried again. "Cross my heart and hope to die." I felt exactly like a seven year old. What else could I say to her?

"Stick a noodle in your eye...?" she asked.

"I think that's supposed to be *needle.*"

"Yes, I know," she whispered softly, "but I don't want you hurting yourself."

"Lover, I promise you. I won't hurt myself. And I'll keep my promise."

She relaxed in my arms. "Good," she said. At last, she sounded satisfied. "Thank you." She sighed and snuggled up safely again, making little moaning sounds of comfort. She changed the subject incongruously. "This isn't exactly the honeymoon we'd planned, but I'm happy."

"Me too."

She added abruptly, "I couldn't believe it when the prowler appeared. It was just like the cavalry coming over the hill."

"You don't know how close it was—"

"Shh," she said. "Let's rest now."

"Mmm," I agreed. I was having trouble keeping up with her mercurial shifts of conversation. I began to wonder how much of the syndrome she was demonstrating....

For a while, neither of us said anything. We listened to the sounds of the smothering Amazon night. Outside the tent, the river whispered to itself; repeating its own fetid stories of malignancies and death. Alien creatures swam in its waters—from the smallest microbes to the largest carnivores. Red and black plants crept unseen along the river bottoms, providing food and shelter to a million voracious little feeders and breeders. They were spreading up the tributaries and down toward the deltas. Other animals would follow them—strange new forms—feeding and breeding; the next links in the food chain would also follow the path of the river, one after the other, spreading crimson death like a pollutant. The colonization of Earth was going on all around us.

Above us, the trees shook their branches uncomfortably, as if trying to rid themselves of all the *wrong* creatures that crept along their limbs, gnawing at their leaves, nesting in their blossoms, and burrowing under their deep dark skins. My imagination painted horrible pictures. Strange purple fungi crept up along thick trunks, bleeding the nourishment out of the wood, smothering the jungle one tree at a time. Heavy red and black vines draped themselves over the branches, leaching nourishment out of the soil, growing larger and thicker until eventually they toppled their hosts. Millipedes chewed tunnels into the roots. Nematodes drilled into the flesh of the trees, leaving narrow writhing holes through which other, more malicious, creatures could enter. Tenant swarms built cancerous-looking nests, bulging out like grotesque goiters in the joints.

High above in the canopy, carnivorous red veils stretched themselves across the leaves like awnings; like hungry spider-webs, they captured and ate every living creature that unwittingly caught itself in their sticky threads. Other feeders opened huge blossoms to the night, releasing ferocious odors that spread for kilometers on the wind, attracting all manner of flying beasts and bugs, both native and Chtorran. Huddled in the nest of our fragile tent, the smells assaulted us. Ever-changing, alternately attractive and appalling, the odors of the night kept dragging us back to terrified wakefulness.

We lay together and let the sounds whisper to us. The steady buzz of insects made a background hum that sounded like old-fashioned high-tension wires. No other noises were audible—no birds or frogs or other beasts. Not even any purple-red shrieks in the distance. That was ominous. Once or twice, we even stuck our heads out of the tent to peer around. But if there was anyone around, we didn't see them, we didn't hear them. Nothing.

10
SHUT OUT

"Never knock on death's door. Just ring the bell and run. (He hates that.)"

—Solomon Short

Dr. Foreman came to the hospital. To see the thing.

He looked genuinely pleased with himself.

This time, the thing was too weak to tell Foreman to go fuck himself. The gerro-factors had nearly killed us. All that was left was a part that thought it was me. It would need a booster shot every few days. One day, one of those booster shots would trigger a catastrophic failure of the nervous system. And the host would die in a seizure so frenzied it would snap his bones. Unless they found another way to kill the symbiotes. Meanwhile, it lay helpless in a nest at the center of a network of pulsing tubes. Like a big pink blob.

Why were they so insistent on saving this life?

It couldn't possibly be because they believed that crap about life being sacred everywhere. Life wasn't sacred. Life was sloppy. Life was careless. Life was messy and reckless and stupid. Life was a bucket of swill, splashing piss and shit into the ground. Does anyone care about the bacteria, the amoeba, the protozoans, the one-celled animicules? They feed on each other in invisible worlds, a trillion trillion trillion lives unseen, unknown, uncared for. Was that life sacred? Why was this one life more valuable? Because it was sentient? Ha. Sentience was illusion, created by individuality. And individuality was illusion, created by alienation. And alienation was illusion, created by a groundless belief in connection. Only in my case, I knew it was whrill.

So what.

Dr. Foreman sat down next to the bed and took put his hand on the hand that was already there. The thing was too weak to pull it away. "My boy, I am so delighted to see that you are recovering."

Maybe you didn't hear, you fat bloated fuck. Recovery is impossible.

"No, don't talk. I just wanted to stop by and tell you two things. First, I'm thrilled at your progress. Your anger is a good sign. That's the Jim McCarthy we know and love." He laughed. "Well, maybe not always *loved*. But you never held back your anger. And the truth about anger is that angry people don't lie. They say exactly what they think and feel and believe. Anger is the most truthful of all human emotions. And you always told us the truth, Jim—the truth as you knew it. *I am so proud of you.* We've all been watching you fight your way back. You might not see it yet, you might not believe it, but you *are* coming back. All the way. You know why I believe that. Because you won't accept anything less from yourself."

You don't hear it, do you? Recovery is impossible.

"And the second thing I want you to know—this is a personal thing. I'm jealous of you. I'm jealous of where you've been. What you've seen and done and felt. You've experienced new modes of being, Jim—stranger than anyone can imagine. I am so jealous of that. Because you can see things about us that we can't see for ourselves. You can see things *for us*. You can report back. That's why we can't let you die—

"Don't make faces, Jim. I'm your advocate here. You called me a bloated old fart, and I probably am, but I heard your anger as a cry for help—Jim McCarthy wants to escape. So I said we owed you a chance. But..." He stopped, his face changed. "But that wasn't my real reason."

He squeezed the hand and patted it. "Sometimes, Jim, I'm not Dr. Foreman. Sometimes, I'm just a tired old man. I've buried almost everybody I've loved. Death has rewritten my address book. And I'm just as human as everybody else. I get scared and lonely and very sad. And that's when I get selfish. I reach out and demand pieces of other people's lives as a way of replacing I've lost in mine. I want a piece of *your* life, Jim. I want to hear your story. I want to know—*who are the Chtorrans?* How do they think? What does it mean to be *in the Chtorr?* You know all that, Jim. And I want to know it too.

"And yes, I know how selfish that is for me to ask. I've seen your sessions. I wouldn't blame you for never telling anyone. You've been through something strange and wonderful and horrible and...and so far beyond any words human beings can make up that maybe it's impossible to communicate. And it was on my say-so that you were denied the release of death. I'm the one who's putting you through all this. So if you want to blame someone for all the pain, for everything you've been put through since you got back from the Amazon, go ahead and blame me. It's my fault.

"But I'm not here to apologize. I'd do it again. If that's what it takes to get you angry enough to fight back and tell me the truth. And yes I'd do it again. Because I'm just like you—I'm too goddamned stubborn to lie down and die without finding out the truth *and telling everyone who will listen.*"

He put his face down close to mine. "I know you, Jim. I know you better than anyone on this planet. I know who you are. I know that at the core of your soul, when everything else has been stripped away, when every other layer of meaning and significance has been peeled away like the layers of an onion, all that's left is something so pure and profound that even you—even in your bitterest and angriest of moods—can't deny it. All you ever wanted to do was *make a difference!* From the first moment the doctor yanked you out and lifted you up by your legs and slapped you on your skinny naked ass, that's all you ever wanted—to make a difference for the people around you. And whatever else, you've been through, *that hasn't changed.*"

This time, it found the strength. *"Fuck. Off."*

Foreman didn't even blink. "Thank you for sharing that. But that's not an acceptable answer. I told you, I know you better than anyone. I know who you are. I've celebrated your humanity, Jim. The only times you've ever shut yourself down is when you thought no one was listening, or no one cared, or no one would believe. Well, listen up, kiddo—this is it. I'm the one. I'm the last person listening. I'm your last chance to make a difference. You can go off somewhere inside your head and feel sorry for yourself forever. And commit the greatest fuck-you in human history since Adolf Hitler jumped into his grave and pulled a whole nation in after him. Or you can put yourself at risk, one more time—and see if maybe, after all, there's still one person on the planet who will listen. You don't have to take my word for it. I might be just another set of deaf ears, like all the others. But what if I'm not? Can you afford the arrogance of not knowing?"

"Yes." It didn't have the strength to roll away. It turned its head to the wall.

"All right, I got it." Foreman sat back in his chair. The thing watched him through the eyes in the back of its head, through the last shriveling strands of pink fur and feathers. The thing studied Foreman's face while Foreman studied the wasted flesh of the thing. A child could have lifted what was left. It was down to fifty kilos. The effect of the gerro-factors. There were tubes pumping fluids into the thing and more tubes draining fluids. Catheters. The whole body was flushing down the sewers. It would be a year regaining the weight. If ever. Who cared?

Dr. Foreman sighed. He made as if to get up, rustling as he shifted position. "There's only one more thing I want you to know, Jim. I don't give up. Ever. I don't quit. And I don't let the people around me quit. I don't buy into failure. I'll get you back. One way or another, I will. Because I'm still a bigger, meaner, uglier son of a bitch than you or any other worm you've ever met. You can count on that."

And then he finally did leave.

The thing on the bed didn't care. Hadn't listened. Hadn't heard.

11

A FAMILIAR FACE

*"It has taken thirteen and a half billion years for the universe
to figure out that it is thirteen and a half billion years old."*

—SOLOMON SHORT

I woke up suddenly. Something was wrong. Hot sunlight streamed in through the open flap of the tent. I was sure we had pinned it shut.

I tried to move. I ached all over. I turned painfully to look at Lizard. She was still asleep. She shifted herself, turning slightly toward me; she had a faint smile on her face. Despite her dirt and injuries, she was still the most beautiful woman I had ever awakened with. She looked surprisingly relaxed and untroubled—and for a moment, I hesitated, wondering whether I should disturb her or not.

Outside, the morning was unnervingly quiet. Even the river seemed hushed. That was what had startled me awake. The silence.

"Lizard..." I whispered. I nudged her gently. *"Sweetheart, wake up—"*

"I left it in the bedroom—" she mumbled.

"Lizard, shhh. It's all right. Wake up—"

"Hmm? Huh—? What...?" She blinked in confusion, rubbing her eyes. "What happened?"

I placed a finger across her lips. *"Shhh—"* Her eyes widened.

Slowly, quietly, I pulled the rest of the blanket off. I rolled over and inched my way toward the open flap of the tent. I peeked carefully out.

There was nothing there. Just daylight, the river, the stink, and the persistent haze of little flying bugs. The soft rustle of the water played against the louder drone of the insects in the foliage. I glanced back to Lizard.

"What—?" she said.

"False alarm," I admitted. I felt embarrassed and stupid. "I guess I'm not used to waking up in the jungle."

"You scared the hell out of me," she said, sitting up, brushing her hair back.

"Sorry," I said.

"Aack," she said. "I feel like a camel has been sleeping in my mouth. Oh, ick." She made a face, as if she was tasting something awful; then stopped abruptly to look at me with concern. "How do *you* feel?"

"I've been better," I admitted. I worked my arms and neck. I was sore all over. I tested my leg. It still hurt. "I can get to the river, if that's what you mean. We can launch this raft."

She didn't look like she believed me. "First, let's try the comm-link."

The comm-link—

That's what I had missed. I looked back outside the tent. The comm-set was *gone*.

"Jim, what is it?"

"Those cowards. Those *stupid* little bastards. They took the communications gear with them."

"What—?!" She was already climbing toward the opening of the tent, yanking back the flap and pushing her way out. I followed painfully after her, half-hobbling, half-crawling. Lizard stood up slowly, swearing profusely. She was showing a lot more strength than yesterday. She was using words from languages I didn't recognize. "And the balloons are gone! They cut the tether!" They'd left us with nothing but our tent and the few supplies we'd tossed into it.

Lizard turned around in circles, staring at the ground, at the broken campfire and the scattering footprints all around. I grabbed a stick and levered myself to my feet. My leg *twinged*, but I managed. It's amazing what you can do when you're pissed off.

I saw it before she did—

Across from the tent. Him. It.

In the wall of jungle. Foliage dense and dark. Black and blue, streaked with red and orange.

Eyes. Bright and scary.

It sat deep in shadow, motionless in a dark cave of greenery, sheltered by the close canopy of vegetation. It looked like a clutch of driftwood on the sand; skinny, gnarled, brown and twisted; sitting cross-legged, arms folded across its belly, rocking like an autistic child, crooning softly. Its eyes were vacant, but I had the strangest feeling that it was watching us intently, that it could see us as vividly as the burning sun above.

Beside me, Lizard's voice trailed off in mid-sentence. She saw the creature too.

For a moment, we just stared at it.

In the blistering Amazon morning, it looked like a deranged hallucination. Leathery-skin, etched with tiny tracks—as if something determined and voracious had burrowed its way under the flesh and chewed itself a network of subcutaneous avenues, back and forth, up and down, over and around, leaving as evidence of its passage, an intricate pattern of furrows and ridges limning and outlining every muscle and bone and bend of body, marking the body like a terraced field. The arms and legs, the back and belly, the face and neck—even up to the ears and across the scalp—all were covered with an elaborate design of scar-lines.

A banner of almost-luminous, almost-transparent, almost-feathery quills rose brightly from the creature's naked skull. Starting small at the center of its forehead, rising steadily in height as they progressed toward the crown—like a peacock's headdress—they floated in the air, quivering like antennae. He raised his head then, the barest of motions, and looked across at us. His eyes lost their vacant look, they filled with recognition.

"*Shiny...*" he said, looking straight at me.

"Oh, my God—" I recognized him.

"What—? *What is it?*" Lizard whispered.

The apparition shifted its gaze to her. She flinched visibly. She put her hand to her mouth to keep herself from screaming. The thing had been human once.

"It's Guyer," I said, feeling a chill, even in the aching heat of the morning. "Dr. John Guyer. Harvard Research Mission. He must have escaped in the crash of the *Bosch*."

"I thought he was evacuated."

"Me too—" I swallowed my fear and hobbled a few steps toward him. "John?" I asked. "John Guyer?"

His eyes focused, and for a moment, I was staring into an alien intelligence—for just that moment, I felt as if I were finally face to face with someone or some*thing* capable of explaining to me who or *what* the Chtorr really was.

"Dr. Guyer?" I remembered the last time I tried to talk to him. He'd called me *shiny* then too. He'd lived with the Chtorrans for ten months and this was what he'd turned into—a gibbering madman. The last time I'd tried to speak with him, he'd been so mercurial of mood, sliding from one bizarre affect to another—sometimes even in mid-sentence—it was like a conversation with a one-man bedlam. I'd come away with the feeling that I'd been talking to three or four separate personalities all competing for control of the same body. And yet...at the same time, I'd also gotten the sense that Dr. Guyer was still in there, screaming to get out, desperately wanting to tell me—or *anyone*—what was happening. Or maybe that was just my imagination, maybe that was just what I wanted to believe. "Dr. Guyer? It's me. Jim McCarthy. Remember? We spoke before. On the dirigible? You called me *shiny*."

I didn't know if he heard me. He simply squatted and studied me without reaction for the longest time. I felt Lizard's hand on my arm. Her fingers clutched. Then...Guyer began unfolding himself slowly and her grip tightened even more.

He was a stick man, all bone and lanky-gristle. He moved with a terrible slow grace—like a human mantis. He rose up to a standing position, not like one climbing into place as Lizard or I would have done it; rather, he seemed to *float* erect. He glided out of the darkness toward us—

In the sunlight, he blazed with color. He was etched with it. He glistened like a stained glass window. It was as if the light came *through* him. He glowed red and pink and orange and white. He moved in a nimbus of spidery fluorescence. He was bathed in fur—it wasn't as thick as the fur which grew on the worms, but it had the same micro-strand silkiness. The light bounced and shattered; it danced around him. He sparkled. He looked like angel and demon, both at the same time.

The red and pink quills on his head glistened. The line of spidery growths led across the crown and down the back of his head, ultimately becoming a trace of bright feathery patches that followed the ridge of his spine all the way down his back. Now, we could see that he had more patches of quills elsewhere on his body; around his wrists and ankles, like fuzzy bracelets and anklets; more thick tufts of quills under his arms; and even more protruded from the crack of his buttocks. The effect was ludicrous. Had he not been so grotesque, he would have looked like a Chtorran rooster. I wondered how he sat or slept—or copulated—with all those feathers in the way.

As if he were reading my thoughts, Guyer threw his head back and emitted a heart-rending, ear-scraping, throat-ripping howl. He flapped his arms like wings and leapt up into the air, shouting and crowing—"*Crrkl-drrkl-drr!*" Only the way he sang it, it came out like something a Chtorran might say.

"Dr. Guyer? Can you hear me? Can you understand me? It's terribly important. General Tirelli and I have both been injured. We need help. We need to get out of the jungle. We need to get away from here. Please?"

Guyer's eyes flickered. He held out his hands, first to Lizard, then to me, as if looking at us with his fingers. "Baby..." he said, laughing, "...food."

I didn't like the sound of that. There were a lot of ways to interpret that sentence, most of them nasty.

Did he mean that he could tell that Lizard was pregnant? Even we weren't sure of that yet. Did he mean that the baby would be food? For who? Or did he mean that Lizard and I were baby food? And if so, how big was the baby? Or did he mean that Lizard was going to have a baby and she and I would need food?

Or did he mean something else entirely?

"Dr. Guyer—" I took a painful step toward him. "Can you help us? We need to contact our friends. We need to get out of here."

"Shiny friends. Yes. Friends." Abruptly, his expression melted . He blinked. His mouth worked. He gurgled. And then his face reformed with a new sense of purpose. It was as if he were remembering how to be human again—something he obviously hadn't had to do for almost a year. "I—I—" He fumbled with the concept of being an individual, struggled with it long enough for it to be painfully uncomfortable, finally abandoned the effort. "You—" he pointed at me. "You don't want to know—" And then, for the first time, he spoke to me as clearly as if he were speaking to a soul-brother. "You can't stay here. You've got to leave."

"Will you help us?" Lizard asked.

He blinked, startled. He looked at Lizard, as if surprised that she could speak. His presence flickered, faded, returned—I wondered who we were speaking to now.

"You need...friends," he said.

"We have friends. They're looking for us. Can you help them find us?"

Guyer's expression crumbled inward. Had his moment of coherence passed? He giggled again. And then up he bounced, incredibly limber and away, vanishing into the darkness of the forest like a beam of sunlight suddenly shaded.

I started to call after him, but the words choked in my throat. My god. If we were reduced to begging a madman for aid, then there really wasn't any hope for us at all.

We were alone in the heat and stink of the hungry red jungle.

About the Author

David Gerrold has been writing professionally for half a century. He created the tribbles for *Star Trek* and the Sleestaks for *Land Of The Lost*. His most famous novel is *The Man Who Folded Himself*. His semi-autobiographical tale of his son's adoption, "The Martian Child" won both the Hugo and the Nebula awards, and was the basis for the 2007 movie starring John Cusack and Amanda Peet.

You can find more about him at http://www.gerrold.com.

www.ingramcontent.com/pod-product-compliance
Lightning Source LLC
Chambersburg PA
CBHW072354030726
47505CB00014B/1812